"You strong boys going to help with these chains, or what?"

Ryan and Jak leaped from the wag and followed Mitch into the shed while Annie remained in the passenger seat. Jak glanced back, making sure that the woman wasn't reaching for the shotgun that was nestled in a rig beside her.

"It's just through here," Mitch stated as Ryan trailed him into the shadows of the outbuilding.

The one-eyed man flexed the muscles of his hand, reaching beneath his coat for the holstered SIG-Sauer. He didn't trust Mitch or the woman, and he cursed himself for getting into this situation. If Mitch could help them, that was fine.

But this felt increasingly wrong.

**Other titles in the
Deathlands saga:**

JAMES AXLER

DEATH LANDS®

Baptism of Rage

A GOLD EAGLE BOOK FROM

WORLDWIDE®

TORONTO • NEW YORK • LONDON
AMSTERDAM • PARIS • SYDNEY • HAMBURG
STOCKHOLM • ATHENS • TOKYO • MILAN
MADRID • WARSAW • BUDAPEST • AUCKLAND

Recycling programs
for this product may
not exist in your area.

First edition July 2010

ISBN-13: 978-0-373-62603-8

BAPTISM OF RAGE

Printed in U.S.A.

Youth is wasted on the young.
                    —George Bernard Shaw
                    1856–1950

THE DEATHLANDS SAGA

This world is their legacy, a world born in the violent nuclear spasm of 2001 that was the bitter outcome of a struggle for global dominance.

There is no real escape from this shockscape where life always hangs in the balance, vulnerable to newly demonic nature, barbarism, lawlessness.

But they are the warrior survivalists, and they endure—in the way of the lion, the hawk and the tiger, true to nature's heart despite its ruination.

Ryan Cawdor: The privileged son of an East Coast baron. Acquainted with betrayal from a tender age, he is a master of the hard realities.

Krysty Wroth: Harmony ville's own Titian-haired beauty, a woman with the strength of tempered steel. Her premonitions and Gaia powers have been fostered by her Mother Sonja.

J. B. Dix, the Armorer: Weapons master and Ryan's close ally, he, too, honed his skills traversing the Deathlands with the legendary Trader.

Doctor Theophilus Tanner: Torn from his family and a gentler life in 1896, Doc has been thrown into a future he couldn't have imagined.

Dr. Mildred Wyeth: Her father was killed by the Ku Klux Klan, but her fate is not much lighter. Restored from predark cryogenic suspension, she brings twentieth-century healing skills to a nightmare.

Jak Lauren: A true child of the wastelands, reared on adversity, loss and danger, the albino teenager is a fierce fighter and loyal friend.

Dean Cawdor: Ryan's young son by Sharona accepts the only world he knows, and yet he is the seedling bearing the promise of tomorrow.

In a world where all was lost, they are humanity's last hope....

Prologue

The warm autumn sun played across Doc Tanner's back, but the cold Nebraska air behind it was heavy with the threat of approaching winter. Tanner didn't mind. There was something enlivening about that chill, the very essence of what it was to be alive seemed contained therein.

Dr. Theophilus Algernon Tanner was a tall man, striking and handsome in his own way. His hair reached down past the collar of his crisp, white shirt, and bright blue eyes peered inquisitively from beneath his high forehead.

He was a man of great learning, with two degrees to his name and a tea chest in his attic that was filled with diplomas and certificates that he had never bothered to display. Tanner knew that the proof of learning couldn't be found in degrees, wasn't awarded on slips of paper. Learning was about understanding, about the application of knowledge in new and interesting and remarkable ways.

Even now, Tanner's mind was working over a hypothesis that one of his colleagues had been discussing with him earlier that day. He had been presented with a theory of time movement, his colleague proposing the ability to actually travel through time as though it were a road with way stations and stop-off points. The theory struck Tanner as preposterous, the stuff of science fiction, and yet he found himself turning the concept over and over in his mind as he made his way along the streets back to the cozy, two-story home that he shared with Emily and his children, Rachel and Jolyon.

Whether possible or not, Tanner realized, the idea of traveling through time held untold fascination. Imagine going back in time to the days of Pompeii or Atlantis or Our Lord Jesus Christ. Imagine if one could go back and halt the crucifixion. Wouldn't that be a quandary for Pastor Richards when the Tanner family listened to his sermon on Sunday at the local church?

Tanner smiled at the thought, before pushing it to one side. No, traveling back in time was fraught with danger; the potential to generate a new history, to create a paradoxical situation, was simply too hazardous. Better perhaps to travel forward, follow the road into the future to see the wonders that man would bestow upon himself in a hundred years or more.

Pushing open his front door, Theophilus Tanner smelled the wondrous cooking aromas coming from the kitchen. "Emily?" he called. "I am home."

A moment later, as Tanner hung his jacket over one of the hooks beside the door, his wife appeared, her long skirts swishing about her as she trotted along the gaslit corridor to meet with him.

"How was your day, my darling?" Emily asked, her voice as soothing as a lullaby.

Tanner nodded. "It was…" he began and then checked himself. "It was but a mere precursor to the wonder of seeing your beauty once more, my heart."

Emily was abashed, waving away his compliment. "You only say that because you smell what's cooking," she chastised him. Even so, she stood on tiptoes and kissed him gently on the cheek.

"Pot roast?" Tanner asked as Emily's lips brushed against him.

"Yes, and it's almost ready," Emily assured him. "Mayhap twenty minutes before it is served. Time enough for you to shave those whiskers." With that, she turned and made her way back to the kitchen to check on the simmering pot roast.

Tanner reached up and stroked his hand along his jowls, feeling the rough stubble that was forming there. Emily had never liked to kiss him when he had evidence of a beard, and so he had always remained clean-shaved for her. He checked his pocketwatch, tilting to see the time in the dull gas-lamplight of the passageway. A quarter of seven. Yes, he could quickly run the razor blade over his forming beard before they sat down to their repast.

Shortly thereafter, Theo Tanner took a boiling kettle of water to the bathroom at the rear of the house and filled the basin there. His shaving equipment, the blade, strop and soap, were held in the cabinet, well out of sight and reach of children's curious eyes and wandering hands. Tanner pushed the mirror to one side and reached for them.

As the water steamed in the basin, Tanner closed the bathroom cupboard door and stood the mirror back in place before it so that he could see himself to shave.

His face looked much older. It was his face, still, but aged, so terribly aged. It wasn't the face of a man in his early thirties, it was the face of a man of perhaps sixty. And, as Tanner watched, his face aged further, the skin tautening around his eyes and mouth, his bony cheeks sinking, becoming dark and hollow beneath the glare of the bathroom lamp, his hair thinning, pulling back from his already high forehead. Tanner watched in horror as the skin on his cheeks showed liver spots and began to rot, and then he could see the inside of his mouth through those cheeks where holes in the flesh— his flesh—had split open.

I am losing my mind, he realized as the face in the mirror continued its ceaseless entropic march. It was the only possible explanation. People didn't age like this, young to old in a matter of seconds. It was impossible.

His bright blue eyes seemed beady now as the hollows around them sunk, almost as though his face was pulling away. His nose had elongated somehow, but perhaps that was an optical trick, a result of his face's withering and receding. Tanner raised his hands, pushing them against his face to try to hold everything in place, to keep from getting any older. But when he looked in the mirror he saw that his hands were just bones, the fingers of a skeleton.

"Am I dying?" he asked. "Is this dying?"

The door opened behind him, and Tanner watched over his shoulder in the mirror as Emily walked in, a vision of youthful beauty to his ancient decrepitude. "Dinner's almost ready, darling," she said, seemingly oblivious to the change in him.

Tanner turned, his skeletal hands still pressed against his rotting face, a picture of entropy. "My dearest," he said, his voice sounding like dried leaves to his ears, "I fear I may be a little late."

Emily saw him for the first time then, the change in him, and her eyes widened as she looked at her husband.

And then she began to scream.

Chapter One

Ryan Cawdor's lone blue eye sprang open and he turned
to locate the source of the sobbing he could hear. He
sat on the floor of a jump chamber, and he could detect
the faint hum of machinery as extractor fans whirred to
clear away the lingering mist in the sealed room.

Ryan was a tall and imposing man with an unkempt
mane of black hair framing his hard, scarred face. A
long scar stretched along his cheek until it ended just
above his left eye socket. The eye itself was missing,
the evidence hidden behind a black leather eye patch.
A dark pattern of stubble shaded his cheeks, the ugly
white streak of scarred skin showing through.

Struggling to keep his head upright, Ryan looked
at the source of the sobbing—a white-haired man just
a little way across from him in the enclosed chamber.
Doc Tanner was huddled in a corner, his head bowed,
his shoulders heaving up and down as piteous, muffled
cries came from his throat.

"Doc?" Ryan asked gently. "You okay?"

Doc looked up with bloodshot eyes, wiping at the
tears that streaked his face. He appeared to be a man
of perhaps sixty years of age, deep lines on his face
and a shock of white hair billowing from his scalp like
steam from an olden-day locomotive. He wore a Victo-
rian frock coat over his smart trousers and white shirt.

The shirt, like the coat, had seen better days. A walking cane lay on the tiled floor at his feet, an ebony stick with a polished, silver lion's head design for its handle.

The old man reached inside his coat and pulled out a blue handkerchief decorated with a swallow's-eye design, carefully unfolded it, then used it to dab at his drying tears. "Must it always begin like this, Ryan?" Doc asked, his usually rich baritone sounding raw with pain.

Ryan shook his head slowly, feeling the cramp in his neck muscles abate with the movement, before rising to his feet and looking around the mat-trans chamber. There were six companions in all, including himself and Doc Tanner. The other four were only now beginning to stir, dragging themselves back into full consciousness after the debilitating jump.

The mat-trans was designed to transport personnel and supplies instantaneously across the United States of America. It was a point-to-point matter-transfer device that stripped an object down to its component atoms before blasting them into the quantum ether where they could be retrieved by a receiver unit.

Traveling by mat-trans took an incredible toll on a person, causing headaches, nausea and vomiting among other side effects, but the most damaging effect was on a person's psyche. It seemed that no matter how many times the group journeyed by mat-trans, they were still unprepared for the hideous jump dreams that it could cause. This time around, Doc Tanner, clearly, had been suffering some hallucination during the deconstruction and reforming of his corporeality.

"Deep breaths, Doc," Ryan instructed as he checked on his other companions, feeling each of their necks in turn for a pulse. "Let it pass."

Doc nodded, mopping the cold sweat from his brow with the handkerchief and pushing his damp white hair back from his face. "I have not had a dream quite that intense in a while," he muttered as he slowly drew a long, deep breath.

Krysty Wroth began to push herself up into a sitting position as Ryan reached for her pulse, stretching her long legs before her and wincing as the muscles protested. Ryan's lover, Krysty was a tall woman, curvaceous beneath the blue denim jeans and cream-colored shirt she habitually wore under her shaggy fur coat. With green eyes and pale white skin, Krysty was a breathtakingly beautiful woman, utterly stunning to look at. Her most notable feature, however, was her vibrant, flame-red hair, which fell about her face like a cascading waterfall. There was something uncanny about Krysty's hair—it seemed to almost have a life of its own. Actually, Krysty was a mutie, and while her mutation was minor by Deathlands standards, it was plainly visible if you knew where to look, for her hair truly was alive. It crackled, it swirled, it shone and it vibrated depending on her mood. That wasn't the only remarkable thing about Krysty, however. Besides being an excellent marksman and hand-to-hand combatant, Krysty held a secret ability in check—her ability to tap into the strength of the Earth Mother, Gaia. This Gaia power had been taught to Krysty by her mother, Sonja, and allowed her to call on incredible, superhuman strength in times of greatest need. But while Krysty could use such abilities to perform astonishing, seemingly impossible feats of might, the boost was short-lived and left her physically weak once it had passed. Like so much in the Deathlands, Krysty's abilities were a curse as much as a blessing.

"Hey, lover," Krysty drawled as her gaze lighted on Ryan. "I was just dreaming about you. You and me and a riverboat made for two."

Ryan shrugged. "Mebbe that's what's waiting for us outside," he said with a smile.

"Mebbe so," Krysty said quietly, pushing her flame-red locks out of her eyes.

There was another woman in the chamber, shorter and stocky, with dark skin. Mildred Wyeth was a medical doctor of some flair. She had been born in the latter half of the twentieth century but, due to a botched operation, had been placed in cryogenic stasis just before the outbreak of nuclear hostilities in 2001. Freed from the cryo chamber a hundred years later by Ryan and his companions, Mildred had thanked every saint that her pastor father had spoken of when she learned that she had slept through the nukecaust and the terrifying skydark that followed. Sneering, the saints had to have deserted her moments after, when she realized that the people who had been killed in those early days had been the lucky ones, and that all that was left was the waking nightmare known as the Deathlands. She had no family, no friends. In time, Mildred had adapted to the shocking new reality, and while her medical skills had been invaluable, it was her Olympic-level abilities with a target pistol that had really helped her come into her own in this shockscape future she had awakened to. Mildred wore black denim jeans and a black T-shirt, with a holster at her hip that held her favored weapon, a Czech-made, ZKR 551 target pistol. A loose-fitting black jacket matched her pants. Mildred shook her head, her beaded plaits swaying about as she recovered from the journey through quantum space. "Aw, damn," she groaned, running a hand over her cheek, "I have sleeping creases on my face. Why didn't somebody wake me earlier?"

Krysty turned to the woman and showed a bright, warm smile. "Such a sleepyhead," she said with a pleasant chuckle, and Mildred joined in a moment later as Ryan made his way across the room to check on his remaining companions.

Leaning against the wall that was farthest from Doc was J. B. Dix, also known as the Armorer. He was much shorter than Ryan, wiry, rather than muscular, and lacked Ryan's regal air. J.B. wore an oversize jacket with capacious pockets in which he kept numerous weapons and caches of bullets. J.B. was a weaponsmith of exceptional knowledge, and his designation as "the Armorer" was well-earned. He didn't simply know blasters, he loved them. Ballistics wasn't a science to him, it was an art form.

J.B. was a little older than Ryan, and the pair had been companions on the road for many years, dating back to the days of the legendary Trader, who roamed the Deathlands in War Wag One. The Armorer habitually wore a battered brown fedora atop his head, the shadow of its brim hiding his eyes the way his jacket hid his arsenal. Round-framed spectacles were perched on the bridge of his nose. J.B. was shortsighted, and without them his targeting ability was significantly compromised.

The final member of the group was Jak Lauren. An albino, Jak's skin was chalk white, and his shoulder-length hair was the color of bone. Jak was a wild child, heading toward the end of adolescence and still as thin as a rake. His face was sharp, its angular planes like blades. As Ryan watched, the young man's eyes flickered open, twin orbs of a terrifying ruby red. Jak wore a camo jacket that was decorated with shards of glass and sharp slivers of metal to prevent anyone grabbing at him unawares. Bits of razor were sewn into the collar. Jak spoke in scattered streams of words, as though his thoughts were too close to the surface to wait for formation into complete sentences. He could kill with blaster or with his bare hands, but he was most comfortable with his .357 Magnum Colt Python and the many leaf-bladed throwing knives he had secreted about his loose clothing.

"Got sicks," Jak murmured as Ryan checked on him, pulling himself to a crouching position and wrapping his arms around his knees. He had been with the companions for a long time, and he knew the feeling of nausea brought on by the mat-trans jump would pass. He just had to wait it out.

As he strode to the door, Ryan checked the breach of his 9 mm SIG-Sauer P-226 blaster, ensuring it was loaded as he spoke. He had another weapon—a scoped SSG-70 Steyr rifle—strapped to his back, and an eighteen-inch panga held in strapped to his leg.

"Everyone looks in one piece," he stated. "We all about ready to move?"

There was a general groan of consent from the companions as they checked their own weapons.

"Right," Ryan continued. "Triple red until we know what's out there." That said, the one-eyed man depressed the door's lever.

FOR ALL THEIR differences in geography, most every mat-trans seemed to be the same. The compact matter-transfer chamber was usually located in a redoubt, an old U.S. military installation occupying a remote location, deliberately hidden from public view. Or in a few cases hidden in plain sight.

Warily, the six companions made their way swiftly through the bland concrete corridors, searching for working armament, ammo and food as they went. The place appeared deserted, but Ryan and his colleagues had learned never to make assumptions like that. When you assume, as J. B. Dix sometimes stated, you made a corpse out of you and me.

Dark water stains marred the gray walls and ceilings, peppered here and there with mould a lime green and vibrant, vomit yellow. Pools of water, no deeper than an inch, glistened on the floor of the corridors as the automated lighting *pop-pop-popped* to life when hundred-year-old motion sensors detected the companions passing through. Obviously there was a breach in the walls somewhere.

It didn't take long to locate the exit, and Ryan and Krysty worked the door controls before cautiously leading the way outside into the balmy evening air. It was raining, a needle-thin, warm drizzle that smelled faintly of sulfur. Acid rain was a major concern. A potent rain could strip flesh from the bone in minutes.

"Nice," Krysty said sarcastically. She tentatively stretched out a hand into the drizzle. Not even a tingle, which meant there was no acid in the rain.

"Come out and play, lover," Krysty teased, turning around and around as the rain spattered on her upturned face, her eyes screwed tightly closed.

The one-eyed man walked out into the shower to join Krysty, reaching his big arm around her back. The others followed a moment later.

Ryan glanced up at the sky and adjusted the time on his wristwatch. "Looks like we've crossed time zones," he said. "Figure we're out east somewhere. What do you say, J.B.?"

J.B. was consulting his minisextant, But the bad weather made it impossible to get a bearing on their location. Mildred spoke up. "We're in Tennessee," she said. As one, the companions turned to her with questioning looks. "I read it on one of the order forms back in the redoubt," she explained with a shrug.

Jak joined Ryan and Krysty at the head of the group and, walking three abreast, the companions made their way along a muddy track and out through a clump of overgrown vegetation. The albino pointed out some vibrant red berries that grew on one of the bushes as they passed. "Hungry?" he asked Ryan.

Ryan nodded, wondering if he should taste the berries, but Krysty was shaking her head in warning. He saw several beetles eating at the berries, their black carapaces glistening with raindrops.

Grinning, Jak shook his head, too. "Chilled later," he explained.

Ryan withdrew his hand and advised the others not to touch the flora. "Poison berries," he said by way of explanation.

Beyond the vegetation that masked the redoubt entrance, the companions found themselves in what looked like another shit-forsaken excuse for farmland. An old road stretched off toward the horizon, its asphalt surface cracked, the open rents bubbling with the putrid rainwater. Around the road were several fields, one containing a few gangly stalks of corn, another a regimented orchard full of dead apple trees, their pointed branches like reaching talons, black nails clawing for the cloud-dulled sky. Several cawing birds, large with dark plumage, braved the rain to swoop into the fields, picking off insects or rodents that their sharp eyesight had spied.

As Jak sprinted ahead, scoping out the area about them, Krysty fell into step with Ryan, sidling close and wrapping an arm around his waist.

"Seems like a nice place," she drawled, looking up into Ryan's good right eye.

"No one's tried to kill us yet," Ryan stated. "I could grow to like that."

Behind them, Mildred was taking inventory of the contents of her medical kit, checking her dwindling supplies as she walked along the churned-up remains of the cracked strip of road.

J.B. and Doc took up the rear, walking beside each other, the older man swinging his lion's-head cane with a flourish as he took each step.

Watching the road with alert eyes, J.B. said quietly, "What was going on back there, Doc?" he asked. "You seemed pretty out of it."

"Old ghosts," the old man replied thoughtfully, "come back to haunt me once again. Emily. My dear sweet Emily."

Emily was Doc's wife, J.B. knew, back from a hundred years before the nukecaust. Doc had a strange life's journey. He had been born in the nineteenth century, and had lived the life of an academic before finding himself the subject of a cruel experiment in time manipulation.

Against his will, Doc had been pulled through time by the scientists of Project Chronos, into the tail end of the twentieth century.

However, those same scientists—"whitecoats" in the Deathlands vernacular—had reckoned without Doc's intellect, and had soon become exasperated with his continued attempts to hinder and outright retard their progress. Using the same time-trawling technology, they had dumped their irascible subject far in the future, and Doc had suddenly found himself in the Deathlands, one hundred years after the nukecaust, fending for himself as a court jester.

But that hadn't been the worst of it. Poor Doc Tanner had physically aged, like a time-lapse film, and found himself a man in his thirties trapped in the body of one much, much older. It had been a cruel fate, and had almost unhinged Doc's mind. For a while, during their early companionship, J.B. had known the old man to snap into visions and memories, convinced he was back home with his wife and children.

"Jump nightmares aren't easy on anyone," J.B. pointed out. "Gotta shake it off, Doc."

Doc sighed his agreement. A part of him had taken perverse joy in seeing his dear Emily again, and he regretted letting the dream fade, however horrific its conclusion had been.

As the companions trudged along the cracked highway, they heard a rumbling in the distance. Fifteen minutes later, a posse of wags, four in all, trundled past them. They were led by two old truck rigs belching putrid black smoke from their upright exhaust pipes. Behind the rigs, a horse-drawn wag bumped over the cracked road, a woman and baby visible inside the rotten shell of the four-wheel drive that the horses pulled, the animals themselves looking tired and hungry, bony shoulder blades close to the surface of their matted coats. Finally, a tractor that had been converted to carry passengers in a covered section stretching behind it puttered along. The companions stood to one side and watched as the convoy made its slow progress along the bumpy road.

"Guess we're on Main Street," J.B. muttered, casting a significant look at Ryan before turning his attention back to the passing wags.

Like most people in the Deathlands, the companions were wary of strangers. Life was a series of rules of survival, primary among them was the simple edict of "chill or be chilled." Communities, little baronies called villes, may work together for the purposes of farming and social cohesion, but outlanders were invariably treated with contempt. Chilling a man for the boots he wore wasn't unheard-of, even if those boots didn't fit and leaked water like a sieve. In the Deathlands, having was better than not having, pure and simple.

"I wonder where they are going?" Doc said amiably, as the wags continued down the broken tarmac.

"Same place we're going, most likely," J.B. replied. "As far down the road as they can until they either find something worth stopping for or die of exhaustion."

The old man snorted with amusement. In that single sentence, J.B. had summed up the motivation that kept the restless companions themselves moving ever onward, mat-trans by mat-trans.

RYAN AND HIS GROUP continued walking along the broken road for another twenty minutes until, as dusk fell and the putrid drizzle continued its relentless assault on the travelers, they spotted a scattering of ramshackle buildings arranged on either side of the blistered blacktop. The wags were just pulling over, placing themselves beside similar parked vehicles, and Ryan could see that they were stopping off in the dirt beside a cluster of three large wooden buildings.

Ryan held his hand up to bring his companions to a halt, and Krysty called to Jak to wait. Then Ryan pulled the scoped SSG-70 Steyr rifle from his back. The one-eyed man rested the butt of the weapon against his shoulder and peered into the powerful magnification lens of the scope.

"Couple of sec men," he said as he studied the clutch of buildings ahead, spotting two well-armed toughs patrolling the area as the wag riders disembarked. Then he spotted another sec man through the scope, and yet another a moment later, both of them brandishing assault rifles with holstered blasters at their hips. "Make that three," Ryan continued in an emotionless voice. "No, four. Sentry post half-buried across to the right of the road, pillbox design. Can see a light there, someone's inside."

"Anything else?" J.B. prompted as Ryan slowly scanned the horizon through the scope.

After a moment, Ryan shifted the rifle from its resting place against his shoulder. "Looks friendly," he announced, relief on his scarred face.

Even as he said it, the sound of blasterfire tore across the fields, cutting through the stillness.

Chapter Two

Ryan peered into the scope again to examine the little settlement. Beside him, J.B. had produced a pair of minibinocs from inside his voluminous coat, while Jak simply narrowed his eyes, using his hand to shade them from the dwindling sunlight of dusk. Behind them, Doc, Krysty and Mildred became alert, checking their weapons in readiness.

Locating the flashes of blasterfire through the magnifying scope, Ryan saw several members of the wag train blasting shots at something he couldn't immediately recognize. Whatever it was, it was the color of shadow and it moved liquid fast and low to the ground as the drizzling rain continued lashing at the soil. As Ryan tracked the dark mass, parts of it broke away, and he realized it was a pack of dogs, or maybe wolves. One of the creatures bolted across the darkening field and leaped into the frightened crowd emerging from the convoy. It moved as a blur across the gun's magnifying lens, and Ryan felt his breath catch as the creature grappled with an elderly man, its powerful forelegs driving its prey to the ground. The hound shook its victim by the arm as he tumbled to the mud, ripping at the man's forearm amid a gush of blood.

Without a moment's thought, Ryan instantly steadied his breathing, calmed his heart rate and gently squeezed the trigger on the Steyr rifle. A bullet sped from the rifle's muzzle with a loud report, zipping through the air and driving into the creature's head where it reared in the center of Ryan's crosshairs. Ryan watched the dark-furred beast topple with the impact of his bullet and roll across the slick ground, away from its elderly victim. Then Ryan felt a sinking feeling in the pit of his stomach as he saw the creature scramble around on the ground for a moment before, remarkably, pulling itself up, a bloody hole pulsing at the right-hand side of its head. The crazy mutie dog was still alive, shaking off the effect of the bullet's impact!

J.B. watched through his binoculars as he stood by Ryan's shoulder, and the one-eyed man heard his friend's incredulous mutter of "Dark night" as the canine stood. A few paces ahead of Ryan, Jak broke from the group, sprinting into the field in the direction of the settlement.

The wolf's long head turned and, for a moment, the dark-furred creature seemed to be peering down the scope of the rifle, its feral, yellow-eyed glare boring directly into Ryan's right eye as its black lips pulled back from blood-washed teeth.

Ryan didn't flinch. Settling himself into a stable, kneeling position on the water-slicked blacktop, he squeezed the trigger again, feeling the Steyr drum against his shoulder as it blasted another bullet at the beast. The slug whipped through the air just above the ground until it met with the monster, directly between its rage-filled eyes. Blood erupted from the creature's face in a red mist, mixing immediately with the drizzling rain.

Ryan didn't stay to try a third shot. He rolled the rifle from his shoulder and turned to instruct his companions. "Some kind of mutie dogs, mebbe wolves," he grunted, getting up and leading the way across the broken highway at a fast trot. The others followed, all except Jak, who had already disappeared into the fields, taking it upon himself to get closer to the action in his own way.

Taking deep breaths as he jogged at Ryan's side, J.B. pulled his M-4000 scattergun from beneath his coat. "Those bastards," he growled, "are gonna take a little something extra."

"Any ideas?" Ryan asked.

The Armorer turned to Ryan, loading the scattergun one-handed as they ran along the slippery, broken tarmac toward the settlement. "Keep your eye open," he instructed with a humorless grin.

As soon as the blastershots rang out, Jak's senses went to high alert. His keen mind was already considering options by the time Ryan blasted his first shot from the Steyr, and he had disappeared among the avenues of high wheat crop before Ryan had pumped his second shot into the monstrous creature.

Jak was closer now, his Colt Python clenched in his bone-white hand, as he weaved through the anemic-looking rows of wheat, making his way toward the shacks. The spindly wheat drooped, weighed down by the raindrops that had settled upon it.

It looked like a pack of wolves—at least a dozen, heavy creatures with muscular legs and lean, hungry bodies. Their fur was fecal brown with black streaks, which made them hard to keep track of in the ebbing daylight.

Even as Jak watched, another of the monstrous creatures sprang away from the pack, rushing at a dark-haired woman holding a baby in her arms. The woman jogged backward as the creature howled as it raced at her, arching its back menacingly. Then it leaped, and Jak watched—emotionless—as its jaws clamped around the woman's neck, rending a hunk of flesh from just below her throat in a dark stain of red. Then it shook its head, tossing her bleeding body aside, blood splashed across its sharp, daggerlike teeth. The woman flopped in a heap on the ground, letting go of her child as she collapsed, mud splattering all around her.

Sec men were scrambling about, trying to frighten away the beasts by firing into the air and firing at the near-impervious monsters themselves, but no one had time—or inclination—to assist in the woman's plight.

She wasn't dead yet however, that was what Jak knew. She wasn't dead, nor was the baby. So Jak ran, head down, arms pumping at his sides, feet striking the rain-soaked soil, rushing to get into a position where he might help her.

Emerging from the field, Jak scanned the scene ahead. The woman was lying still, just a few feet from the monstrous wolf as its jaws widened around the bundled baby that lay wailing on the ground, its pink blanket splattered with mud. The other people from the caravan and three sec men of the ville were running about, desperately fending off the rest of the pack, ducking behind the sheltering walls of the nearby buildings. Jak spotted the bloody remains of another sec man beside the pillbox sentry post, two of the gigantic wolves feasting on his entrails as he kicked and screamed.

Sprinting through the field, Jak turned his attention back to the woman with the baby. He raised the heavy revolver in his hand, sighting down the length of his arm and pulling the trigger as he ran. There was a boom, a flash and the smell of cordite hung in the air as his first shot blasted into the wolf's flank. Staggered, the foul creature turned its long-muzzled head to face Jak, the baby still clamped, drooping from its jaws.

Jak stopped, his boot heels sliding momentarily in the wet soil, and he reeled off three more shots at the wolf as it began to race toward him, its feet striking the earth in a drumming tarantella, its pace increasing with every step. The first .357 Magnum bullet merely clipped the monster's ear, but the second and third found their target, drilling into the beast's right eye, exploding the eyeball and powering onward into its brainpan.

The dark-furred monstrosity staggered a moment, its legs giving way under it like a ville drunk on free hooch night, before opening its jaws and dropping the child to the ground with a thump. The child rolled over and over, howling in shock, and the beast followed, its body sagging into a clump at Jak's feet. The albino teen warily watched the creature's legs spasm, kicking out in awful jerking movements as its dying form lay in the soaking, muddy earth.

Then he leaned close, placing the muzzle of the Colt flush against the side of the monster's head, and pulled the trigger once more. After that, the hulking thing stopped twitching.

Leaning down, Jak picked up the baby. The pink blanket that it was wrapped in was stained with mud and disheveled from the creature's attack, but the child seemed intact, its eyes screwing up as it wailed. Jak rocked the baby back and forth as he made his way toward the wounded woman who was lying in the mud.

WITH A FINAL BURST of speed, Ryan raced ahead of his companions, the scoped Steyr rifle slapping against his back where he'd slung it, his 9 mm SIG-Sauer P-226 blaster now clenched in his right fist. The Armorer raced to keep up with his longtime friend, sweeping the area with the Smith & Wesson scattergun as the pack of wolves lunged at the locals with the savagery of a raging river bursting its banks. As soon as the pair reached the half-buried pillbox, their weapons spit fire, blasting shot after shot into the crowd of mutie hounds. The dismembered sec man lay there, an explosion of blood where his torso had once been.

A little way back, the remaining companions took up static positions on the cracked blacktop. Doc wielded his deadly LeMat, an ancient percussion pistol that had been adapted to include an additional shotgun barrel capable of unleashing a single, devastating .63-caliber shot. To either side of the white-haired man, Krysty and Mildred were scanning the fields along the sights of their own handguns. Krysty favored a small revolver, a .38 Smith & Wesson Model 640, a stubby gun with plenty of stopping power. Across from her, Mildred had her double-action ZKR 551 targeting revolver in her hand.

Mildred's heart was pounding, and she steadied her grip by placing her free hand tightly beneath the wrist of her right hand. In her other life, a hundred years before, Mildred had been an Olympic free-shooting silver medalist, and she valued the need for a still mind and a steady aim when facing a target, even one as savage and unpredictable as the oversize wolves.

There was a risk that more of the pack were hidden in the crops surrounding them, and the two women were meticulous as they eyeballed the fields in the ebbing light.

"Incoming!" Doc shouted suddenly as four of the muscular beasts broke from the pack at the shacks and scampered across the rain-slickened blacktop toward them, their large paws slapping against the cracked tarmac.

Krysty and Mildred swung around, aiming their blasters at the oncoming creatures as Doc unleashed that cacophonous .63-caliber wad of shot. The result was dazzling in the twilight, a bright explosion of light and fury. Twenty feet ahead, the lead wolf was eviscerated, exploding in a burst of guts and flesh, its head crumbling to the ground as two uneven hunks of flesh and bone.

The other wolves slowed their pace for a moment, a tremulous whine coming from one of them, before racing once more toward Doc and the women. Mildred had their height now, and she snapped off a steady stream of bullets into the left-most member of the group, almost casually, such was her unhurried manner. To Doc's right, Krysty held her Smith & Wesson tightly, her finger softly stroking the silver trigger as she waited for the shot. In an instant, she squeezed the trigger, pumping it repeatedly and launching 9 mm bullet after 9 mm bullet at the wolf to the right of the group.

Both wolves dropped simultaneously, sinking to the ground as the streams of bullets snagged them. They were still alive, their bodies thrashing, but chunks of their heads and bodies were missing now, bloodied strips of bone visible in the one to the left where Mildred's attack had struck at the same point repeatedly.

The mutie in the center continued its charge, its head down, jaws slavering as it powered toward Doc and the companions, ignoring the harsh fate of its brethren. Its shotgun capacity exhausted, the LeMat in Doc's hand spit fire from its standard barrel, driving a shot into the creature as it sprang off the ground toward him. At the last possible instant, Doc simultaneously ducked and sidestepped, letting the heavy form of the wolf sail over his shoulder, so close that he could smell the foul stench of the flesh that had been caught between its blood-soaked teeth.

The beast landed heavily behind Doc and the companions, its feet hitting the slick tarmac with a thud before it scampered around to face the three friends once more, kicking up rainwater as it turned. Its dark lips peeled back and it loosed a low, angry snarl as it glared at the white-haired old man.

Krysty and Mildred began blasting shots at the monster, but it was already moving, its padded feet slapping loudly against the cracked and broken blacktop of the road.

"Dammit, it's too fast," Mildred spat. "I can't get a bead…"

To Doc's other side, Krysty muttered something in agreement, but he ignored both women and timed the creature's movements in his head. All he could do was keep out of the monster's way. The hulking mutie barreled at him, howling as it ran, and Doc spun on the heel of his boot, pulling the sweeping tails of his dark blue frock coat to one side like a matador taunting a charging bull.

"By the Three Kennedys!" Doc cried as the monstrous hound passed him, its meaty shoulder knocking into his leg as he struggled to step out of its way. It had been a glancing blow, barely a tap, but the speed and power of the wolf was such that it had crashed against Doc's leg with the impact of a jackhammer. Even as he cried out, the old man felt his balance waver and suddenly he went tumbling to the ground.

He looked up as he struggled to recover, and saw that the wolf was running in a tight circle, doubling back to lunge at him again with those fierce, snapping jaws. Mildred was trying to shoot the monster, but most of her shots were going wide because the hellish hound moved so fast. As well, those shots that did hit seemed to leave no impression on the enraged beast whatsoever. Still struggling on the ground, Doc saw that the nightmarish creature was almost upon him.

But the dark-furred beast never reached the old man's fallen form. A thin, pale hand lunged out and grabbed the wolf by the ankle of its hind leg. The beast yelped in surprise as it was pulled back, its leap abruptly curtailed.

Everything was moving so fast that Doc had to recover his thoughts before he could process what it was he saw. Krysty had the hulking wolf by the ankle of its right hind leg and, as it snapped its jaws at her, her other hand whipped out and slapped it across its snout. Even with the sound of drizzle washing against the road, Doc heard the sharp noise of cracking bone when Krysty's hand hit, and the monstrous wolf whined. Its jaw was misaligned now, Doc saw, and wouldn't close properly on its hinge. The wolf's putrescent yellow eyes were wide with terror.

As Doc and Mildred watched, Krysty swung the dark-furred form down on the ground, letting go of its ankle as its spine cracked against the hard tarmac. The beast shuddered on the ground for a moment, struggling to stand. Krysty swung her leg back and punted the hound in the face with the pointed toe of her silver-capped boot. Doc felt his breath catch in his throat as the creature's face—remarkably—caved in with the tremendous force behind that kick.

And then Krysty took two wavering steps before sinking to her knees before the bloody carcass of the mutie wolf. She had used the power of Gaia, the Earth Mother, Doc knew, a remarkable spring of power that came from the earth itself, infusing Krysty with incredible, superhuman strength for a very short period of time. The Gaia power was brief, a firework burst of energy, and, as its glow faded, it left Krysty as weak as a kitten.

Mildred was already crouching beside Krysty, concerned, checking that the remarkable redhead was all right. Beside them, the huge wolf lay still, its once proud snout now a concave mess of shattered bone.

"Thank you kindly, my dear Krysty," Doc managed to say as he struggled back to his feet and retrieved his lion's-head cane from the ground.

THE SCATTERGUN BOOMED as J.B. launched another blast at the wolf pack that had rounded on the little clutch of buildings. The pack was wary now, having lost several of its brethren to these lethal newcomers. A little way behind J.B., Ryan skipped backward, his SIG-Sauer blaster held before him, nearing the struggling group that had emerged from the caravan of mismatched wags.

"Everyone okay?" Ryan asked in his authoritative voice, peering over his shoulder for a snap second before turning back to the circling mutie hounds.

"We have three wounded," someone—a young man's voice—explained from over Ryan's shoulder.

Jak's familiar voice called from behind Ryan then, providing a little more information in his strangely abrupt manner of speech. "Baby and Ma, not look good."

"Just get everyone inside, Jak," Ryan commanded, not taking his eyes off the feral creatures before him. "They'll be safe there."

As he spoke, one of the wolves made a break for it, lurching forward on its wide paws, picking up speed as it rushed at the retreating group of humans. J.B. leaned over his M-4000, firing three thunderous shots at the monstrosity while Ryan unleashed a flurry of bullets at its feet, as though daring it to come closer.

The wolf turned, scampering back to the pack, its tail low. Watching the creature scramble away, a tight smile on his lips, J.B. held his ground a moment before taking a single pace forward and blasting another shot from the shotgun. The blast ripped into the creature's back, knocking it over itself as the explosion rocked its hind legs. It struggled a moment, then got back on its feet and continued to run away, limping a little as it disappeared

among the soaked shafts of wheat. The wolves around
it watched, their heads low, snarling between clenched
teeth before finally turning tail and running.

J.B. and Ryan blasted off several more rounds, accompanied by Jak, who now stood at Ryan's side. They
watched as the creatures weaved through the high fields
of wheat and disappeared from sight.

"Come back, reckon?" Jak asked, his heavy revolver
still trained on the field where the monsters had run.

"Bastard sure of it," Ryan growled. "We should find
some cover of our own."

Ryan turned to peer around them, giving the little
group of shacks the once-over before turning his gaze
down the road to where his other companions were hurrying to join them. Doc had loaned his ebony walking
cane to Krysty, who was now using it to aid her progress
on weakened legs. Mildred brought up the rear of the
group, her ZKR 551 target pistol poised in a straight-
armed grip.

"Krysty?" Ryan asked, jogging over to be at her side.
"What happened?"

Krysty looked up at him between sweat-and-rain-
dampened strands of her red hair, and a wonderfully
innocent smile crossed her face. "Just a little bump and
grind, lover, nothing to get jealous over," she assured
him with good humor, but her voice sounded weak.

Ryan shot the others a meaningful look and Doc took
that as his cue.

"She called on Gaia," Doc said. "Saved this very
grateful man's life in so doing."

Ryan nodded. He knew the Gaia power affected his
most precious companion. He knew, too, that she would
come back around again, back to full health in a little

while. It just took time, and right now, standing out here waiting for another mutie wolf attack was about the least smart way to spend it. "Let's everyone get inside," he instructed, putting his arm around Krysty's waist to help her across the road to the nearest wooden building.

A wooden fence stood waist-high with a gate that caught on a simple latch, the kind used to stop farm animals getting out or wildlife—like mutie wolves— getting in. Beyond that, a two-story shack waited, and piano music drifted from inside.

A bewildered goat was tethered outside the rotting wooden shack, soaked through and bleating miserably in the downpour. The words *Traid n Post* had been carved into a sign beside the building's front door with a smaller sign below that read *Good Eaten*. Music drifted from inside as someone pounded at the keys of a badly tuned piano.

The goat bleated as the six travelers made their way past it to go inside, and Jak stopped to marvel at the sorry-looking creature. He felt an affinity for the animal as it looked up at him hopefully, its satanic red eyes matching Jak's own, white fur and tuft of beard in imitation of Jak's colorless skin and pure white stubble. The goat rested on a square of rough plywood, with two wheels on an axle running beneath it. Its hind legs had been removed high on the shoulder, not even the hint of a stump remaining, and Jak could see the jagged black thread lining the animal's white fur where the amputations had been sewn closed. As Jak looked at the beast, its fur matted with the awful drizzle that was still lancing at the ground with needle-thin precision, they heard a bleating and two more goats, a nanny and her kid, came prancing around the corner. Each of them wore a collar with a short length of rope tying one to the other, preventing them from moving comfortably without butting into each other. All three sorry creatures looked hungry.

The first animal bleated again, shaking its head from side to side as Jak turned away and followed his companions into the building. The goat scrabbled forward with its remaining forelegs, the rest of its body following on the wheeled base, until the tether line pulled taut at its neck and halted its progress. It let out another sorrowful bleat as it watched this kindred spirit disappear through the dirty, burn-streaked door.

Jak smelled the air as he entered the run-down shack and a smile touched his pale lips as he scented rich cooking spices.

The room that the companions had entered was roughly twenty feet square, encompassing the full length of the building. To one side, on a raised platform, stood the badly tuned piano, played by an attractive, dark-haired woman wearing a low-cut dress and a single incisor tooth in her open mouth.

Two young women, scantily clad and with collars at their necks, danced lethargically to the clanking tune of the piano, entertainment for the patrons of this trading post. The women, like the goats outside, were tethered together by their collars so that they could go no farther than two feet apart. Also, much like the goats, they looked hungry. Much like the dancers, the patrons seemed to be mostly disinterested, more concerned with feeding their own bellies than watching this lackluster floor show.

Tables were dotted across the room, twelve in all, and customers from all walks, young and old, sat at them, eating and drinking, passing the evening. These were traveling men, like Ryan and his companions, just passing through on their way to pastures new. The group from the caravan had taken up a couple of larger tables to the right of the room; twelve of them in total, plus the baby. They were tending to the wounded mother and her child, bandaging the old man's bloodied arm. The mother had a wadded bandage across her throat now, but apart from looking pale with shock, she seemed to be all right. With Ryan busy checking on Krysty's well-being, J.B. touched his index finger to the brim of his hat in acknowledgment as he passed the group. One of them, a man in his fifties with a shaved scalp and peppering of white stubble on his chin, nodded and offered a few words of thanks, but he was drowned out by the poorly tuned piano, and, regardless, J.B. hadn't bothered to stop and listen. The man with the shaved scalp continued to watch the companions as they made their way toward the main service counter.

A large mirror lined the far wall, overlooking a long countertop that served as bar and trading area. The counter was crowded with things for sale—fur pelts and ammunition, religious symbols and homemade lucky mascots, a writhing box of maggots that was labeled as "live bayt"—all of it presided over by a fat man sitting on a high stool, picking at his teeth with a splinter of wood. The whole lot probably didn't amount to much of value, even out here in the middle of nowhere, Tennessee, and it was obvious that the trading post's main trade was in food, drink and the scrawny excuse for gaudies that were currently dancing for the passing trade.

In one corner of the room, at the end of the long countertop, stood a lean-looking, skinny girl of maybe fourteen, stirring a big metal ladle in a steaming pot as big as a bathtub. She wore her dark hair long, and her arms were bare where the burgundy sleeveless T-shirt she wore didn't cover them. Scars were pitted down her arms, from burns and perhaps blades, it was hard to tell. An open fire cracked and spit beneath the huge pot, casting its fractious, flickering light across the room.

"Well." Doc clapped his hands together, looking at his companions with a bright smile on his face. "Who's up for some dinner?" He turned to Krysty, thinking that, after drawing upon the Gaia power, she would be ravenous.

The companions looked at Doc as he stroked his chin unconsciously and his eyes lost focus, seemingly in deep thought. "Though with our journeying of late, mayhap it is lunch. It can get so frightfully confusing when one is ever hopping about from place to place."

Mildred stepped over and took the older man's elbow, smiling up into his clear, blue eyes. "Let's break our fast, you old fool," she said affectionately.

Doc nodded, smiling agreeably. "Breakfast it is," he announced before leading the way over to the countertop where the fat man continued picking at his teeth.

As Doc, Mildred and Jak stepped up to the counter, the remaining companions headed for an empty table on the farthest side of the room from the door. The table allowed a good view of the whole room, and J.B. pushed one of the wooden chairs far back until it was pressed against the wall. Once it was, he sat down on it, the brim of his fedora low as he silently scanned the room. Exhausted, Krysty wearily sat beside him while

Ryan took a seat facing him, his chair at an angle so that he might turn easily if he was required to face the room.

The patrons seemed a mismatched bunch. Some were quite clearly local farmhands, others just traveling through. There was a sense of hostility, all too familiar in the Deathlands, but it came from the raucous conversations and lewd floor show more than any specific antagonism between parties.

"Lots of ordnance in here," J.B. said quietly, "not all of it on show."

Beside the Armorer, Krysty was beginning to regain her usual healthy appearance, the color returning to her cheeks. Her green eyes were sifting through the weapons she could see tucked beneath the tabletops. "Nothing out of the ordinary," she decided, telling of her findings in a low mutter. "Guy left of the door looks like he has a flamer maybe."

"No," J.B. corrected her. "That's a crop duster, sprays pesticide."

With his back to the room, Ryan glanced up at the mirror behind the bar, searching for the man in question. "Would it work as a weapon?" he queried.

"Depends what's in it," the Armorer admitted. "A face full of bug spray could blind you, burn the skin off your face, or worse."

"What's worse than that?" Krysty asked, furrowing her brow.

"Put some industrial-strength shit in there, and you'd be tripping the rest of your short life, see the flesh peeling from your skull whether it was really happening or not," J.B. explained disinterestedly, his eyes still scanning the room.

At the counter, Doc was addressing the proprietor in his rich, sonorous voice. "Your sign outside promises good eating, sir," he began, "perhaps you would care to explain what delicacies you have to offer to a band of weary—and hungry—travelers?"

Behind the counter the round man's tiny eyes widened at Doc's elaborately phrased request, and he worked his spike of wood with his fingers, pulling something from his teeth, before he spoke. "We got meat," he said, gesturing to the alcove where the teenage girl was stirring at her large pot, "fresh today and stewed up all nice and tender. That do you an' your trav'lin' buds?"

Doc glanced across to the girl in the alcove and nodded, scenting the air in an effort to determine what meat it was. "It most assuredly would," Doc told the barman. "We would like six bowls of your finest stew. It smells delicious," he added, turning to check for the approval of his companions.

The overweight barman went over to talk to the rake-thin girl at the bathtub-size cooking pot, and when Doc turned back, he was returning to his post as the girl began reaching for bowls and wiping each with a cloth before placing them in turn on the table beside her. As Doc checked through his pockets for some jack or spare ammunition that might serve as currency—nothing was more valuable in the Deathlands than a live round—the bartender gestured for him to come closer. Leaning forward, Doc bent close to the bar, looking at the bartender curiously as the fat man spoke.

"What's up with whitey there?" the barman asked, not looking at Jak Lauren. "He a mutie? We don't much like serving their kind in here. Not for me, y'understand, just that the locals get sore about it and it's liable to bring trouble."

"No," Doc said, shaking his head, "Jak's as normal as you or I." Doc considered explaining the nature of albinism but thought better of it. "He just stays out of the sun, that's all," Doc finished somewhat lamely.

Which wasn't to say that they didn't have a mutie among their band. Few people picked up on Krysty's mutations, despite her prehensile hair being on show for all the world to see. Doc smiled to himself. In two hundred years, humankind hadn't changed so very much. People would look past a lot if you were that rare and wonderful combination of facets—tall, striking and a woman.

The man behind the counter told Doc to find a table and his daughter would bring the meals over. As the three companions shuffled past the group from the caravan, one of its crew called to them. The companions turned, and Mildred accompanied Doc as he strode a few paces to join the group. Wary, Jak watched for a moment before slipping through the other patrons and making his way across the room to join Ryan's table.

A sturdy-looking man addressed Doc as he walked closer, standing up to grasp his hand in a firm, friendly grip. The man looked to be in his fifties, with thinning white hair atop a tanned face and a patchy white beard on his chin. He looked to Doc like a farmer, a man used to working outside.

"You were out there with those what saved us," the man said, smiling gratefully. "You an' your friends took some risks there, and we're mighty grateful."

"You are very welcome," Doc said agreeably, as he disengaged his hand from the man's firm grip.

"My name's Jeremiah. Jeremiah Croxton," the man told Doc, gesturing to a free seat at the table. "Why don't you come sit with us, Mr....?"

"Tanner," Doc replied automatically.

"Mr. Tanner," Croxton continued, looking around the shack for other seats. "We would be most honored, if you would come eat with us, both you an' your friends." As he spoke, several of his party stood, shuffling their seats along to make more room at their tables.

Doc smiled again. "That is very gracious of you, Mr. Croxton, but we would not wish to intrude."

"'Intrude' nonsense," the old farmer dismissed with a hearty laugh. "I thinks we may just have us something to interest you, Mr. Tanner. I couldn't speak for your friends there, but I'm pretty sure you'll be glad you loaned me your ear for the two minutes or so it will take."

Intrigued, Doc looked across the table at its inhabitants as Croxton introduced himself to Mildred. The group seemed normal enough, mostly older folks, tired-looking with that hard, leathery skin that suggested long hours toiling in the sun. There were two youngsters among them, besides the wounded baby. One was a girl, perhaps seventeen or eighteen, sylphlike with just a little puppy fat on her pretty face, long, ash-blond hair cascading down her back. Across from her, his eyes on the door, sat a young man of perhaps twenty, hair the same color as the girl's and with a light dusting of beard on his chin. He seemed hungry to Doc, predatory eyes scanning the room and the door, a bow and quiver of arrows resting at his feet. The next in age was the baby's mother, who appeared to be perhaps forty years old—it was hard to tell as she was clearly in shock from the attack. A dark-skinned woman with graying hair was gently cleaning the wound at the woman's neck using a rag dipped in a bowl of water. The water held the pinkish tint of diluted blood.

"Well," Doc decided, "perhaps just for a moment."

Beside him, Mildred touched Doc's sleeve to get his attention. "Doc, I think our dinner is almost ready," she said, giving him a significant look. Mildred's time in the Deathlands had taught her that strangers, however kindly they appeared, were almost never to be trusted.

His back to the farmer and his people, Doc gave a sharp nod and mouthed, "It's fine," before he spoke aloud. "Perhaps you would alert me when our waitress arrives with our meals, Mildred," he said.

Mildred rolled her eyes, hoping that Doc knew what he was getting involved in, then walked across the hard wooden floor to speak to Ryan and wait for the serving girl.

As Mildred strode away, a chair next to Croxton was vacated at the table and Doc was invited to join the group. The empty chair was also beside the blonde girl, and Doc offered her a polite bow, little more than a courteous nod, before he sat. She giggled just a little, covering her mouth with her hand as a blush rose across her cheeks. The girl smelled sweet and musky, delicately scented with woman's perfume. Her youth and long blond hair reminded Doc of another girl, one he had been close to not so very long ago. A treasure of a girl called Lori Quint, who, like everything else in the Deathlands, had been tainted and spoiled and ultimately killed by the unforgiving world around her. Doc pushed Lori's bittersweet memory aside, as he realized that the bearded farmer, Croxton, was talking.

"The reason I asked that you join us, Mr. Tanner," Croxton was saying, "is that I do believe we have a little proposition that may be of interest to you."

Doc inclined his head, inviting the man to continue.

"You see Daisy there," Croxton said, indicating the fresh-faced, blond-haired teenager. "Pretty as a picture, am I right?"

Nodding, Doc began to feel slightly uncomfortable, concerned that he had come across yet another exercise in an old man whoring his children. "I would say so, certainly," he replied, amiably enough.

"Would you like to guess how old she is?" Croxton asked, his blue eyes shining, his tongue running across his teeth as a playful smile appeared on his lips. It was the smile of a gambler, someone used to fooling people, and to judging them from their body language.

Shaking his head, Doc pushed his chair back and began to stand. "I am sorry," he said, "I am really not interested in what I believe you are offering, kind though that offer most certainly is…"

The girl—Daisy—spoke, her voice rich like treacle. "I'm seventy-an'-six, Mr. Tanner," she said.

Caught halfway between standing and sitting, Doc almost fell over. He reached out and grasped the side of the table before him as his chair crashed to the floor.

"Seventy—" Doc began, the words choked in his suddenly dry throat.

Daisy shrugged her bony, girl's shoulders and blew Doc a kiss. "I look good on it though, don't I, sir?"

Chapter Three

"Do you remember what it was like to be young, Mr. Tanner?" Daisy asked, as Doc regained his composure and sank into the chair beside her.

Her voice was low, intimate, with a sweet, rich quality like molasses. Her eyes, a shade of blue so light they appeared almost white, peered at him, the tiniest creases appearing at their edges where she smiled. Her mouth was smiling, too. Her wide, flawless teeth were a dazzling shade of white even in the indifferent, gloomy light. Looking at that friendly, inquisitive smile, Doc felt himself drawn to the girl. There was an intimacy here, created by her soft voice, by the half-light of the room, by the wall of noise all around them as other people continued with their meals and conversations, oblivious to the two of them sitting there discussing the nature of youth.

Realizing that the pretty young girl was waiting for him to answer, Doc nodded slowly. "Oh, I remember," he intoned. "Long summer days, running simply because you could, running until you fell down with giddiness."

Doc's head was still nodding, a smile on his lips, as he looked back at Daisy. He would guess that she was perhaps sixteen or seventeen. Her skin was smooth, crinkles forming and disappearing as she flashed that wonderful, dazzling smile at him, the flesh on her cheeks a ruddy pink in the flickering light from the cook's fire. He looked at her more closely, trying to see the old woman that she had once been. Her face was round, as though she was predisposed to smile for any occasion, a little chubby around the rounded cheeks, dimples appearing as she smiled. She was pretty, but not beautiful. It was the prettiness of youth, Doc realized, of innocence, the way that only a child could be pretty.

Daisy's hair was long, falling past her shoulders and ending halfway down her back, a cascading wave of silvery-blond. It was fine hair, wispy and prone to tangle, and she would shift the tangled bangs out of her eyes as she spoke, an unconscious movement, long practiced and harboring no sign of irritation.

As Doc watched the girl, Daisy continued to smile at him. "That's not it," she said in that slow drawl that didn't seem to quite form the hard edges of the words, instead mushing them into a flowing sound, like a song. "That's—what you are talking about—that's what you *think* youth was, because you don't really remember it. You think it was this thing that was all about being a kid, but that's nothing like what being young is. That thing that you described, that's what I thought it was before I was—" She stopped, her eyes wandering as though searching for the rest of the sentence.

"Changed?" Doc suggested after a moment's pause.

"Youngered," the girl responded. "Like the way I used to get older, so I guess I got youngered by the pool. That make sense to you, Mr. Tanner? You seem like a man o' learning, is all."

Slowly, Doc nodded once again, intrigued despite himself. "Youngered it is," he replied with a smile.

Daisy glanced up for a moment, and Doc followed her glance. She was looking across the table to where Jeremiah Croxton, the aging farmer, sat. He had spread out an old, dog-eared map across the table and was deep in conversation with the person sitting to his right, another outdoors type. When he saw Daisy and Doc looking at him he smiled in acknowledgment before getting back to his cartographical calculations.

When Doc turned back to her, the blonde girl was holding her hand up before his face, palm toward him, fingers upthrust. "Look at my hand, Mr. Tanner," she said. "Go 'head, it won't bite none."

Doc peered at the girl's pink hand, wondering at the strange request.

"You can touch it, if you want," she told him encouragingly.

Doc looked at her quizzically. "What am I looking at?" he asked.

"The scars," Daisy told him, her lips upturned in a smile. "There's no scars there, not now. I worked the fields for almost sixty years with my father and then with my better half, the lazy good-for-nothing. But the scars have healed, they disappeared. You wouldn't know that they was ever there."

"No, you wouldn't," Doc agreed, wondering what else he could say, suddenly aware of his own hands, old and wrinkled.

"That's being young, Mr. Tanner," Daisy said with certainty. "No scars, no shooting pains deep in your bones fucking with you when the first frost comes. Not running about in the summer, that's just some—I dunno—song words, troubadour crap. *This* is being young, Mr. Tanner—" she flexed her fingers before him "—*this* right here."

Doc found his eyes following Daisy's slim hand as she reached for the glass that sat before her on the wooden table. Behind her, and all around, the other members of the wag train were laughing, drinking and eating, watching the tawdry floor show, enjoying themselves.

Daisy took a drink from her glass and Doc was amused to see that it was a swig, a gulp, not the delicate ladylike operation that one might associate with an adult. "You taste this?" Daisy asked, holding the glass out to Doc.

Doc shook his head, waving away the proffered glass. "That's very kind," he stated, "but I should really be getting back to my friends."

"You should taste it," Daisy encouraged. "Just a little nip. Won't hurt you none. It hasn't chilled me," she said.

Doc took the glass from her and sniffed at its contents. It smelled of sweetness, some blended fruit concoction. Warily, he held the rim of the glass against his lips and tipped it until a tiny dribble of liquid washed past his teeth and into his mouth. "It's nice," he assured Daisy, passing the glass back into her waiting hand. "What is it?"

Daisy's baby blue eyes were watching him intensely, and the fire of challenge colored her words. "You tell me," she drawled.

"It tastes like…" Doc began thoughtfully. "I'm not sure. Perhaps cantaloupe? Cantaloupe and some spices perhaps?"

As though performing a show, Daisy placed the glass against her lips, all the while watching Doc, her eyes locked on his. Then she closed her eyes and tipped her head back to drink, her neck arching into a beautiful, pale curve of flawless flesh. As Doc watched, Daisy drank the whole glass, her throat bobbing just a little as she swallowed the last of it. Finally, her eyes popped open—still locked on Doc's—and, licking her lips, she placed the empty glass back down on the table. "Cantaloupe, raspberry, a hint of berry to add tartness," she told Doc, "and the spice you could taste—that's the tiniest fleck of cinnamon."

Doc looked mystified by this performance. "A tasty concoction," he assured her when it seemed that she was waiting for him to say something.

Daisy leaned forward, bringing her lips close to Doc's, speaking low despite the hubbub all around them. "That's what I tasted, Mr. Tanner," she whispered. "I could tell each of those wonderful tastes in my mouth, savor every last drop. And that's what it is to be young."

The girl pulled away, and turned to speak to the person on the other side of her—a man in his midfifties with the haunted expression of a professional chiller. "You mind, Charlie?" she asked. After a moment, the man—Charlie—got up and made his way to the bar counter to order more drinks.

When Daisy turned back to Doc, who was still puzzling over the meaning of her display, she spoke in a less intense manner, friendly and buoyant once more. "You get old," she explained, "and things die. Parts of you die. Your taste, your hearin', your eyes, your sense of smell. You lose things, senses, and you don't never even notice. Because it takes such a long time to happen, you don't never see it till it's too late. You go back, you get youngered and it all comes back, Mr. Tanner. It all comes back and you wonder how you ever managed without it, like some cripple who can't even dress himself. Those stories about being superhuman—they're not stories. That's what it is to be young. The longer you live, the less alive you are."

Doc looked at her, this simple farming girl, old yet young, wondering at her words, marveling at them.

"Giddy," Daisy continued, "running in the summer until you fall down—that's not it at all. You just got too old to remember what it's really like, is all."

Doc nodded thoughtfully. "I remember now," he said, "or, at least, I begin to."

He sat there, lost in his thoughts as Daisy wrapped her delicate fingers over the new glass of fruit punch that had been brought over by the man with the haunted expression. Jeremiah Croxton leaned across to Doc, tapping him gently just below the shoulder. Doc glanced up, and seemed surprised for a second to find himself looking at the man.

"Mr. Tanner," Croxton began, "I would like to discuss a proposition that I feel would be of mutual benefit."

Turning to the old farmer, Doc listened intently to the man's words.

Chapter Four

J.B. peered over Ryan's shoulder at the pair of wide tables across the other side of the room, where Doc was held in discussion with the people from the convoy. "What the heck is Doc up to?" he muttered, shaking his head in disbelief.

Mildred was just walking across the room to join Ryan and the others, her brow wrinkled with concern. Ryan peered up as her shadow fell across their table. "What's happening, Mildred?" he asked.

Still standing, Mildred leaned close, keeping her voice low so as not to be overheard, even in spite of the clashing chords emanating from the piano. "Those travelers we helped out invited us all over to offer a few words of gratitude," she explained.

"Tell them thanks," J.B. growled.

"The spokesman," Mildred continued, "that old boy you see there, he says he has a proposition that may interest Doc. Perhaps the rest of us, too."

Ryan looked nonplussed. "Which is?"

"Search me," Mildred said lightly. "Seems he wanted to run it by Doc first."

"What's your impression?" Ryan asked.

"They seem normal enough," Mildred stated. "Mostly old folks. Couple of young ones, too, nothing out of the ordinary."

Krysty was scanning the strangers from her position against the wall. "They're only lightly armed," she observed. "Real lightly for traveling folks. Kind of stupe."

Sitting beside Ryan, Jak nodded. "Not travelers," he said. "Farmers. Smell it."

J.B. nodded once in agreement. "Jak's right, those folks don't look much used to hard road trekkin'. Probably why they got caught short against those mutie hounds outside."

Shortly after Mildred had taken her seat, Doc strode to the table, followed by the thin serving girl with the burn scars along her arms. The girl was balancing four steaming bowls on a tray, and she smiled and shook her head as Doc kindly offered her a hand.

The old man took his seat as the girl set the bowls in front of the companions and began placing mismatched cutlery before them. "I'll be back in a second with the others," she drawled, curtsying briefly before she went back to her cooking alcove.

As the serving girl walked away, Doc related his conversation with Jeremiah Croxton to the companions. "They were all tremendously impressed with—and grateful for—our assistance outside," Doc explained, "and Mr. Croxton has asked if we might avail our services for the duration of their journey."

"As sec men, you mean?" Ryan asked.

Doc nodded, idly brushing a hand through his white hair as the serving girl returned with two more bowls of the aromatic stew. "Thank you, my dear," Doc said to the girl. The bowls steamed as she set them down on the table before Doc and Ryan.

"If ya's need anything else," the girl said, "j'st holler an' I'll come right over."

Jak was already working a spoon through the thick gravy in his bowl, and he looked up at the girl with his unearthly smile. "Good," he said. "Meat's good."

Disconcerted, the girl thanked Jak and the others before scurrying back to her nook at the side of the bar. She stood there, her eyes on the strange young albino, watching him warily.

"What sort of meat is it, Jak?" Krysty asked as she pushed the contents of the bowl before her around with a fork.

Jak chewed for a moment, working the spiced meat around his palate. "Goat," he decided, grinning contentedly.

Once the companions had started on their own bowls of stew, Doc continued relating Croxton's request. "They have got a two-day journey ahead of them," he said, "or so Croxton thinks. They have been on the road over a day, hard going, too, I should think."

Ryan peered up from the contents of his bowl. "Where are they heading, Doc? Did he say?"

"A little ville called Baby," Doc said.

Ryan's eye flicked across the table to J.B. the custodian of the group's maps and navigation equipment. "Heard of it, J.B.?"

After a few seconds thought, the Armorer shook his head. "Name like that would surely stick in my craw tighter than dynamite in a pesthole," he said. "New villes are popping up and falling down all the time, Ryan. Just 'cause I haven't heard of it doesn't mean it's not there."

Ryan nodded. "I didn't say it wasn't," he agreed, before turning his attention back to Doc as the old man picked his way carefully through his stew with a bent-handled spoon. "So what's your angle on this, Doc? They putting up a lot of jack?"

"No," Doc said between mouthfuls, shaking his head. "Something far more interesting than money. They're promising youth."

"Youth?" The word came from three people at once, as Mildred, Krysty and Ryan all uttered it with incredulity.

"The pretty little blonde girl over on the left-hand side of the table there…?" Doc said, looking up but not pointing. "Says she's seventy-six years old. Came out of Babyville to spread the word. Seems they have the secret of eternal youth there."

J.B. barked a short laugh at Doc's words. "And you believe this horseshit they're feeding you?"

Doc looked at the glistening sheen of grease on top his half-full bowl before slowly replying in a considered, deliberate voice. "I neither believe nor disbelieve, my dear John Barrymore. My natural inclination is to disbelieve, of course, for such a thing would seem fanciful, not to say impossible. But the old fables are full of youth-giving potions, immortals and the rejuvenating effects of such-and-such mixture of herbs. The fountain of eternal youth may very well be a story, but might we suppose that it could have been rooted in fact?"

J.B. shook his head in disbelief, while Ryan and the others sat considering the white-haired man's words.

Krysty was the one who finally broke the silence. "We have seen some mighty strange things in our travels," she said, "most of them not a blamed bit of use to anyone. Who's to say that Doc's youth fountain doesn't actually exist somewhere?"

"It's impossible," J.B. observed. "Doc just said so himself."

"Implausible, perhaps," Mildred said, "but not impossible. Back in the days before skydark there were drugs, antiaging creams, hormonal injections, numerous ways to make people look and feel younger. In my day there was a lot of emphasis on appearance and youth."

"But a girl," Ryan said in a low voice, "of, what, sixteen saying she's really seventy-something?"

"There are chemicals in the atmosphere," Mildred considered, warming to her subject, "that can strip a man to his bones in a shower of rain. You don't realize how upside down the world is right now, because it's all you've ever known, Ryan. And Krysty's right. We have seen an awful lot that is more unbelievable than what Doc's friends have described to him."

A moment passed in silence as the companions considered Mildred's words. She was talking about a world they had never known, a world they could scarcely imagine. But they knew that she was also an educated woman, a trained doctor with a mind that was attuned to scientific inquiry, not flights of fantasy.

Pushing thick gravy around her bowl, Krysty spoke thoughtfully, her words slow and deliberate. "There are plants, too, that make people healthier," she said. Krysty's knowledge concerning the properties of plant life was almost encyclopedic, although she rarely had cause to call upon it. "Isn't being healthier really just another type of being young?" she asked.

Several of the group around the table muttered their agreement, but to Ryan's ears Krysty sounded like she was trying to convince herself; he knew her so well.

Doc looked earnestly around the table at his companions. "The usual fee for entering Baby is much of an individual's worldly possessions, I am told. If we were to go there in the capacity of bodyguards, Mr. Croxton and his people would vouch for us, perhaps allowing us indulgence in the operation for free."

"Which would still be too damn high a price," J.B. grumbled.

Doc turned to the Armorer, rising anger turning his face a darker shade. "Might I enquire, John Barrymore, how old you are? Might I ask how long you have lived in that body?"

J.B. looked at Doc, taken aback by his question.

"Is it perhaps forty years, mayhap forty-five?" Doc continued. "Forty years of bones forming and hair and nails growing, of skin tautening and cracking and repairing? Of eyes growing slowly dim behind your spectacle frames?"

J.B. looked emotionless as he replied, "Hurry up and pull the trigger, Doc."

"What you see before you, my friend," Doc said, "is a thirty-year-old man, give or take a few summers. Yet, I am stuck in this creaking set of limbs because some morally repugnant scientific scrutinizer decided it would be beneficial to shunt a man through time, to shunt *me* through time. I lost my dear wife and my two sweet children, and everything that meant anything to me, and those wounds, I assure you, will never heal. But this body, this old fool I see every time I look in the mirror to shave his white whiskers from his wrinkled chin—this is something I was cursed with to make that cruel joke all the more bitter."

"Doc—" Ryan began, but the old man held up his hand to halt him.

"Allow an old man time to gather his thoughts, if you would," Doc said, a bitter edge to his voice. "Oftentimes have I dreamed of returning to my home, to hold my dear Emily, Rachel and Jolyon once more, and every time I have been there in my mind's eye, it has been in this wretched old man's frame. It has been something I have resigned myself to, something I believed could never be changed.

"This opportunity," Doc continued, "however slight it may be, is a fleeting glimpse of something I thought I could never have. Something that was stolen from me most cruelly."

J.B. leaned close, looking Doc square in the eye. "And if it turns out to be a bust, do I get to say 'I told you so'?" he asked, the trace of a smile forming at the corners of his mouth.

Doc felt his rage subside and he glanced at his other companions before meeting J.B.'s fierce stare once more. "If it turns out to be a bust, John Barrymore, I will royally insist that you do."

Ryan turned, casting his single-eyed gaze from one companion to the next, making sure that everyone had said their piece. Finally he turned his blue-eyed gaze on Doc and offered him a single, curt nod. "Then it's decided," he said.

For several more minutes, the companions ate the goat stew, joking a little to ease their own tension, reminiscing over old victories and occasional, temporary defeats. Once they had finished their meal, Ryan pushed his chair back from the table and, with the lanky Doc at his side, strode across the wide room to where the caravaners were enjoying drinks and the hospitality of the overweight bartender. Ryan left his lengthy Steyr rifle with Krysty, and she placed it beneath the table, out of sight. The two chained girls were still dancing on stage, swaying to the sound of the piano like somnambulists. Ryan ignored them as he walked past, his one keen eye focused on the group of travelers as they continued their raucous discussions. Doc looked at the dancing girls, feeling a sick sense at the pit of his just-fed stomach at the way their ribs pushed against the skin beneath their nearly naked breasts.

The old man that Doc had pointed out as their leader, Jeremiah Croxton, was talking to a couple who had entered the building with a younger man—they were at least sixty, and he had almost certainly seen his fortieth birthday. The barman, who had been speaking with the group of travelers, looked up at the newcomers' approach. A moment later, once the other three had left, Ryan leaned down to speak with Jeremiah Croxton.

"I hear you're in the market for some traveling sec for the next two days," Ryan began. His glance flicked around the table, taking in the dozen patrons that sat there. The youngish woman who had been attacked had wrapped a tourniquet around her throat, and looked to be numbing any lasting pain with a pathological intake of alcohol. Her baby was snuffling in sleep, doubtless having imbibed a nip of brandy to keep it from waking. The older man who had been attacked by another wolf had a bloody gash across his arm, but, cleaned up, the wound looked superficial and he seemed to be having fun in a lively conversation with a middle-aged gaudy slut wearing a none-too-flattering dress with a low neckline that she seemed to be struggling to artistically flail out of. A couple of the others at the table had rudimentary weapons, a remade revolver here, a single-shot rifle there. They appeared companionable enough, seemed happy to enjoy the delights that the trading post offered with food, drink and, for one bald and wrinkled old man at the far side of the table, the company of the awkward girl who had served Ryan and his companions dinner. The girl looked uncomfortable as she endured the old man's attention.

Croxton looked at Ryan for a moment before he spoke, assessing the man's wide-shouldered frame, the wide chest beneath his shirt. "Yes, that we are," he said finally. "Our little escapade with the wolf pack out there was a surprise, an' I ain't so sure we'd have coped without your timely intervention. Showed us that mebbe we could do with a little extra muscle, if you are interested in that line of work."

Ryan nodded. "Name's Ryan," he said as Jeremiah shook his proffered hand, "and you've met Doc here already."

"That I have," the old farmer acknowledged, looking down at Ryan's hand as he released his grip. "You have a few old scars showing there, if I may be so bold," he said.

"That comes with the territory," Ryan said. "When do you plan on setting off?"

"We'll bed down here," Croxton said in his warm, friendly voice, "and look to move out a little after dawn. Will that suit you and your crew?"

"We'll be ready," Ryan assured him. "We'll meet you by your wags at dawn."

"Might be one extra from what you saw," Croxton added. "Been spreading the word a little."

Ryan nodded. "We can protect six if need be. Beyond that, we may need to consider adopting another strategy before we set off."

The farmer thanked Ryan and Doc, and the two companions made their way back to their table.

"First impression?" J.B. asked as Ryan took his seat.

"Underarmed, naive and frightened as hell," Ryan said. "As long as we keep them in line they won't bring any trouble down on us."

Jak's ruby eyes flashed eerily in the flickering light of the fire. "Trouble come," he assured Ryan and the others. "Always do."

DAWN ARRIVED WITH A whimper, the sun struggling over the easterly horizon as dark, bloated clouds full of rain and chem did their best to stifle its rays.

Ryan and his companions waited in the vicinity of the parked wags, weapons on show as much for effect as protection. They had spent the night sharing three rooms in an old shack that doubled as an inn, just a little way along the road from the so-called trading post. Ryan had relished that brief opportunity to be alone with Krysty in a real bed, reaffirming their devotion to one another. Now, the companions were rested and renewed.

Before leaving the trading post the night before, J.B. had swapped some spare ammunition he had found in the redoubt—of a gauge that didn't fit any of the companions' weapons—for a pack of locally made, hand-rolled cigars. The pack itself was constructed of thin balsa wood, glued together with a little hinge mechanism in the top, and the Armorer admired the craftsmanship as he pulled one of the stubby, brown cigars from it, intending to have a quick smoke before Mildred spotted him.

Standing beside him, Doc watched the man light the cigar with a butane lighter, inhaling deeply until the tip glowed orange. J.B. spluttered as he tasted the heavy smoke for the first time, pulling the brown cigar from his teeth and glaring at it. He felt somewhat lightheaded, as it had been a while since his last smoke.

"'Tis a bracing morning, John Barrymore," Doc said as the Armorer took his second drag on the homemade cigar.

J.B. breathed thick smoke from his mouth, wisps coming from his nostrils. "Nothing a little fire in your lungs won't stave off," he assured the old man. J.B. offered Doc a cigar, but he politely declined.

As they continued waiting for the caravan travelers, J.B. began checking the wags, peering at their wheel housings and running his fingers along rust spots he found, making sure that the wags would stand up to the continued abuse of hard travel.

Across from the wags, Mildred leaned against the side of a wooden shack, checking the contents of her olive-colored satchel while Jak crouched on the curb, sharpening the leaf-shaped blade of one of his throwing knives, his Colt Python resting on the sidewalk beside him, just inches from his busy hands.

"Shit, I'm running out of supplies," Mildred muttered to herself.

Jak looked up at her, a querulous expression on his stark, ghostlike face. "Meds?" he asked.

"Yeah," Mildred replied. "I don't know about the secret of eternal youth, but if this Babyville has a stash of ibuprofen and acetaminophen it will be a miracle worth visiting."

Jak just smiled, choosing to keep his wisdom to himself.

Standing in the lee of one of the tall truck cabs, Krysty was telling Ryan a tale from her days as a child in Harmony. Ryan had heard the story before, but marveled at the way that Krysty related it, the idyllic, carefree existence she had had in her early life in contrast to his own, more formal upbringing, in Front Royal as the son of a baron. Midstory, Krysty inclined her head subtly and, in a low tone, informed Ryan, "They're here."

Ryan looked up, and saw Jeremiah Croxton leading his mismatched crew—now grown from twelve to fifteen—into the sunlight from the weather-beaten shack that served as an inn for travelers.

The bearded old farmer looked satisfied as he approached the one-eyed man. "Bright an early as promised, sir," he bellowed. "I like to see good timekeeping in a man. Shows a determined spirit, sure as hell."

"Said we'd be here at dawn," Ryan reminded the man. "You'll find me and my people keep our word, Croxton."

"I am sure you do." Croxton laughed. "Now, we got us five wags and there are six of you. How you see splitting this? I'm seeing a man on every wag." He turned his gaze to Krysty for a moment. "No offense, ma'am."

"None taken," Krysty assured him, the rising wind catching her long hair and blowing it across her face for a moment before she swept it back with her hand.

"You have room for us scattered like that?" Ryan asked.

As Ryan spoke, J.B. sauntered over to join the discussion, the cigar wedged in his mouth. "He's right," J.B. added, talking around the stub of cigar. "Some of these wags look pretty worn."

Croxton nodded favorably, smiling at the Armorer. "The wags'll hold up, and we'll make room," he assured them. "We'll be moving out in ten minutes. You okay with that?"

Ryan nodded. "The sooner the better."

Croxton looked thoughtfully at Ryan, picking his words with care. "It's mighty gen'rous of you to accompany us like this," he said. "We're just sod busters. No real money worth speaking of, nothing much of value. Can't pay you for what you're doing."

Ryan remained emotionless as he listened to the man relieve his conscience.

"But mebbe you'll find something you need in Baby, too, right, Mr. Cawdor?" the farmer continued. "I don't rightly know what the healin' properties of this spring are, but mebbe it'll be able to fix your scars. Not so sure it can replace that there something what you have lost."

Ryan realized that the round-faced farmer was looking not at him but at the leather eye patch he wore over the empty socket of his left eye. "I'm not much of a believer in miracles," Ryan told Croxton shortly. "I've seen too much horror with the one eye I have."

"Then what you are doing is that much more brave, sir," Croxton said gratefully, before turning to organize his own people.

Shaking his head, J.B. turned to Ryan. "This whole setup stinks worse than a gaudy on threesome-special day," he muttered.

Ryan agreed, but all he said was, "Doc's been a good friend to all of us." It served to remind J.B. of where their loyalties had to lie.

RYAN HAD CONSIDERED how to distribute his people the night before, lying in bed with Krysty sleeping in his arms, his lone eye staring at the ceiling. Like J.B., he was skeptical of the miracles that Babyville promised. However, he held a great deal of respect for Doc, and he could see that this was a dream that the old man needed to follow. Indeed, Ryan suspected that Doc would have gone alone with the travelers, rather than miss the incredible opportunity that Croxton had presented.

Before dawn, Ryan had taken Mildred quietly aside while Doc busied himself with his morning ablutions.

"I trust all of you," Ryan had said firmly, his voice low. "Couldn't ask for better companions for the long road. But I know that a man can get to thinking and obsessing if he's left too long on his own with too heavy a weight on his mind, and I don't want that to happen to Doc."

Mildred had nodded, understanding what Ryan was getting at.

"You keep an eye on him for me," Ryan continued. "Make sure his head stays in the here-and-now. Okay?"

Mildred nodded again.

Doc came striding out of the inn's bathroom at that point, his hair combed and his chin shaved. "Are we all ready to experience a miracle?" he asked cheerfully.

"Count me in on that, Doc," Mildred replied.

Ryan just turned away, fidgeting with an ammo cartridge as he awaited the dawn rendezvous. At least Mildred was open-minded to Doc's dreams, he thought. She wouldn't rattle the old man without due cause.

The other crucial choices for Ryan were who would sit up front and who would protect the rear.

The Armorer took backstop, well-armed and mean-tempered enough to ensure that any attack from the travelers themselves could be averted or swiftly curtailed. It was always a risk traveling with strangers; people played a lot of tricks to get what they wanted out there in the middle of the Deathlands, where trust was in short supply. Still, it appeared that the convoy was only lightly armed and was what it appeared to be—a group of elderly farmers looking for the miracle two youngsters were promising.

Ryan had asked Jak to guard the front vehicle, despite his urge to take the position himself. Jak's keen eyes and preternatural senses made him an ideal scout; he would pick up on things quicker and spot indicators that others in Ryan's team might miss.

Chapter Five

In silence Jak observed everything through the windows of the lead wag. It was a six-wheeler truck rig, preskydark technology, and it belched foul black smoke into the atmosphere as it trudged along the wreckage of the old roads. The ancient vehicle had been patched up using items from numerous sources, including metal drain pipes and bottle glass. The open drain hole from a bathtub could be seen in the right-side door, where Jak rested his knee. Sometime in the distant past, the engine had been retrofitted to run on moonshine, though it grumbled at the effort of pulling the monstrous weight of the rig up any significant incline, mostly managing a top speed of no more than twenty mph and howling like a banshee the whole bastard time.

The driver, Jeremiah Croxton, kept his eyes firmly on the shattered roadway as the wag bumped over ruined blacktop, and the worn suspension offered little comfort as the vehicle thundered over each pothole and crevice. Beside him, resting against the far door, Jak watched the dry landscape pass by through the dirt-smeared side window, frequently peering ahead to see what was coming. After a while, Jak drew his blaster—a .357 Colt Python—and began taking it apart so as to oil its inner works using a finger-size bottle of oil he carried in his jacket.

From behind Jak, sitting in the cubbyhole in the rear of the cab, surrounded by what amounted to all of Croxton's negligible belongings, the blond-haired Daisy peered over the back of Jak's seat. She was watching Jak's practiced, economical movements as he field-stripped his weapon.

"What ya doing?" Daisy asked, her languid voice close to his ear.

Jak ignored her, glancing ahead at the low rise that the broken road poured over, past the last of the emaciated wheat fields.

A half minute passed in silence before Daisy spoke again. "Hey, mister," she drawled, "I asked what ya doing? You deaf as well as weird-looking? Don't see much point in a deaf sec man."

Jak turned to face her, his ruby eyes boring into hers. "Here guard, not jabber," he told her.

At the steering wheel, Croxton guffawed. "Boy's got a point, Daisy," he said, not bothering to look behind him.

"I was just trying to make nice," Daisy whined. "Thought a weirdo like him would 'preciate that."

Oiling his blaster, Jak ignored her. But his mind was considering Daisy's words carefully—not because they hurt, Jak was above such petty concerns, but because of the way in which she phrased them. It nagged at him that the girl had called him "mister."

THE SECOND WAG IN THE convoy was similar to the first, a rusty old truck rig that had been converted to run on moonshine. Krysty had taken the shotgun seat next to a dark-skinned woman called Nisha Adams, who looked permanently tired. Nisha's husband, Barry, a man in his midforties, with the tanned, leathery skin of someone used to working outside, drove the rig with an easygoing nonchalance, remarking on things that caught his attention at the roadside, keeping his hands in a four- and eight-o'clock grip on the rig's large wheel.

Three other people shared the cab, sitting in the sleeping compartment behind the main seats—another older couple called Julius and Joanna Dougal, and the old farmer who had been attacked by one of the hounds outside the trading post and now wore a bandage across his wounded arm. The five of them seemed to get along well—they were old friends, full of anecdotes and not above teasing one another in a lighthearted way.

Krysty sat quietly, her green eyes watching the cracked strip of road and the surrounding landscape as they lumbered along, following Croxton's rig at a steady pace.

"So, where are you from, long and tall?" Julius asked from the back of the cab.

Krysty turned and gave the man a brief smile. He was about fifty, dark-skinned and carrying a few extra pounds around his middle and on his jowls. Whatever he had farmed before he'd downed tools to go on this crazy quest for eternal youth, it had kept him strong and well-fed. "Name's Krysty," she began. "I come from a ville called Harmony. Have you heard of that?"

Julius looked thoughtful for a moment, then shook his head. "Can't say I have, Krysty."

"It's in the past," Krysty said with a shrug. "You folks come from a long way?"

"Couple of days on the road so far," Joanna explained. Like Julius, she was a dark-skinned woman carrying a few extra pounds. She wore a machete at her hip, its blade notched here and there from use.

"Worth it though," Julius added. "Imagine, being young again. You live in this hellhole so long and suddenly someone offers you a chance to be young all over again. Strong and healthy again. Can't even imagine it, I'll bet, young'un like you."

Krysty laughed. "I grew up fine and strong, Julius," she said, "but I still miss some of the things I used to be able to do."

"Like what, child?" Joanna asked, encouraging Krysty to continue.

Krysty glanced back at the road through the windshield, her eyes scanning the back of the wag ahead and peering at the dead terrain all around. "Dreams," she said wistfully. "I miss being able to dream the way I did when I was a little girl. That feeling of security that lets you dream just about anything."

From the back of the rig, the old farmer, Paul Witterson, loosed a loud, braying laugh. "Ha. You're still a little girl, sweetie," he said. "Having curves in all the right places don't change that."

Krysty smiled, flattered by the old man's observation. "Thanks for the kind compliment."

"Compliment nothing," Witterson stated. "Facts is facts, Red. Facts is facts."

Gazing through the window to her right, Krysty wondered what the facts were about the spring of eternal life.

THE THIRD VEHICLE in the convoy was a broken-down, American-made four-wheel drive that had survived the nukecaust but not much else. It was patched together with mismatched doors and sheets of metal, and the roof wore the acne-scar evidence of acid raid erosion. The engine had been removed, and that space was used for additional storage, containing almost all of the occupants' possessions. Despite displaying mutie musculature, the two weary horses that pulled the vehicle looked to be struggling with the weight.

Doc had taken the passenger seat beside the driver, a man in his middle fifties called Charles Torino, whose face was more scarred than the roof of his automobile. Mildred sat in the back, across from Doc, beside Mary Foster, checking the bandage that had been applied to the wound where her shoulder met her neck. A dark-haired woman in her late thirties, Mary was the woman who, along with her baby, had been snagged by the mutie wolf when the companions had first intervened. She was rocking the baby in her arms as Mildred dressed her wound, replacing the bandage.

"Ryan and J.B. think I am crazy, do they not?" Doc said, breaking the silence inside the vehicle.

Mildred looked up from her gentle work on the woman's wounded neck. "No," she replied, "don't be silly."

Doc's smile was genuine as he answered. "Do not try to kid an old man, Mildred. I have known you too long. And I know what I saw in their eyes. They think I am out of my mind."

"Well," Mildred admitted, "no more than normal, I'm sure."

Doc looked ponderously out of the missing windshield for a moment before he continued. "How about you, Doctor?" he prompted. "Do you think this old fool is crazy?"

Mildred cast a significant look at the other people in the automobile before she spoke. "Doc, I hardly think now's the time to…" she began.

"It may be false hope," he told her, "but you understand what would happen if I did not pursue it. I would not have been able to live with myself knowing that this opportunity may be out there."

Mildred leaned forward and touched Doc's shoulder reassuringly. "I know, Doc," she said, "we all do. No one thinks you're wrong or loopy. We just worry about you."

The driver, Charles Torino, spoke in his hoarse, strained voice then, looking over his shoulder through the headrests to take in Mildred as well as Doc. "You folks think this is a wild-goose chase?" he asked.

Mildred shrugged. "I don't know. It sounds pretty amazing. I guess we have doubts."

Charles nodded, peering back at his mutie horses to see that they were still on the right track. "I seen it happen," he said. "Old guy come through our ville two months ago, decrepit, looked like Old Father Time hisself limping along on that bad foot of his. He come and told us about this young-making spring he heard about out east. Said he was going looking for it. Six weeks later he came back."

Mildred and Doc looked at the man, hanging on his every word.

"He was just a kid," Charles said in his strained voice. "I mean, mebbe twenty years old, I dunno. Still had the limp he come to the ville with all them weeks before, but he looked young. Real young."

"And it was the same man?" Mildred asked.

Charles nodded. "I'd swear to you it was. Mary?"

The younger woman holding the baby nodded solemnly. "Same eyes, same jawline," she said. "S'funny, he looked kinda handsome as a young man."

"Yet he still had his limp," Doc wondered.

"Oh, the spring cured that, too," Charles said with a throaty laugh. "Idiot was so busy dancing with joy he trod on a nail, went right through his boot. Put him pretty much back where he started at, I guess."

Doc and Mildred both laughed at that, too, feeling a curious sense of relief.

"Me," Charles continued, his eyes glazing over as he considered his words, "I'm hoping it can cure something a bit meaner than a broken foot."

Mildred peered at the man and gently asked what he meant.

"I got me the black lung, miss," Charles said with that throaty voice of his. "The big black crab inside me, making it a blamed chore to breathe."

Cancer, Mildred realized. The man was looking for a cure for cancer.

RYAN WAS ACTING AS SEC MAN on the fourth vehicle in the convoy—a canvas-covered wooden wag with large wheels, pulled by four weary-looking horses. He sat at the front of the wag, his 9 mm SIG-Sauer P-226 ready at his hip, the Steyr rifle resting at his side. In silence he mentally reviewed his concerns. The whole quest seemed foolish, and yet he felt loyalty to Doc. The man deserved this chance, however unlikely it seemed.

And there was something else. There was a part of Ryan that, blast it all, wanted it to be true. The whole world, it seemed, had been turned against humankind, making every day a battle of desperate survival against astonishing odds. The plants, the wildlife, mutations and even the weather patterns had become poisonous, dangerous or downright lethal to man, and that was before considering the brutality that people inflicted on one another. To discover one bright hope, one good thing in the landscape of badness—that would be nothing short of a miracle.

Ryan and his companions had trekked a long time hoping for a miracle, seeking somewhere to settle, to call home. Babyville wasn't it, Ryan was sure of that, but it just might rejuvenate the sense of hope that was sorely ebbing deep inside him.

Ryan's companions in the wag were a family of three—the Cliffords—whose youngest was forty-three years old. A much younger man called Alec shared the back of the horse-drawn wag with the family, apparently shifting across from Croxton's own wag. Alec was the blond-haired young man Ryan had noticed at the table in the trading post the night before. Alec looked similar to Daisy, the miracle girl who claimed to be over seventy years old, and Ryan suspected that they were brother and sister, or perhaps cousins. Their physical similarity nagged at him. Despite the layers of clothing that Alec wore for the trip, Ryan could see that the lad was rake-thin. Where Daisy still had puppy fat, Alec's face was slender and bony, sharp planes and narrow, predatory eyes. He had the wispy beginnings of a beard on his chin, which he had clearly cultivated, though its ash-blond color made it seem insubstantial.

While the Clifford family members argued with one another in that way that families will, Alec remained silent, observing everything without comment. In that, Ryan saw something of Jak Lauren in the young man. Jak was a fine man to have on side, Ryan reminded himself, but he was a dangerous foe to turn one's back on. Ryan wouldn't be letting his guard down around this blond-haired young man.

J.B. HAD BEEN POSTED as sec man in the final wag in the train. This wag was a converted farm tractor, belching thick, tarry black smoke into the air behind it from two exhaust pipes as it gobbled up a sweet-smelling fuel made from sugar solution. A canvas shelter had been strung across the engine, and a boxed-in trailer had been tagged onto the rear. The Armorer sat in the trailer, watching the road behind them through the aft half-door. Sitting beside him, working his way through an illustrated instruction manual, was Vincent White. Vincent was a man in his midfifties, and he left his wife, Maude, to drive the sputtering vehicle. A naked lightbulb had been wired up into the side of the trailer, and was running off the engine to cast a dim, yellow light inside the box on wheels. He used a magnifying glass to read the print in the booklet he held. The man was desperately farsighted.

The road behind them bumped along, trailing off into the distance, the tragic fields with their skeletal plants sweeping away toward the horizon. J.B. watched the skies where a peppering of carrion birds followed the wag train. Were they simply being hopeful, he wondered, or did the convoy and its passengers have the mark of death upon them?

THE SEARING, NOONDAY SUN beat against the battered, rusting four-wheel drive, highlighting every streak and imperfection scarring the old, broken windshield. Doc sat comfortably in the passenger seat, watching the light playing across the cracks. Beside him, Charles Torino held the reins, urging his tired horses onward with occasional words of encouragement. They were somewhere still in Tennessee. It was scrubland here now, where once farms and thriving towns had been. Crows flew above, cawing discordantly to one another, swooping down to perch on the struggling saplings that had emerged from ashlike soil. When they landed, the soot-feathered crows seemed so heavy as to almost topple the scrawny, young saplings. The crows waited, watching the convoy of wags pass like a jury deliberating its verdict on the accused as they were paraded before them.

Doc closed his eyes, feeling the yellow warmth of the sun beating down through the cracked windshield, painting patterns on the inside of his eyelids. The heat was good, a simple delight harkening back to a more innocent age. Charles was saying something beside him, speaking to his horses, but Doc ignored him, tuning out the man's throaty voice. Behind him, in the back of the wag, Mildred and Mary were talking about the wildlife, about favorite things, foods and beverages, meaningless stuff to pass the time. Baby Holly snuffled now and then in her sleep.

They were getting slowly closer to Babyville, and its mythical pool of rejuvenation.

Doc thought back to the conversation he had had with Ryan that morning, after he had finished shaving in the dingy bathroom of the inn, and then back to the discussion in the trading post with its tethered goats and tethered dancing girls. The conversation played out in his mind's eye, Doc himself trying to justify his need to pursue the promise of Babyville.

DOC WAS EXPLAINING Croxton's proposition to his companions, but J.B. kept dismissing his words, waving his hand in front of his face as though swatting at a fly.

"Nobody's getting any younger, Doc," J.B. said gruffly.

Angered, Doc looked around the table for support from his other companions. Ryan Cawdor's single blue eye seemed to stare right through him, noncommittal. Mildred was shaking her head apologetically and, beside her, Krysty Wroth had her hands in her mutie hair, brushing at it as though disinterested in the whole discussion. As he watched, Doc saw chalk-white dust falling from her hair, peppering the table like the falling snow.

Doc turned to the last seat at the table. A beautiful blonde woman sat there, gazing back at him, affection and devotion in her crystal-clear blue eyes. Beautiful and shapely, the woman was still so young, a child's innocence characterizing her face.

"I believe you, Doc," the woman said, her voice holding that musical quality that he thought he had forgotten. "I'll follow you."

Lori Quint.

"Not like I follow Keeper," the blonde woman— Lori—said. "I follow because you're so good to me."

Without even realizing, Doc was reaching over the table then, reaching for Lori, pulling her toward him, enveloping her in his arms. It had been so long since he had seen her. Why was that?

But she wasn't Lori now. She was the old-young girl from the convoy, Daisy, smiling up at him with her round, puppy-fat face.

"I believe in you," Daisy-Lori said, gazing at Doc with wide, innocent eyes, her long hair falling across her face.

With tenderness, Doc pushed the sun-yellow hair out of the girl's eyes. As he did, he saw his companions watching him, disapprovingly.

But they were no longer the companions he knew. These were older, skeletal, no skin left on their bones—just fleshless, dead things. Fleshless dead things with staring, judgmental eyes boring into his. Krysty's red hair fell away from her white skull in clumps as her bone hands brushed through it. Mildred slumped in her seat as her neck bones crumbled to dust with the way she was shaking her head back and forth in disagreement. J.B. Dix's jaw worked up and down, up and down, saying nothing, only the noise of creaking bones wearing against one another, crumbling to powdery dust.

And then there was Ryan, his face a skull, an eye patch beside an empty socket.

Doc turned back to the girl in his arms. Daisy seemed older now, her cheeks hollow, dark rings under her eyes, her fine hair becoming patchy. There were things in her hair now, too; living, squirming things—maggots and worms, the purifiers of the dead.

"I believe you, Doc," Daisy said, her voice still young. "We can grow old together. Arm-in-arm."

And a dog started barking, the noise loud in his ear.

SUDDENLY, DOC'S EYES snapped open. Beside him, Charles Torino was coughing, hacking up a thick crust of phlegm, his cough sharp and loud as the barking of a mongrel dog. Torino spat out a wad of phlegm through the open side window, and turned to Doc, an embarrassed smile on his face as the old man was startled awake. "The sooner we get to this miracle pool the better, huh, brother?" he said.

Doc nodded his silent agreement, still feeling the icy tendrils of his horrifying dream. Lori was dead, he reminded himself. She had been dead a long time.

The train of wags continued bumping along the old country lanes and broken, ruined highways, lurching and halting as though they were suffering epileptic seizures. Eyes open, Doc watched the countryside pass them by, keeping his thoughts to himself.

THEY JOURNEYED THROUGH emaciated fields and beyond, traveling into waste ground and through skeletal forests of deadwood trees, evergreen pines now ever dead. The wags kept up a steady pace, the weary horses looking miserable as they breathed in the exhaust from the lead trucks. The roads were patchy at best, and Doc described them to Mildred as "hit and miss, though most often miss, I fear."

In the late afternoon, as the white winter sun dwindled in the sky, they found some improved roads that hadn't just survived the ravages of the nuclear Armageddon, but looked to have been repaired in the interim. Jeremiah Croxton turned the wide steering wheel of his wag and bumped up onto the sturdy-looking tarmac.

Beside him in the cab, Jak eyed the road ahead. It was surrounded by bushes and a smattering of anemic trees, their branches overhanging the road, but the strip of blacktop itself looked empty and clean. A little way in the distance, he could see a small ville, but there were no lights coming from it and it was hard to tell if the place was inhabited or deserted. Jak peered at old man Croxton as he urged the wag along the smoother strip of tarmac.

After a few moments, Croxton became aware that Jak was watching him. "You got a problem, boy?" he inquired, turning to pierce Jak with a blue-eyed glare.

"Not like," Jak explained, nodding to the open strip of road.

"Me neither," Croxton said, "but someone's laid this thing so we may as well use it since it's here."

Jak shook his head. "Easy route never easy," he assured the old farmer.

The train of wags continued onward, getting closer to the ville. The ville itself appeared to be an old, predark town and Jak, though not the best reader in Ryan's party, spotted a tumbled road sign that identified it as somewhere called Tazewell. He wondered what the hell a Taze was and why it would be well. From a distance, the settlement seemed deserted, with a few old, dilapidated farm buildings on the very outskirts, well-weathered and falling apart with age.

As they closed in on the little town, Croxton's wag seemed to suddenly lose pulling power, the engine whining harshly as the vehicle puttered forward.

Jak looked at Croxton as the older man downshifted gears. "Problem?" the albino asked.

Croxton wrestled with the gearstick, grinding the gears until the engine picked up speed once more. "Lost traction for a second there," Croxton explained, "like we was going uphill or something."

From behind them, Daisy yawned and peered over the seatbacks. She had been asleep for most of the afternoon, wrapped in a patchwork woollen blanket. "Where are we?" she asked, her breath smelling of sleep.

"Taze'll," Croxton said.

Daisy glanced up at the view through the windshield, peered out of the dust-smeared windows to either side. "Seems fucking lonesome," she said.

Just then, there was a groan from the engine and the wag shuddered to a halt. "Dammit!" Croxton spat, pulling his hands off the wheel and clenching them angrily into fists.

Jak watched as the old farmer turned the ignition key, his foot pumping the accelerator. The engine turned over but, after traveling just a few more feet, began howling in complaint.

"Switch off," Jak instructed in an emotionless monotone. He had already unholstered his Colt Python, flipping off the safety.

"What are you talking…?" Croxton began, but he stopped, realizing that Jak wasn't listening.

His hand on the door handle, the albino teen had pushed the door open a crack and was peering at the low buildings at the side of the road. Jak's red eyes were working back and forth, his senses on high alert. There was no one about or at least no one that he could detect. He turned back to Croxton and Daisy, catching them with his penetrating stare. "Stay," he instructed. "Keep down." Then he shoved open the door and dropped out of sight, down to the road surface, just the trails of his white mane of hair visible as his figure disappeared below the level of the windows.

Agitated, Daisy asked Croxton what was going on.

"Engine's stalled," Croxton explained. "But something ain't right here."

"You said we had enough fuel," Daisy said anxiously.

"We do," Croxton said. "Sure of it. But the engine just ain't pullin'."

Outside, Jak stood close to the truck cab, blaster raised, scanning the surrounding area for signs of movement. Rapid footsteps came from behind him, and he turned to see Ryan and Krysty approaching. Both of them were brandishing their own blasters and they looked warily around as they raced up to join with their companion. Ryan was no longer carrying his Steyr rifle, Jak saw. Presumably he had left it in the wag he was tasked to guard. At the far end of the wag train, Jak could make out the figure of J.B., now standing guard beside the final wag.

"Told the others to stay put," Ryan said. "What's going on, Jak?"

Jak pointed to the wheels of the wag, and Ryan saw that they had sunken almost to their midpoint into the tarmac. "Quicksand trap," Jak explained.

"Mebbe the tarmac just got laid," Krysty suggested doubtfully.

Jak scented the air. "No one around."

Ryan looked down the road, peering at the darkened buildings. They were still on the outskirts of town; the final wag wasn't even up to the first building where the devastated remains of Tazewell began.

"We'll go back," Ryan decided, and he jogged around the front of the wag and clambered up the ladder at the driver's side. The tarmac beneath his boot heels compacted, feeling mushy and soft, definitely spongy beneath his weight.

Croxton opened his side window. "What's going on, Ryan?" he asked.

"The tarmac here is freshly laid," Ryan explained. "It's got caught up in your wheels. You'll need to reverse."

Croxton cursed. "Knew it was too good to be true, seeing a road like this," he snarled. "You think I can just back out?"

Ryan looked down at the half-buried front wheel, back up to Croxton. "Worth a try." He shrugged. "If not, we'll use some tow cables. I take it you have some."

"We'll manage to rig up something," Croxton grumbled with a sigh of resignation. Then he started the engine up and shoved the wag into Reverse, while Krysty instructed the other wags to move back and give them some room.

Clinging to the side, Ryan felt the cab shudder as power chugged through it. Croxton held the emergency brake down, letting the revs build before he tried to move. While he did so, Krysty worked her way back to the other wags to pass on the instructions.

"What's goin' on, tall and slim?" Paul Witterson asked as Krysty explained what they were doing to the driver of wag two.

"This road's no good," Krysty said.

Nisha, who was now sitting in the driver's seat with her husband, Barry, in shotgun, looked concerned. "No good how?" she asked.

"It won't take the weight of the wags," Krysty explained before moving on down the line.

The people were agitated, Krysty realized. Night was falling and they were starting to get jumpy. Not good at all.

Once the roadway behind the foremost wag had been cleared—the others having backed along the road by twenty feet or so—Croxton took off the emergency brake and let the wheels free. The truck cab lurched back with Ryan standing at its side, pulling away from the spongy tarmac for a moment. Then its wheels began to spin as it lost traction, and Ryan saw that the back wheels were sinking into the tarmac as they spun.

"Fireblast," Ryan snarled, holding his hand up in clear instruction for Croxton to halt.

Croxton switched off the engine and looked out the window hopefully. "No good?"

"You're jammed both ways," Ryan told him. "We're going to have to tow you out, after all. Otherwise it's just going to get worse." Ryan didn't like it. Night was descending rapidly now, and he wanted to either be moving or, preferably, holed up somewhere safe before some kind of crazy or other came at them from out of who cared where.

From the other side of the cab, Ryan heard Jak hiss for his attention. Ryan looked at him, a querulous expression on his face.

"Company," Jak stated, pointing along the blacktop strip toward the center of town.

Ryan looked down the road, sighting the horizon and peering at the darkened buildings on either side of the road. He couldn't see anything, and all that could be heard was the wind and the occasional popping and ticking of Croxton's engine as it cooled. But, as Ryan watched, he became aware of a noise carrying from the distance. It sounded like an engine.

Instantly, Ryan pulled his compact SIG-Sauer blaster into his hand, waiting to see what was coming. He called up to Croxton, his voice adopting an authoritative tone. "Turn off your engine and keep hidden," he said.

Gradually, the rumbling became louder until the silhouette of a wide wag could be seen making its way along the blacktop from the far side of town. The wag was trailed by a cloud of exhaust and trundled along at a pace not much faster than jogging.

Holding his blaster casually at his side, Ryan glanced across to Jak. The albino youth was standing, his own blaster clenched in his right fist, masked from the approaching vehicle by his body. Ryan nodded, then walked forward, leaving Jak alone beside Croxton's wag.

Ryan walked down the road toward the slow-moving wag, his blaster held loosely at his side. The wag was a fixer-upper. Once upon a time it had been a combine harvester. It had large wheels and a belching smokestack. Something glowed in its heart, a fire raging like one of the old-fashioned ovens that Ryan had grown up with back at Front Royal. There were two seats, placed high up to either side of the burning ovenlike tender, and Ryan saw the figures of a man and woman sitting there.

"Can I help you?" Ryan called as the wag trudged closer.

With a defiant splutter, the wag belched another cloud of smoke and slowed, shaking as it pulled up beside Ryan. The man peered down from his high seat, an ingratiating smile on his lips. He was thin and scrawny, with the beginnings of a beard on his chin and the patchy sprouts of hair of the rad-affected. He looked perhaps thirty or forty, but it was hard to tell in the dwindling light. "I was about to ask you the same question," the man said, his voice warm and friendly.

Ryan watched in silence, keeping pace with the vehicle as it slowed.

"Thought you might be needing a ride or a place to stay," the man continued. "Or mebbe you want to negotiate a towing." He chuckled, his teeth glinting with the glow of the hearth beside him as he reached for something that rested at his side.

Ryan's arm snapped out then, grabbing the man by his lower leg and yanking him down from his seat. The driver fell, yelping as he crashed to the hard tarmac of the ground, a rebuilt Colt Anaconda six-shooter tumbling from his grip. "Hey, what th—?" he began, but his words were cut off abruptly as Ryan rammed the heel of his boot against the man's throat.

His foot held against the base of the man's throat, Ryan leaned forward, pointing the muzzle of his blaster at the man's forehead. "Yeah, let's negotiate," he snarled.

Chapter Six

"Black fire!" the scrawny excuse for a man gasped as Ryan pressed his booted foot against his throat. "What the devil has gotten into you?"

Ryan looked at the man beneath him, his expression tense. "Did you set this up?" he demanded, the muzzle of the SIG-Sauer never wavering from the man's forehead.

The man screwed up his eyes as Ryan's foot pressed harder onto his windpipe, sputtering out a rasping cough. "No, sir," he said, his voice straining to be heard.

Suddenly, over the sound of the steam-powered truck's engine, Ryan heard a shotgun being cocked in readiness. He turned his head, ducking a little and training his blaster on the other rider of the truck. He saw now that it was a woman, and she had climbed out of her seat to stand on the metal bridge beside the belching, ovenlike engine. As thin as her companion, with straggly long hair, she held a sawed-off Mossberg M9200A1 shotgun pointed at Ryan. The 12-gauge weapon was over a foot in length, and could blow a hole clean through a man. "You want to get the fuck off my husband, sweetheart?" she demanded.

"You think you can shoot me before I break his windpipe?" Ryan countered, pushing his toe deeper into the man's throat until the fallen driver groaned in pain.

As the woman considered that, a whistle sounded up ahead. She looked up and saw J.B. holding his M-4000 scattergun on her from the head of the wag convoy, with Jak and Krysty standing to either side of him, leveling their own blasters at her. J.B. strode forward, the hefty scattergun trained on the woman, never wavering, his expression grim.

Slowly, shaking her head in disbelief, the woman lowered her weapon.

As she did so, Ryan raised his foot from the driver's throat, allowing him to breathe. The man spoke, his voice sounding strained. "Black fire, you're wound tighter than a new gaudy on deflowerin' day," he muttered, reaching up to rub at his aching throat. "I mean, what the crap are you trying to do?"

Blaster still held on the driver, Ryan stepped back, warily assessing the scrawny man. "Our wag here got stuck in some shitty excuse for a road," he explained. "Seems mighty convenient you coming along like this with a tow truck."

The driver sat up and rubbed at his neck and shoulders. "Just coincidence, friend," he stated. "Happened to be heading along this way to our home is all. Don't go aiming your blaster at good luck."

"I don't get much good luck," Ryan rasped, still holding his blaster on the man.

The man began to laugh and, after a moment, his wife joined him. "See how hard we're laughing?" he said. "It's just coincidence, man. Just a flaming coincidence." After a few seconds, the man dusted himself off and began to get up. "You, um, you mind?" he asked Ryan, casting a significant look at the blaster in the one-eyed man's hand.

"Go ahead," Ryan said, the SIG-Sauer still poised at the man as he struggled up from the blacktop.

Standing, the man held his hands loosely at his side, making it clear that he meant no harm. "Name's Mitch," he said, "and that there is Annie. Didn't meant to frighten you or whatnot."

"It'll take more than your junk heap to frighten me," Ryan assured him.

"So," Mitch began, "you want us to give you a towing or you want us to just piss off on our way like we never saw you? I'm easy, friend. Ain't worth it to me to get shot over your predicament." The man had made no attempt to recover his blaster.

Gradually—warily—Ryan lowered his blaster, clicking the safety back on. "You think you can pull us out? That's a heavy wag," he said.

Mitch stepped forward, walking a few paces to get a better look at the truck that was sinking into the spongy tarmac. "Oh, I can get it out," he said with certainty. "It may take some doing, but there ain't nothing my old 'junk heap' won't tow." He emphasized the words that Ryan had used to describe his vehicle, saying them as though they were a curse.

Billows of smoke belched from the smokestack atop the man's strange wag, filling the air with a sickly stench. Ryan looked past the smoke and gazed up at the darkening sky. Up there, stars were beginning to twinkle—full night would be upon them before long.

"How long will it take?" Ryan asked, conscious of the approaching night.

Mitch shrugged. "A half hour, mebbe a little more," he admitted. "I got some chains back at my garage, 'bout five minutes away is all. Hook them up and you'll be good to go in no time."

"We've got tow ropes," Ryan told him.

Mitch shook his head. "Nah," he said, "your wag there looks like—what?—five tons?"

Ryan shrugged.

"You need proper chains," Mitch explained. "Won't break, see?"

Years before, after he had escaped Front Royal and the insanity of his brother's reign of terror, Ryan had traveled across the Deathlands with a man known as the Trader. The Trader had taught Ryan a lot about vehicles, as well as other things, including survival. What this man, Mitch, was telling him about using chains sounded sensible. Inconvenient, perhaps, but sensible just the same.

"Five minutes, you say?" Ryan confirmed.

The scrawny driver smiled. "Ten," he said. "Five there, five back. You don't trust me, do ya?"

A ghost of a lopsided grin crossed Ryan's scarred features. "I don't trust anyone, Mitch," he said.

"Yeah, good way to be," Mitch agreed. "Look, you come back with me and Annie, see we're all straight and aboveboard. No funny business. Then we're all square, right?"

Ryan looked at the scrawny woman atop the steam-powered wag, the one who had pulled the shotgun on him. That was understandable, he acknowledged, only natural that she'd try to defend someone who attacked her husband, whatever the reason, and there was nothing unusual about Mitch wanting to be armed when he met with strangers, either, not out here in the middle of a ruined world full of predators. Still, it didn't sit well with him that they had happened along—with a tow truck no less—at nearly the exact time that Croxton's wag had been caught in the quicksandlike tarmac. Perhaps the tarmac was freshly laid, perhaps it was poorly mixed or had been damaged by the toxic rain that had hit the day before. The bottom line was, it was a problem and a convenient solution had presented itself too easily for Ryan's comfort.

"Do you expect payment for this?" Ryan asked, holstering his SIG-Sauer back at his hip, pulling his dark, heavy winter coat over to disguise it.

Mitch and Annie laughed in unison. "We won't take your jack," Annie explained. "Good deeds is their own rewards."

Ryan nodded, before walking toward J.B. and his other companions. Doc and Mildred had remained hidden inside Charles Torino's horse-drawn wag, while Krysty was crouched in the shadows beside the second wag. As Ryan joined them, Krysty rolled out, Smith & Wesson in hand, allowing herself to be seen again.

"What do you think?" Ryan asked, addressing J.B. and the others.

"Nothing good," J.B. said, shaking his head.

Ryan indicated their lead wag, the one driven by Jeremiah Croxton. "The road's not holding the wag," he pointed out. "Our man there is sinking deeper every minute. We'll have a hell of a job pulling him out now."

"We could just leave the wag, Ryan," Krysty suggested.

"Be a better idea," J.B. agreed.

Ryan was thinking about Mitch and Annie and their steam-converted harvester. "The newcomers' wag could get it out," he stated. "It's certainly got pulling power."

Reluctantly, J.B. nodded. "It has at that," he agreed. "Leave Doc and Mildred to guard the wags," he suggested. "Your new friends haven't seen them, so they won't be any the wiser."

Ryan thought about it. "Me and Jak will go," he decided. "If they see us leave the place without sec men, they'll get suspicious."

J.B. nodded, deferring to Ryan's judgment.

Turning, Ryan walked back to where Mitch and his wife had parked their strange makeshift wag, Jak keeping pace at his side. Mitch had placed his Colt Anaconda back in its holster, strapped low to his right leg.

"I'm Ryan and this is my friend Jak," Ryan explained to Mitch. "We'll be coming with you, unless you plan on having any objections."

Mitch hacked up a gob of phlegm and spat it at the blacktop over the side of his wag. "You'll have to hang on," he told them. "She's a boneshaker."

MITCH WASN'T KIDDING. The wag had no suspension to speak of, and it leaped over every bump in the road like a horse vaulting fences. Ryan and Jak had taken up positions at the rear of the vehicle, hooking their hands through the ribs that made up its skeletal structure as it trudged past Croxton's group. After a few moments, Mitch turned back to them and shouted over the chugging engine, "Gonna go off road now." With that, he turned off the nominally smooth blacktop and onto a dirt track.

The wag continued bumping along the track for a few minutes, traveling at a top speed of perhaps fifteen miles per hour, until a large farmhouse with a wide outbuilding came into view. From her position in the passenger seat, Annie pointed to the buildings and shouted something over the noise of the engine. "That's where we live," she explained.

The buildings were dilapidated. As they got closer, Ryan saw that one wall had caved in and there were numerous holes in the roof of the main house, while the outbuilding was a large barn or shed with a set of double doors that looked as if they were rotting where they stood. In the fields to the right of the house, Ryan could see the wrecked remains of other wags, salvage that had been left to rot. "Nice place," he commented as Mitch pulled the wag up beside the open doors of the outbuilding.

Ryan peered at the house as they passed it, noting that, despite its general decrepitude, it had been patched with sturdy sheets of metal that acted as cladding for the whole of the first floor. The surrounding trees had been cut down, leaving large trunks along one side of the building, enough to protect them from attack without providing much cover for the attackers. Beyond that, however, the wilderness threatened to overwhelm the area.

Mitch pulled one of the long levers before him and the wag shook as the brakes were engaged and the engine powered down. It remained there, ticking over, as Mitch got out of his seat and climbed down from the wag.

"You strong boys going to give me a hand with these chains or what?" he asked, peering up at Ryan.

Ryan nodded, and he and Jak leaped down and followed Mitch into the shed while Annie remained in the passenger seat. Jak glanced back, making sure that the woman wasn't reaching for her shotgun that was nestled in a leather rig beside her. She smiled at him, a nasty, spiteful thing on her bony face, keeping her hands on show.

"It's just through here," Mitch was saying as Ryan followed him into the shadows of the outbuilding.

Ryan flexed the muscles in his hand, reaching beneath his coat for the holstered SIG-Sauer. He didn't trust Mitch or the woman, and he cursed himself for getting into this situation. If Mitch could help them, that was fine. But this felt increasingly wrong.

Jak was walking a few paces behind Ryan, his ruby eyes shifting back and forth, his nose wrinkling as he sniffed at the air. There was something here, he was sure of that. The whole place held the smell of meat, like a butcher's. It was ingrained in the wood of the walls. Jak's fierce eyes peered into the shadows, trying to discern something in the pitch-blackness at the far side of the barn.

"Much farther?" Ryan asked. "I can't see shit in here, Mitch."

A few steps ahead of him, Ryan heard Mitch pulling something from his pocket, and his hand automatically clutched the butt of the holstered SIG-Sauer. A series of brushing noises, flint against flint, and the tiny flame of a lighter came to sputtering life.

"Here you go," Mitch answered, holding the flame out before him. "Don't get much in the way of visitors out here," he explained with a charmless smile. "No cause to rig up pretty lights."

"No problem," Ryan assured him, his hand still clenching the butt of the blaster at his hip.

The flame of the lighter cast a minuscule amount of light in the barnlike building. Ryan saw over a dozen lengths of chain hanging from one wall, attached by a series of hooks that had been pushed into the wooden wall. There was farm machinery in here, too, he saw— rusty, old plows and tillers with churning blades, the kind of things you tied to a horse or mule so that they could work the fields for you. A crossbeam ran along the side of the barn, about eight feet above them, and the whole structure was almost two full stories in height, with a single, simple light fixture—really just a naked lightbulb—attached to one wall, though it had been left switched off. A deep blue sky and twinkling stars could be seen through several gaps in the dilapidated roof.

"You do a lot of farming?" Ryan asked, trying to be conversational as he peered into the shadows beyond the little pool of light.

Mitch reached up and detached one of the longer lengths of rusted chain from a hook. "Some," he admitted. "Been tryin' to grow us some… Ah, I don't know what it's called. Leafy things, taste like water."

Ryan watched the man wrap the first length of chain in on itself. "You have seeds then?" Ryan asked.

Mitch bundled the length of chain in his hands and offered it to Jak. "You think you can make yourself useful, whitey?" he asked.

Jak looked at Mitch and shook his head. "You carry," he said.

Mitch looked at the strange-looking albino teen quizzically, then to Ryan. "I can't carry everything back to the wag without making three trips. And there's three of us right here," he whined.

"Point out which chains you need us to take," Ryan instructed, "and give me the light. We'll follow you."

Mitch nodded and handed Ryan his little lighter, its flame popping and wavering in the breeze from the open door. "One in from the right," he explained, indicating the wall of hanging chains.

Ryan reached for it, looping the chain around itself in a spiral.

"Last one is over the far side," Mitch explained, "on the floor. Nice, sturdy length. Be just right for you fellas and your predicament."

Ryan inclined his head, indicating that Jak was to collect the other length of chain as Mitch made his way to the double doors. Ryan waited while Jak crouched and pulled at the chain on the grimy floor of the barn.

As Jak pulled at the chain, unhooking it from a thick rivet in the wall, the two of them heard a sudden, low growl from the shadows. Something stirred.

Ryan glanced back, just in time to see Mitch and Annie pushing the double doors closed, the moonlight peeking through the cracks between the boards. Even as Ryan tossed the chain aside and began running to the doors, he heard the shunting of wood against metal as a heavy bolt was locked in place.

"Fireblast!" he cursed, slamming a palm against the door and finding it stuck firm. From outside, beyond the door, he heard the cackling laughter of Mitch and his wife. Ryan turned back to where Jak remained crouching near the back of the barn. A moment later, a lightbulb illuminated overhead, dim wattage working off an oil supply, but enough to light the center of the room.

From its place in the shadows, Jak and Ryan heard movements as the growling, snarling thing at the end of Jak's chain stirred. And, from beyond the locked doors, they heard the whooping sounds of laughter.

Chapter Seven

"Jak," Ryan demanded, his voice steady, "what have we got?"

Jak was carefully backing away from the rear of the barn, leaving the chain back where he had found it on the floor. "Meat eater," he said. "Can smell it."

Figures, Ryan thought irritably.

Jak stepped closer to where Ryan stood, pulling his .357 Magnum Colt Python from its holster and pointing it, one-handed, into the shadows at the far side of the barn. Ryan had doused the flame of the little lighter, and the low-wattage bulb above did little to illuminate the large barn, leaving most of it still in deep shadow. The angry growling continued.

"How many?" Ryan asked. "Can you see?"

Despite his albinism, Jak had incredible eyesight, and his other senses were so attuned that he could often locate enemies by hearing or smell as easily as another person might with his eyes. "Not know," he answered, trying to see what it was that made the noise.

Suddenly, a blur appeared from the darkness, a leaping shape, a long body and dark hide. The chain was attached to the creature, whatever it was, clanking against the floor of the barn as the thing charged at them.

Jak pulled the trigger of his blaster, and for a moment Ryan saw the thing in the bright flash of gunfire. It was big—as long as he was tall, with a barrel-shaped body covered in coarse, black fur, a short, curling tail at its rear. The thing was squealing, a high-pitched shriek that sounded like a hideous corruption of child's laughter, and it was then that Ryan realized what it was that they faced. It was a boar of some kind, as big as a man and as heavy as two.

From outside, beyond the barn doors, gales of laughter came from Mitch and Annie, the simple-minded pair enjoying the cruel entertainment they had created. Ryan knew then that the wags outside weren't salvage—they were from the previous victims of this sick little game. Most likely, Mitch and Annie had set the tarmac trap and had been forced to improvise when they found five wags and over a dozen people waiting for them.

The mutie boar slammed into Jak, knocking him off his feet as Ryan tracked it with his SIG-Sauer. Jak rolled to pull himself out of the way of the enormous black boar, as Ryan unloaded a full clip into the thing's hide. It squealed angrily, shaking its head and turning to face the one-eyed man.

Laughter came from beyond the barn doors and the woman's voice—Annie—mocked Ryan's efforts: "Come on, stud, big strong man like you can do better'n that."

Ryan loaded a fresh clip, never taking his eye off the horrible, piglike creature. It had a wide face, dark, leathery flesh covered in coarse, black hair and just a hint of pink peeking through around its blubbery lips. It had twin, upturned tusks at either side of its mouth, stretching almost the full height of its squat head, curving up in daggerlike points. Its eyes were dark pools, a watery black like a spider's. Along its flank, circles showed where the bullets from Ryan's blaster had caught it, but there was no blood. The boar had so much blubber that the bullets had lodged somewhere within its body without hitting any major organs.

Jak was coming around Ryan's rear, his blaster held ahead as he tried to discern what else was in the barn. He seemed fine, just a little surprised at the speed with which the creature had charged at him.

"This it?" Ryan asked. "Is this all there is?"

Jak strained his ears, but all he could hear was the braying laughter of Mitch and Annie just outside the doors. Looking back, he saw them watching through knotholes in the barn doors, laughing at the antics inside. "Chill light," he instructed Ryan, blasting an angry shot at the door.

Without a second's pause, Ryan discharged a shot from the blaster in his hand, and the bullet shattered the bare lightbulb. It could put them at a disadvantage, Ryan knew, but it might be acting as a beacon for the monstrous mutie boar as much as it was helping them right now. And Jak had called it right. Without lights, Mitch and his scrawny lover wouldn't be able to enjoy their perverse "entertainment."

For a moment the whole barn seemed plunged into utter darkness, and Ryan sidestepped to the right on silent feet in the hopes that, if the boar tried anything, it would charge at where it had last seen him. That was assuming that the hideous thing wasn't nocturnal, wasn't in fact better able to see in darkness. So many unknowns, so many variables, Ryan felt his frustration—and his anger—rise.

Annie's whining voice came from the barn doors. "Fuckers ruined all the fun, honey. I can't see shit now." With a tinge of satisfaction, Ryan ignored her and turned back to the matter at hand.

Jak's voice came out of the darkness behind Ryan's left shoulder. "'Nother," he said.

Damn. This party was becoming overcrowded.

The two men listened as the grunting and snuffling sounds came from around them, trying to locate multiple swine in the enclosed space of the barn.

BACK AT THE CONVOY, the travelers were becoming restless. They had journeyed for most of the day, and this unplanned stop had made them tired and anxious. Several had left their wags, against the advice of Ryan's team, to stretch their legs and get some fresh air.

"Stay in sight of the road," J.B. had instructed. He was keeping one eye on the horizon, wishing for Ryan and Jak to hurry back. It didn't do to be waiting around like this, a whole damn brace of sitting ducks waiting to get shot.

Mildred had joined the personnel in the second wag, where Nisha Adams had taken the wheel from her husband, and was dressing Paul Witterson's wound from the night before. The wound was scabbing over nicely, and his arm seemed to be working fine. Nisha seemed dignified, almost stately in her mannerisms, but held no edge of snobbery. Mildred chatted to her a little as she dressed Witterson's wounds.

"Oh, we didn't come from a ville," Nisha explained as her husband dozed in the seat beside her. "Just farmland where we were. Had a smallholding, did our best but that soil out west is tough and unyielding. Tough to grow much, year in and year out."

"It wasn't always like that," Mildred said wistfully. "Tennessee used to be all farms, when I was a girl. Cattle as far as the eye could see."

Nisha peered querulously at her, and Mildred became aware that the other members of the vehicle were watching her, too.

"I, um," Mildred began, "that's how I heard it anyway." She didn't want to explain how she was a freezie, awakened a hundred years after the end of the world. She got back to tending to Witterson's wounded arm.

Standing with one foot resting on the front bumper of Torino's 4WD, J.B. tilted his wrist to check his chron in the starlight. The sun had set, and the area around the stalled wags was almost entirely hidden in the darkness.

"You need a light, brother?" Charles asked, leaning his head out of the driver's window. "The head beams run off a little battery pack if you need to see."

J.B. shook his head, thanking the man solemnly. "Best we stay hidden," he explained. "I don't like the thought of what's out there so much."

"Me neither," Charles agreed with a throaty laugh. He drew back from the window and reached for the glove box by Doc's seat, pulling out a stubby cheroot from among the amassed possessions therein.

In the passenger seat, Doc eyed the contents of the glove box in the near-darkness. It contained a handful of stubby cigars and a tinderbox, which Charles reached for to light his stogie. Doc also detected the glint of metal, and realized that there was also a small handgun tucked in the compartment, its barrel about half the length of Doc's forearm.

"I see you're carrying a little strategic defense," Doc whispered to Charles as the man lit his cigar.

The man looked at him, the creases around his old eyes showing in his scarred face as he smiled. "A smart man doesn't go looking for trouble, Doc," he said, "but he also doesn't run away when it comes knocking."

Doc agreed with the sentiment. "Wise words, Mr. Torino," he said.

A little way from the horse-drawn automobile, J.B. worked his way down the line of waiting wags, a grim expression on his face. He made his way to Krysty, who was standing close to the lead wag, examining the entrenched wheels with Jeremiah Croxton and the young-old Daisy.

The Armorer gestured to his watch. "That's ten minutes," he said, "and I can't hear their engine making its return trip."

Krysty looked anxious. "Ten minutes isn't much," she reminded him. "That's how long the guy said it would take."

"I'm not feeling much patience for these dirt farmers," J.B. growled. "It just doesn't feel right."

Krysty agreed but she didn't tell J.B. that. "Ryan will handle it," she said firmly.

IN THE DARKNESS, Ryan began to make sense of what he was looking at, discerning shadowy shapes around him as he stepped lightly across the hard floor in a slow, circular pattern. Off to his left, making a similar circular pattern, Jak emerged, just a dark silhouette against a slightly darker background. Ryan saw the dark, hard-edged mound of the farming equipment across from him, wondered if he might somehow use it to his advantage.

The laughing outside had stopped. Presumably Mitch and Annie had become bored by the new events now that they could no longer see them.

"Why have you stopped laughing, Mitch?" Ryan taunted. "Why don't you and your woman come in here and we'll all play 'chill the pig'? Afraid we'll mistake her for one of them?"

There was no answer from beyond the doors, just a grim silence.

And then they heard the scrabbling on the floor, and Ryan saw one of the boars flit across his vision as the creature charged at him, squealing as it ran. This one was smaller, still just a piglet really, but it had already grown large enough and powerful enough to force a man to the ground, Ryan was sure.

"It's a mother and her brood," Ryan told Jak as he ran to one side, out of the angry creature's path. "No wonder she's so bastard riled up."

Ryan blasted a shot from the SIG-Sauer, then another as he saw the monster in the flash of light. There weren't just two of them—there were six, maybe seven, and they had surrounded Jak and himself as they waited in the darkness. Intelligent pigs, stalking their prey. It was lunacy, but a kind of lunacy that made a perverted kind of sense; pigs had long been proved to be intelligent animals. Probably a whole lot smarter than the laughing pair outside, Ryan thought bitterly.

Behind Ryan, Jak was loosing shot after shot from his Colt blaster, watching the bullets rip into the tusked swine and cursing that they just kept coming. As Jak fired a fifth shot, one of the younger boars charged into him, knocking the teen off his feet. He staggered, spinning in place before crashing to the hard floor of the barn.

Hearing his comrade fall, Ryan turned, watching in horror as the boars swooped down at him in the lightning flash of his gunshots. *The bullets are having no effect on these hard-skinned bastards,* he realized. Ultimately, they were just going to wear him and Jak down, wait until they had run out of ammo and then kill them unless the companions took some drastic action.

On the floor, Jak was rolling out of the path of the attacking boars. One of the animals stepped on him, high on his left arm, and Jak bit back a cry of pain as the boar's full weight dug into him. He rammed the muzzle of the Colt under the monster's jaw and pulled the trigger. The recoil drove through Jak's hand, pushing his forearm back so that his elbow slammed painfully against the wood boards of the floor. Above him, the young boar squealed once more as a mush of blood and brains and flesh exploded from the top of its wide, fat head.

Jak saw a flash of blasterfire as, standing over him, Ryan fired another shot at the encroaching pack of animals. Then the big man was next to him, wrestling the boar away with his bare hands. He saw that Ryan had grabbed another length of chain from somewhere—one of the hooks, perhaps—and now he whipped it around the monster's neck, cinching it tight as he straddled the foul animal. With a strained grunt, Ryan yanked the chain toward him, pulling the boar backward, up off its feet, as the other squealed and butted at him. The boar struggled against the length of chain, grunting and whining as the metal links dug into the thick folds of flesh around its neck.

Ryan continued to pull at the chain, dragging the boar backward against its will, hefting it away until it was out of reach of Jak's supine body, while its enraged brethren squealed and grunted maniacally. Jak seized the opportunity to blast further shots from his Colt Python, spitting bullets at the surrounding mother and brood as they closed on Ryan and the piglet.

Then, as Jak watched, something flashed in Ryan's hand in the darkness, and he realized that the foreboding, muscular man was using the razor-keen edge of his eighteen-inch-panga blade to carve a deep cut into the squealing boar's side. A moment passed, and Ryan's figure was suddenly standing in the darkened barn, the mutant pig flopped lifelessly at his feet, a trail of guts and blood spewing from the wound in its side and the hole in its head. All around, the monstrous mutie pigs were squealing louder and louder, but whether it was in fear or anger, it was impossible to tell.

"Come on, Jak," Ryan bit out, breathless, "let's get out of here."

Jak rolled his left shoulder, feeling the pain of the forming bruise as he struggled up from the floor. They were surrounded, and these creatures were so bundled in their rolls of fat that they appeared near-impervious to bullets. "How?" Jak asked.

With a light shove, Ryan pushed Jak toward the silhouette of the rusting plow that his eye, now adjusted to the darkness, could make out lurking in the barn. "Up," Ryan explained, and Jak stepped onto the raised surface of the plow, just two feet off the ground. Behind Jak, the one-eyed man was blasting another clip of bullets at the angry pigs as they stomped toward the retreating men. A moment later, Ryan was with Jak, balancing atop the plow.

The pigs snarled and snuffled, bashing into the plow with their sharp tusks, making the rusted, rotten piece of equipment shake. Ryan and Jak swayed, managing to keep from falling back to the floor. For a moment, as he balanced atop the plow, Ryan thought back to the game of "pirates" he would play as a child in the vast rooms of Front Royal, leaping from sofa to armchair, onto the rug then grabbing the mantel and hanging from it, Harvey at his side, trying to keep from the sharks they imagined were swimming all about the floor. That was a long time ago, back when Harvey was still some kind of brother to him, before the madness had set in.

After a while, the boars gave up on their attacks, turning their attention instead to their fallen colleague and, though it was hard to discern in the darkness of the barn, Jak and Ryan were sure that they were eating the corpse.

Crouched up there, tottering on the narrow bar of the plow, Ryan whispered instructions to Jak while they reloaded their blasters. Ryan indicated the lengths of chain that hung from the hooks on the wall as he outlined his plan. Jak nodded in agreement, his eyes fixed on the boars, watching their dark, bulky shapes as they feasted on their brother, the mother on her son.

Once he felt certain that the boars were occupied, Jak stepped very lightly back onto the floor of the barn, placing one foot silently down on the wooden planks. The boars continued at their awful meal, barging one another aside as they tore away bloody hunks of the warm flesh. Slowly, silently, Jak walked across to the chains that hung against the wall, the Colt Python back in its holster. Standing there, watching the boars, Jak weaved his left arm behind the chains, wrapping one around his wrist and getting a firm grip upon it. Then, with a remarkable economy of movement, he pulled himself from the floor, muscles straining as he took his whole weight on one arm. Once he was off the floor, Jak kicked his feet forward and scrambled up the wall, his legs running to power him up until he could reach the little wooden ledge that ran around the barn, roughly eight feet above the ground. Below him, the strange mutated boars circled, grunting and squealing, feasting on their fallen sibling.

The crossbeam that Jak found himself on was very narrow, barely half the width of his foot. Jak remained composed, his innate sense of his surroundings kicking in, calmly balancing as he made his way along the ledge toward the barn doors.

Two or three minutes passed, and the boars began to quiet down. From outside, Annie's screeching voice came loudly to their ears. "I think they may be chilled," she said.

Then they heard the sound of a slap coming from beyond the door, flesh on flesh. "You see how I'm laughing, Annie? No way," Mitch's voice replied. "Those boys'll take more punishment than that. They just bought themselves a tempor'y breather is all."

Standing atop the rusted plow, Ryan waited in the silence, his SIG-Sauer gripped firmly in his hand. He could see the rotting double doors to the barn. And there, above the doors, his boot heels flush against the wall on the narrow wooden ledge, Jak waited with the

Colt Python glinting in his pale hand. The light of the fire from Mitch's wag could be seen through the cracks and knotholes in the doors, fizzing and spitting with the inconstant redness of living flame, casting a slight, eerie glow into the barn itself.

A shadow appeared across one of the knotholes, blocking the light, and Annie's whining voice came through the doors once. "I can't see nuthin' in there," she said, keeping her voice quiet but still audible to Ryan and Jak. "I think it's just the pigs that are a-living."

Mitch's voice came through the door then. "You think? Shame about them dousing the light. Was a good show while it lasted. Not as much fun as a scalie fight. Them dumb sons of bitches don't bust our light. Guess even muties know good entertainment when they sees it."

There was some rustling from outside, and Ryan waited, keeping his breathing steady as he watched the illuminated holes in the doors for further movements.

"Don't gimme that look, woman," Mitch said, his voice rising in anger. "I ain't opening up. Not till morning now. Make sure they're good and dead. I ain't no idiot."

"But I want to see," Annie whined. "I want to see what the pigs did to the big one, I reckon he put up a hell of a fight."

"I reckon he did, too, Annie," Mitch said, and there was something in his voice, an edge that was like a taunt.

Ryan watched the doors as shadows crossed the knotholes once more, and then the barn doors shook. *They're opening them, after all,* he thought. But no, the doors weren't moving. They shook a little with the pressure as a body was pushed against them, and Ryan realized, with a twinge of disgust, that the couple were making out, right there, against the door; turned on, presumably, by the thought of the bloodshed, the sadistic play they had created by locking Jak and himself in the barn with these savage carnivores.

Both Mitch and Annie were busted in the head, Ryan knew, the flame of their mutual concupiscence only sparking when they hurt others. Whatever the nuclear eschaton and the rise of the Deathlands had done to humanity, it was no excuse for people like this. In any world, on any day, they were sick—corrupt in their thought processes, corrupt in their very souls.

The sounds of kissing, the murmurings of lust, of wanting, drifted through the doors. Without another second's thought, Ryan squeezed the trigger of his blaster, driving a 9 mm Parabellum bullet through the rotten wood of the door and into the human body that rested against it.

There was an agonized scream, and the shadow figure fell away from the door. Below, on the floor of the barn, the boar mother and her children began snuffling, agitated by the sudden explosion of light and noise.

"Saint holy crap—" Mitch's voice was raised in shock "—what the hell just happened? Annie? Annie!"

Annie's voice sounded weak, and Ryan couldn't make out the words.

Mitch was cursing then, calling Ryan and Jak every name he could think of as he tried to recover. Ryan and Jak silently waited. Then, things outside went quiet once more.

Standing atop the farm machinery, his lone eye locked on the barn doors, Ryan whispered his instructions for Jak into the darkness. "He'll come now," he said. "Get ready."

Standing against the wall, Jak bent and unbent his knees, keeping the circulation going, preparing himself for the final assault.

It took about two minutes, but finally they heard the engine of the boneshaker wag that Mitch drove splutter back to life. The engine of the heavy wag rumbled louder, and then the pitch changed and Ryan waited for the inevitable. In a moment, the light grew brighter through the splits in the wooden doors, a shotgun blast drilled through the door, creating another split in prelude to what would happen a moment after. Then the doors caved in as the wag crashed into them, knocking the rotten doors aside as Mitch plowed his wag into the barn. The boars squealed, running from the colossal crashing shape of the vehicle as it drove through the splintering doors. Ryan could see two figures lit by the fires of the engine. Mitch was in the high driver's seat again while Annie was slumped in the passenger chair, the shotgun resting awkwardly in her hands.

As Ryan watched, Annie raised the weapon and began blasting, but the assault lasted less than a second. Above her, Jak leaped from the crossbeam ledge that ran high over the barn doors, the ball of his booted right foot crashing into the barrel of the shotgun, knocking it free of the woman's grip.

Running, Ryan kicked off from the rusty, rotten plow, pouncing forward, letting gravity feed his momentum as he barreled at the approaching wag. He landed on the high front plate of the awkward-looking wagon, charging forward as Mitch raised his Colt Anaconda and snapped off a shot. The bullet flew wide, and Ryan gave him no chance to try another. He was already upon him.

With a powerful grip, Ryan pulled the scrawny sadist from his seat, slapping the blaster out of his hand. Mitch was muttering some words in complaint, but they seemed nonsensical now, as if he had lost his ability to comment, to speak properly.

"You should have stayed outside," Ryan barked at the disheveled driver.

Across from the driver's side, Jak reached up and unhooked one of the lengths of chain from its place on the wall as the old, patched-up combine harvester trudged past them. The fight appeared to have left Annie, and a bloody wound could be seen on the right side of her chest just below her collarbone—Ryan's bullet had driven through her from the back, and she was losing a steady stream of blood now.

Jak whipped up the chain, knocking the woman's jaw with its tail end. She toppled from her seat, looking dazed. "Up," he told her. One word, an angry instruction.

The woman crawled across the curved surface of the wag, trying to get away from Jak.

The wag continued on, traveling slower than walking speed but shunting everything in its path aside.

Across the other side of the wag to Jak, Ryan had yanked Mitch from his seat and he rammed the barrel of his blaster into the man's stomach, driving it upward—hard—as he held the man by the collar of his shirt.

"You don't have the guts to chill me," Mitch said. It was a ludicrous thing to say, the kind of moronic bluff only an idiot would try.

"What?" Ryan asked, his voice grim. "Do you think I'm going to leave you to your pets, some kind of poetic justice?"

Mitch nodded, wincing as the one-eyed man before him shoved his blaster harder into his soft gut. "Yeah, that's the ticket, Ryan," he said, his voice strained and breathless. "Poetry justice, just like what you said."

Holding the man in place, Ryan turned his head, watching the grunting, squealing boars scramble aside as the wag trudged onward through the darkened barn on its trundling wheels. Lit by the fires that powered the heavy wag, Ryan saw that there were bones there, both human and animal. Mitch and Annie had locked other people in this barn for their perverse entertainment, doubtlessly laughed as they heard them scream and die, screwing each other senseless as they reached their insane form of ecstasy.

"Poetic justice?" Ryan snarled. "Do you see how hard I am laughing, Mitch?"

As Mitch began to answer, Ryan pulled the trigger of his blaster, drilling a bullet up into the man's gut and beyond. Mitch spluttered, a thick line of dark red liquid oozing from his mouth.

Across from him, Annie was scrambling away from Jak as the albino teen brandished the chain. She had heard the muffled gunshot as Ryan blasted her husband, and she looked up, shrieking with disbelief.

"No!" she cried. "Mitch, my darling. My darling."

Ryan let go of Mitch's body as it went limp in his hands, and watched as it tumbled from the wag and down onto the wooden slats of the barn floor. In the firelight cast by the stokehole, Ryan saw the boars circling, watching their fallen owner with dark, malevolent eyes.

Jak made to tie up Annie using the length of chain, but Ryan held his hand up, stopping the albino youth in his tracks. "Let her be now," he instructed, his voice drained of all emotion.

Annie leaped from the wag, down to where her husband lay, blood pooling around his stomach wound. She pulled his thin figure close to her, cradling the man's head in her lap and kissing him on the forehead. "Mitch, my darling, darling brother," she sobbed as the family of angry boars closed in on them.

Above her, Ryan swung into the driver's seat and began yanking at the levers, gunning the engine and aiming the vehicle toward the still-solid back wall of the barn. Across from him, Jak was settling into Annie's seat at the side of the stoked fire.

"Hang on, Jak," Ryan instructed as he picked up speed.

Jak braced himself as the wag lurched forward, increasing speed until it smashed through the far wall of the barn and out the other side, splinters of rotted wood crashing about them like rain. With a shift of levers, Ryan swung the mighty wag around and drove past the outbuilding and the dilapidated house, heading back along the dirt track toward the town of Tazewell.

Chapter Eight

J.B. pulled the binocs from his pocket and squinted into the eyepieces. He could make out the trees and run-down buildings all around them, stark lines against the darkening night sky, but he could see little else. There was something moving out there, he was sure of it, could feel it in his bones. He stashed the binoculars in his pocket and strode swiftly back to where Krysty perched at the side of the road.

"Krysty," he said, his voice low, "I want everyone gathered up and back in the wags right now."

Krysty cocked a thin, red eyebrow as she looked at him. "Did you see something out there, J.B.?"

"No," he replied, "but I can feel it. Sure as shit, something's out there watching us."

Krysty nodded. She had known J.B. a long time and felt no desire to question his instincts. He might not be as in tune with his surroundings as their half-feral companion, Jak, but the Armorer wasn't one to jump at shadows, either.

J.B. checked the load in his M-4000 scattergun, eyeing the edge of the road as Krysty went off to gather the various passengers of the wag convoy. Then he reached to a hidden loop inside the back of his coat, pulling out the 9 mm mini-Uzi he had stashed there. "Come on, you sneaky bastards," he muttered, "let's get a look at you. Prove me right."

Beside the convoy, Krysty was giving out instructions, swiftly ensuring that everyone was back in their own wags and under cover. Mildred leaped out of the truck cab that was the second wag, her work on Paul Witterson's wounded arm complete, and chased after Krysty as the taller woman made her way along the road to instruct the other vehicles.

"What's going on?" Mildred asked, keeping her voice low.

"J.B. says there's something out there," Krysty explained before turning to Charles Torino, the amiable driver of the third wag in the train. "Everyone here who should be here?" she asked.

"All present and accounted for, sister," Charles replied with a friendly smile. "You got trouble?"

"Not yet," Krysty told him, "but we may be expecting us some."

Torino nodded once. "Let me know if you need a spare hand," he told her.

Beside Charles, Doc pushed open the passenger door and stepped out of the car. "You'll have to excuse me, I'm afraid," he told Charles and Mary Foster, who sat with her baby in the back of the wag, "but 'twould appear that duty calls."

A moment later, Doc took up a position in the shadowy fields by the edge of the road, the modified LeMat in his hand. He tapped the old weapon against his leg anxiously as he waited for whatever it was that J.B. had sensed.

As Krysty hurried Maude and Vincent, who had left their tractor while they answered their respective calls of nature, a sound howled through the trees. "Go!" Krysty instructed them. "Back to your wag. Quickly now."

The couple didn't need to be told twice; they rushed away, peering behind them as they climbed into the back of the converted tractor.

All around it was dark, the sky a deep indigo now, dotted here and there with stars. Wisps of fog, rainbow-tinted like spilled gasoline, wavered across the sky on the far horizon, more of the ceaseless fallout from the devastation that had begun a hundred years before and yet never seemed to end. There were noises, the irritated tsk-tsking of crickets' legs, the distant baying of dogs, the whispering flutter of wings. Krysty walked back along the road, sticking close to its edge, her Smith & Wesson in hand.

A little farther up the road, standing between two stationary wags, Mildred waited with her ZKR 551 target revolver held low to her body. She had removed her satchel of medical supplies, tucking it down on the ground beneath one of the wags.

Doc stood close to the edge of the tarmac on the far side, his blue eyes narrowed as he tried to discern something among the withered trees and scrubby grass that surrounded the blacktop. It was impossible to tell—there might be nothing at all, or there could be a hundred men staring at him, unmoving, just feet away. It was too dark to see. He strained his ears, stilled his breathing, picking through the natural noises of nocturnal life and trying to do the impossible, to find something that—just maybe—didn't belong. But all he heard was the ticking over of wag engines, the uncomfortable shuffling of their passengers. He cursed himself for an old fool; it was like hunting for a needle in an auditory haystack, he knew, but there weren't exactly a wealth of options presenting themselves to him at this moment.

Out at the front of the line of stationary wags, a blaster in each hand, J.B. picked his way forward slowly, scanning the horizon. He could hear something, but not really hear it. Smell it, mebbe. Leastways, he could sense it. Something was waiting just out of reach. Something that came out at night, something that knew its prey was stranded.

Slowly, reluctantly, J.B. began to walk backward, his eyes darting this way and that, searching for that telltale sign of movement.

Back at the lead wag, the one that had become buried in the tarmac, J.B. called up to the driver. "You got some lights in that rig, Croxton?" he asked.

Croxton assured him he had. "Couldn't travel by night without them, J.B.," he said. "It'll take a little time getting the generator up and running though."

"Do it," the Armorer instructed firmly.

Croxton turned the ignition key and the wag's engine rumbled back to life, chugging contentedly as it spit black exhaust through the upright pipes. He let the engine idle for thirty seconds before reaching for a switch on the dash, a makeshift junction box with an old-fashioned light switch on its top. As the engine ticked over, Croxton poked his head from the window and tried to locate J.B. in the darkness around them. After a moment, he gave up and simply called out his instructions. "J.B.," he said, "I'm turning on the lights in five seconds."

Unseen by the old farmer, the Armorer nodded. He was waiting on the spongy tarmac at the front of the sunken wag, stood between the headlights of the cab, the scattergun and Uzi poised like natural extensions of his arms. He narrowed his eyes to slits, barely leaving himself any vision at all, as he counted down from five to one in his head. Then the headlight beams burst into life, bathing the area before the wag in a flickering, yellowish glow.

J.B. saw them immediately, and so did Croxton and the girl-crone Daisy.

Scalies.

Hundreds of them surrounded the convoy.

"Dark night," Dix murmured.

"WAG'S GOT A LOT of pull," Ryan explained as he wrestled with the controls of Mitch's converted harvester, urging the heavy vehicle away from the farmhouse and its outbuilding. "More than enough to get Croxton's wag out of the tar."

Jak nodded as he sat in the passenger seat and reloaded his .357 Magnum Colt Python.

Ryan grimaced, yanking the levers on the old wag, urging it to speed. The patched-together wag bumped across the fields and hurried toward the road.

THIS WASN'T THE FIRST time that J.B. had seen scalies. In fact, Ryan's disparate group of companions had crossed paths with scalies on numerous occasions in their long trek across the shockscape. Indeed, the actual term "scalies" was a disingenuous one, for it referred to several different types of mutation that the group had encountered in the Deathlands.

The group that emerged from the trees, fields and buildings all about them seemed to be very mutated, with hard, crustlike skin on their upright, naked, repellently deformed bodies. There had to be at least fifty of them, the Armorer realized. And that was just the ones he could see. Even as he watched, more scalies poured from the shattered buildings along the main street. Many of them carried weapons, clubs and knives, and J.B. ran his eyes across the group, picking out a few blasters among them. They had to have been nesting there, waiting for the night.

Nocturnal scalies, Dix thought. It explained something, of course—just why Mitch and Annie had been in such a rush to get home as dusk turned to night. Which brought another question to mind—just where the heck were Ryan and Jak? They should have been back by now.

The Armorer stood between the headlights of Croxton's lead wag, knowing that he was perfectly hidden as he stood between the dazzling beams. Raising his voice, he called to the approaching scalies, thinking there might be a few of them intelligent enough to understand him. If they were smart enough to carry weapons, maybe they could listen to reason. "Attention, locals," he called. "We're just passing through. Don't mean you no harm. You let us pass and we'll be out of your way before you know it, that I promise."

The scalies continued to surge forward from the wrecked structures, a slow, building wave that was searching for a shore to crash into. Was it possible, J.B. wondered, that the scalies had set the slushy tarmac as a trap for anyone passing through Tazewell? Ensnare wags and then pick them off at their leisure? It seemed a complex plan for muties, but not an impossible prospect.

Movement caught the corner J.B.'s eye, and he peered across just in time to see something hurtling through the air toward the lead wag. Off-target, the thing fell short and to his left, and he ducked his head behind a hunched shoulder as the object—a homemade grenade—exploded.

"Playtime's over," Dix murmured, turning the M-4000 scattergun and the Uzi on the crowd and holding down the triggers. The scattergun boomed in his right hand, while a steady stream of bullets spurted from the mini-Uzi in his left, mowing down the front line of scalies in the direction of the gren thrower. From behind him, J.B. heard his compatriots begin their own defense against the onrushing mutie army.

In quick succession, J.B.'s blasts knocked down a dozen approaching scalies, felling them like saplings. He held his position and reloaded, first the Uzi, then the scattergun. His first volley had made the scalies slow down warily, but that wouldn't last long. Outnumbered, he needed a miracle.

The Armorer's mind was racing. They needed to pull back, form a tight defensive perimeter, somehow halt the scalies' advance. The sheer weight of numbers would be overwhelming unless they could figure some solution. *Nocturnal scalies?* his mind asked. *What the hell do you do against nocturnal scalies?*

As his scattergun boomed in another explosive flash that lit the road and its surrounds, a savage smile crossed J.B.'s features. Light. That was the answer.

The scalies weren't closing in on him, but it wasn't simply because of the stream of bullets he was feeding them—it was the light. The lights of the old truck rig were holding them at bay. He just needed a big enough light.

.

NEAR THE MAIN GROUP of the parked wags, Doc held his LeMat steady as he tracked the movements in the trees around the road. There were human shapes moving there, scalies choosing their positions in the darkness.

Even as Doc watched, the fronds of a bush parted and three leather-skinned scalies pounced out into the road, boldly showing themselves at last. Standing his ground, Doc depressed the trigger and blasted a bullet through the skull of the leader, dropping him in a shower of blood and bone. The two remaining muties halted, looking at their fallen colleague, wondering what to do. Doc didn't hesitate. He pulled the trigger again, driving his next bullet through the skull of the mutie to the left.

From somewhere behind him, Doc heard the horses whinnying, spooked by all the noise and explosions. He paid it no attention, trusting Charles or someone would calm the horses.

As his second comrade dropped to the floor, leathery hands over his destroyed face, the final scalie turned tail and ran back into the woods, glancing fearfully over his shoulder as Doc held his weapon on his retreating form.

This first skirmish had been successful, but it was a lucky escape, Doc realized. If they weren't careful, the sheer weight of numbers would overwhelm them.

SUDDENLY, A NOISE came from the roadside bushes just beside Krysty, where Maude and Vincent had been urinating just minutes before. Krysty spun, training her Smith & Wesson on the space between the trees. "Stay in the wags," Krysty ordered, not bothering to check on her charges.

Krysty took a step closer, her blaster steady. The bushes were blobs of darkness on darkness. There could be people or creatures there for all Krysty knew. It was damn hard to see, as there was barely any light; just what little came from the stars overhead, the sliver of waxing moon.

"Who's there?" Krysty challenged, her voice loud.

No answer. Nothing.

"Who's there?" Krysty repeated, inching closer to the bushes, her feet leaving the hard artificial surface of the road and squelching on the muddy soil.

Again, there was no answer. Just the wind rustling the spiny leaves of the bushes, the shadowy branches of the trees above.

The blaster held firm before her, Krysty looked swiftly to the left and right, trying to make out something in the gloom all around. Her green eyes flicked to the ground below, back up to whatever was ahead of her. And then she looked above her head, and as she did so something moved, dropping from the branches overhead, a dark shape, black on the ink sky.

Krysty fired, more of a flinch reaction than a planned effort, and the .38 flashed to life, lighting the darkness all around as the bullet raced from the blaster's barrel. In that half-second flash, Krysty saw the creature that dropped towards her. It was humanoid, but not human. It wore no clothes, and its skin was hard and leathery, callused plates like armour crisscrossing its chest. The thing was completely hairless, bald with a long, angular face. Its mouth had been open, displaying a jaw filled with needle-thin teeth like the spines of a porcupine. Its eyes were wide, saucer-shaped with a black splodge of pupil amid a yellow base; they reminded Krysty of a cat's eyes, or those of an owl. The eyes had reacted in that flash of light, dilating, and the mutie had given out a noise, a breathy grunt of pain like the hydraulic brakes of a bus.

Even as Krysty's brain raced to process what she had seen in that half second, the creature landed beside her on all fours, thudding into the spongy earth. Krysty turned toward it, ducking her head as she swung the blaster she held at the mutie's face.

And then it was upon her, barreling into her like a runaway wag. Krysty's blaster went off again, though she didn't know if she had meant to fire it or if it was an automatic reaction, it all happened so fast. By then she was falling, the breath blurting out of her as the creature crashed against her ribs.

Krysty grunted as she hit the ground, her arm twisting under her where she landed. Above her, inches from her face, the creature's head bobbed in the darkness, its breath sickly sweet like spilled gasoline. For a moment, its head reared back and Krysty heard it snort with apparent contempt. Then, before she could move, it came at her, head-butting her squarely against the forehead, making her ears ring.

Without thinking, Krysty pulled her blaster's trigger again, the bullet going off into the trees in a lightning flash of propellant. Above her, the mutie flinched, ducking away from the blaster as it went off. It wasn't fear of being shot, Krysty thought. It was more basic than that—a fear of noise, of bright light. She fired again, blasting another shot into the night as the mutie struggled above her.

CROUCHED BETWEEN two stationary wags, Mildred narrowed her eyes and watched the shifting shadows that moved between the trees that lined the road. She could hear the frantic firefight that was occurring farther along the road, where J.B. and Doc were holding the army of scalies at bay, and Krysty was blasting them amid the trees. They were swarming, she realized, and it was only a matter of time before they made an attack on these wags.

Holding her ZKR 551 steady, resting her grip on her free hand, Mildred squeezed the trigger and fired a single shot into the gap between the trees, just as a shadow crossed the space there. The shadow halted, tumbling over with a yelp as Mildred's bullet drove through its head. Mildred watched the gap as three more shadows appeared, stopping there, presumably to examine what had just happened. Her breath was coming faster now, shallow, as Mildred pulled the trigger again and again, launching bullets at the enemies. Two of them fell, but her third shot missed its target, embedding into a tree with a burst of splinters as the scalie moved aside.

Suddenly, the scalie raced across the road, a thick branch in its stubby hand, looking this way and that as it tried to locate its hidden attacker. Mildred waited in her hiding place as the scalie approached the clutch of parked wags, watched as its stump of nose twitched. This thing was so very nearly human, Mildred realized, just a twist of DNA away from her.

As it stepped between the wags, Mildred stroked the trigger on the ZKR 551 and a bullet embedded between the creature's eyes. She watched from her hiding place as the mutie dropped the club in its hands and then sagged to the ground, hitting the tarmac of the road with a hideous, bone-cracking thump.

Then Mildred spun, hearing something approach from behind her, desperately hoping she could get her revolver up in time. Another scalie, this one larger with skin like batter, was running at her across the blacktop. It had to have spotted the flash of her gunshots, giving away her position.

Mildred lifted the ZKR, her heart drumming faster in her chest as she aimed the weapon at the approaching monstrosity. As she did so, something blurred across her vision, and the scalie dropped to the ground like a tree struck by lightning.

Rising slightly from her crouch and peering to her left, Mildred saw Alec, the blond-haired teen from the other wag, standing with a bow in his hand. Nocking another arrow, he gave Mildred a nod in acknowledgment before turning back to his vigil, scanning the area.

"Thanks," Mildred whispered, the sound no louder than her breath.

KRYSTY LAY ON THE DAMP soil, struggling beneath the weight of the mutie as it clambered upon her, holding her down. The nightmare thing flinched as she fired another blast from the Smith & Wesson .38, fearing the noise, the brightness. As the mutie flinched, Krysty put all of her effort into rolling it from her, scissoring with her legs to dislodge the monstrosity as it reached for her. Jarred by the movement, the horrible creature swayed above Krysty, and she rolled her hips.

Entwined, they tumbled over and over, Krysty and the scalie, one on top of the other, like some perverse, pornographic dance from another era. In a blur of motion, Krysty found herself on top of the fiend, and she swung her blaster at it, smashing its butt into the creature's head.

The mutie howled, and Krysty felt the strength in its body as it tried to shake her loose. With her left hand, the redhead clutched at the armorlike skin at its throat, feeling its hard sharpness cutting at her flesh. She held on to the creature as it swung and rolled; it was like hanging on to a bucking bronco, the wind in her ears, the rustling of leaves from all around.

With a determined flick, the creature tossed Krysty from it, braying in victory as she tumbled backward, slipping on fallen leaves and sliding down onto her flank with a heavy crash. Even as it cried in victory, Krysty swung up her Smith & Wesson and blasted another shot at it in midmotion. A dazzling flash in the darkness, and the bullet knifed through the air and straight into the creature's forehead, abruptly cutting its howl with chilling finality.

Still lying on the ground, Krysty watched as the creature sank back, a dark shadow amid other shadows. Once it dropped, Krysty let out a deep breath that she hadn't realized she had been holding, and brought the still-warm blaster back down to her side.

A moment later she stood, brushing the dirt off her pants' legs and the back of her shaggy fur coat. Even as she did so, Krysty became aware of other noises, of movements all around her. She swung out the cylinder of her blaster and swiftly reloaded, conscious that she was being watched from all around.

As she reached the surface of the blacktop, Krysty's jog became a sprint as, behind her, the bushes parted and a dozen more scalies raced after her.

"I need backup," Krysty shouted, trusting someone from the wags would hear.

She spun, blasting off three quick shots over her shoulder as the nocturnal scalies rushed after her. Then something boomed from up ahead, and one of the chasing scalies fell. The others jumped over it, leaving their companion to its fate.

Before her, Krysty could see Doc and Charles standing close to Torino's wag. Torino's head was lowered as he watched the side of the road. In his hand he held a stubby blaster, and as Krysty watched he reeled off two more shots, felling more of the attacking scalies. Beside him, Doc picked off another three scalies as they began emerging from all around.

"Keep running, Red," Charles called. "We got your back."

Krysty kept running.

NEIL CLIFFORD, forty-three years old with the start of a middle-aged paunch from too much good eating, peered out of the canvas leaves that covered the old wagon. The terrified horses, a team of four healthy mares, were fretting as the shots whizzed all about them.

Neil turned back, keeping his voice low as he spoke to the two other occupants of the shaking wag. "Ma, Pa," he whispered, "I got to go calm down the horses."

"No, Neil—" his father's voice, urgent "—it's dangerous out there and the redhead said we were to stay right here."

"Screw that," Neil spat. "Those horses are 'bout the most valuable thing we Cliffords ever owned. I ain't seeing them panicked or stole or shot."

Before his father could argue any further, Neil ducked through the partition in the canvas cover and stepped out onto the road. If he had been from a different age, he might have thought it was a fireworks display—explosions and wads of shot flying this way and that as the crazed scalies descended on the stalled convoy. Instead he knew it for what it was—a war zone.

Neil dashed forward, his head twitching as another blast went off close by, and got in front of the nervous horses. Chestnut-brown, with deep, chocolate-colored button eyes, the foremost horses were of mixed blood but mostly Thoroughbreds, magnificent beasts in any era. Just now, sweat foamed on that chestnut hair, and their eyes rolled in wide, white pools.

Neil grabbed for the rig that held the horses' reins, and began talking in as calm a voice as he could manage as another explosion went off in the nearby trees. The horses resisted, turning this way and that, threatening to topple over because of the way they fought as they were harnessed together, but Neil looked his favorite—Charlotte—in the eye, urging her to calm down. "It's just some big ol' explosions is all it is," he assured her, knowing that the words didn't matter, just his tone. "In a coupla days we'll go out riding, just the two of us. We'll put all this madness behind us."

Something boomed just over Neil's shoulder, and he ducked so quickly that he thought for a moment that he would fall. The horse, Charlotte, watched him, whinnying in fear, her lips pulling back from her teeth.

"It's okay, girl," Neil assured her breathlessly. "It'll all be okay."

Another blast, and something flew past him. A second later, he saw the dark-skinned woman from the sec crew—Mildred—running toward him down the road, a blaster in her hand. She was shouting orders, but with all the noise—not least the frantic beating of his own heart—Neil Clifford couldn't make sense of her words.

The muzzle of Mildred's blaster flashed, and Neil heard the shot amid other explosions all around him. Her bullet streaked past him, and Neil turned in time to see a man topple to the ground just feet away from him. No, not a man, he realized, a mutie.

A similar creature was following, running out of the bushes at the side of the road, something raised in its hand. It was female, Neil saw, with naked, pendulous breasts swaying in the moonlight. The creature, the female, was running at him, swinging whatever the hell it was in her hand, swinging it down in an arc, aiming straight at his head. The blade of an ax glinted as it caught the moonlight, and Neil closed his eyes as he felt something warm splash down his legs. He realized he had lost control of his bladder.

Eyes closed, hanging on to the leather reins with a grip so tight that his own fingernails cut into the palm of his hand, Neil waited for the killing blow to strike.

Miraculously however, the ax didn't hit him. Cowering, Neil opened his eyes. The mutie woman with the pendulous breasts was gone, her ax no longer poised to cleave his head from his shoulders. He stood up straighter, blinking back tears as he looked around.

Mildred sprinted past him, her legs kicking out and eating up serious distance as she made her way down the road, blaster blazing. "Keep down," she instructed, as she continued past the wag and the horses.

Neil watched her for a moment, then something on the road before him caught his eye. The mutie woman lay there, her arms splayed. There was blood across her ugly, punched-in face where a bullet had drilled through it, and the blade of the ax was embedded in her thigh where she had misjudged its swing.

Neil breathed a long, slow sigh of relief. Behind him, Charlotte and the other horses clip-clopped on the spot, frantically wanting to be elsewhere. The firefight raged on around him as Neil turned back to calm them.

J.B. HELD DOWN THE TRIGGER of his mini-Uzi, spraying the scalies until the blaster clicked on empty once more. Seven of the muties dropped, red blood bursting from their demolished bodies.

As his blaster clicked empty, J.B. spun, walking briskly along the side of the old wag until he stood beside the driver's door. The terrified faces of Jeremiah Croxton and the young-old girl Daisy peered through the window, their eyes glistening in the darkness.

"Get out," J.B. instructed. "Quickly. I'll cover you."

Croxton's eyes widened, but he pushed the door open and called down to J.B. "What's your plan?"

The Armorer blasted an approaching scalie with the scattergun, tracking it with the gun's muzzle as the foul human-form fell to the earth. "Get out, bring anything you can carry," he instructed Croxton. "We're going to have to leave the rig."

"No can do, friend," Croxton bellowed, fighting to be heard over the sounds of the continuing firefight. "I can't leave my rig."

J.B. turned to the man. "You can and you will. Our best chance of survival is to retreat, and we can't move the wag. You want to live, don't you?"

"But…" Croxton began, but J.B. had turned away, holding his Uzi in his outstretched arm and blasting a stream of bullets at a pair of rushing scalies, sweeping their legs out from under them.

A swift plan was forming in J.B.'s racing mind. It was rudimentary, he knew, but their options were becoming more and more limited by the second. He reached into his coat, pulling out two explosive charges no bigger than the palm of his hand, and a timing pencil. Quickly, he slapped them against the truck rig at his back, glancing up to see if Croxton had seen what he was doing. The old farmer was still inside the rig, collecting whatever belongings he thought were necessary. Good, Dix thought. The old man wouldn't like this part of the plan one iota. They had only minutes to get clear.

A moment later, the driver's door was pushed open wide, and Croxton leaped from the rig, a stuffed backpack hanging over one shoulder. He stood there beside J.B. as the Armorer reeled off another lethal blast from the scattergun, and reached up to assist the blonde girl's descent from the cab. Daisy had brought a leather satchel crammed with her own belongings, he saw.

"What now?" Croxton asked as J.B. eyed the landscape around them.

"Go to the other wags," J.B. instructed. "Find some space for you and the girl there."

Croxton looked irritated. "I really don't think—" he began but Dix cut him off.

"We are badly outnumbered," J.B. snarled, "and two of my people are lost right now. You have asked me to keep you alive, and that's what I'm going to do. How I go about that is my business. We clear?"

Croxton dipped his head once in acknowledgment and then, with their heads down, he and Daisy rushed down the line of stalled wags until they were lost to the shadows. Once the pair was out of sight, J.B. walked backward in the direction that they had retreated, blasting the M-4000 scattergun at anything that moved in the shadows of the trees as he retreated from Croxton's wag. From somewhere behind him, J.B. noticed, arrow shafts whipped into the foliage, felling any scalies that tried to make a break for it to get closer to him. J.B. counted off fifteen paces, blasting the scattergun at regular intervals to keep the scalies at bay.

Seconds later there was an explosion and the truck went up in flames.

J.B. turned away, bringing his arm holding the Uzi up to shield his face as the charges ignited. Several scalies were caught up in the blast and instantly turned to flaming torches. And then the second ripple of explosions began, as the flames caught the moonshine in the gas tanks of the wag, setting it to flames.

The old wag shuddered as the explosions ripped through it, shaking this way and that, amid the inferno. Scalies were like burning torches running about as the flames licked at their hard skins. Others had been thrown to the ground, the flames dancing all around them, spits of fire fizzing on the blacktop of the road.

Those that still stood, or struggled to do so, were moving away, trying to escape as smoke and fire blossomed from the melting shell of the wag.

Shaken, J.B. stumbled back a few paces, watching the flames lick at the dark sky. He chuckled to himself as the scalies retreated from the sudden illumination. It had worked.

Krysty ran to join J.B., a wisp of smoke puffing from the barrel of her .38-caliber Smith & Wesson. "They're holding back," she stated, "but my guess is it's a temporary reprieve."

"Yeah," J.B. agreed, "won't take them long to regroup. We need to get out of here now."

Krysty looked at him, a challenge in her fierce eyes. "What about Ryan?" she asked. "And Jak?"

J.B. thumbed the round-framed spectacles on his nose, before swinging the Uzi back to cover the shadows. "Nobody gets left behind, Krysty, you know that," he said. "We'll go find them."

As J.B. spoke, there came a grumbling noise like thunder, and he and Krysty turned to see the glowing red flames of the engine of Mitch's bizarre wag as it jounced across the fields. Before their startled eyes, the wag leaped onto the road, its engine howling like an animal caught in a trap. In the light from Croxton's burning wag, J.B. and Krysty saw now that it was Ryan at the controls, with Jak riding shotgun.

"Looks like I'm too late to help out," Ryan called as he pulled up the wag beside J.B. and Krysty.

"You're not," J.B. hollered back. "We need to get out of here right now."

"What the heck have you been doing without me?" Ryan asked, gazing in astonishment at the burning wag.

"Had us a little barbecue, lover," Krysty explained, pulling herself up to stand beside Ryan on the high decking of the patchwork wag.

Ryan peered past the flames into the darkness. "Cooking anything nice?" he asked, though there was little humor in his tone.

"Scalies," Krysty explained. "A whole damn army of them."

J.B. took another shot with the lethal scattergun, blasting off into the shadows. "They're coming back," he growled. "Mebbe we can outrun them if we get moving right now."

In the high driving seat, Ryan worked at the controls and scanned the dark woods all around. Figures were moving there, humanoid in proportion but hunched over. On the other side of the burning grate, Jak was taking aim with his Colt Python.

"Move now," Jak spat, drumming bullet after bullet at the moving figures.

Ryan reached down for the lever that stood beside his knee, grinding the wag into gear and powering the engine. With a pained howl of complaint, the haphazard vehicle lurched forward and turned toward the trees heading back in the direction they had just come from. To Ryan's side, still clinging to the wag, Krysty secured her position and began picking off scalies with her Smith & Wesson.

On the road, J.B. scrambled back toward the remaining wags that were waiting at the side of the trees. In the flickering illumination of the burning rig, he recognized the gangly form of Doc standing beside the passenger door of one of the horse-drawn wags.

"Start 'em up," J.B. barked, indicating a looping route with his hand above his head. "Follow Ryan."

Doc leaned into the open door of the wag and passed the instruction on to Charles Torino, who was back at the reins. "Make haste, Mr. Torino," he explained. "We are leaving momentarily."

Torino yanked at the reins and shouted to his horses, urging them to a gallop. Hanging from the open door, one foot on the floor of the automobile, Doc reeled off one last cacophonous blast from the shotgun pipe of the LeMat before ducking back into his seat. A bush burst into flame under the impact of Doc's parting shot, and the figures of three scalies could be seen running from the destruction, their bodies speckled with burning flames.

In the seat behind Doc, Mary was rocking her baby gently. The child was wailing in fear, its screams so loud that they seemed to be inside Doc's head.

As Charles spun at the wheel and pulled the horses' reins, turning the wag around to follow the path that Ryan and Jak were carving through the fields, he flicked a glance at Doc. "Where are we going to go now?" he asked, urgency in his tone.

"Keep Ryan in view," Doc instructed in the calmest tone he could muster. "He will see us clear." With that, Doc turned his attention to the scalies that were rushing along beside the wag. Resting the LeMat's barrel on the sill of the open window, Doc took careful aim and blasted the two nearest muties, dropping them to the ground as the wags sped away.

Farther down the road, Mildred leaped into the canvas-covered wag that Ryan had been guarding and shouted instructions. "Get this thing moving," she hollered.

The driver, Patrick Clifford, glared at her, vexation on his creased brow. "Where?" he asked.

Mildred pointed to the right, where Ryan and Charles were bumping across the fields. "Follow the leader," she urged, "and make it quick."

Already, the other truck rig was doing a reverse turn, and its driver, Barry Adams, was gunning the moonshine-fed engine. The sturdiest of the wags that they had left, Barry would bring up the rear until they were out of this Venus flytrap.

In the tractor, Maude White was urging the engine to a reasonable speed as Alec took shots at the scalie mob out of the open canvas doors with his bow and arrow. He snagged two in the legs and a third in the neck as the tractor picked up speed and lurched off road.

Running a diagonal path, J.B. caught up to the tractor as it bumped into the field, blasting the Uzi in a wide arc to stave off further attacks. As the wag raced past, he flagged it and driver Maude pumped the brakes.

"Keep going!" the Armorer shouted. "Keep your speed up!"

Maude turned the wheel, feeling it shake through her grip as the tractor bumped over the uneven ground. As she passed him, J.B. grabbed the side of the covered part and hauled himself up. Hanging there, blasting short bursts of 9 mm bullets at the scalies, he repeated his instruction to Maude. "Keep going! Don't slow down!"

J.B. watched as the final wag joined the convoy, accelerating to get away from the rampaging mob of muties.

LEADING THE CONVOY, Ryan wrestled with the awkward steering system of Mitch's wag, cutting a path through the moonlit fields. The wag had the appearance of a converted harvester, and it handled like a drunkard, tottering this way and that despite his best efforts to control it.

Krysty had pulled herself on board, crouching behind Ryan's seat and picking off scalies as they tried to board the wag. She was reloading her blaster, while Jak kept up the stream of covering fire from his position on the other side of the wag, when her urgent shout came to Ryan's ears. "Ryan, eleven o'clock!"

"I see them," Ryan rasped, urging the complaining engine to even greater speed.

Up ahead, a group of scalies was waiting, clubs and blasters in their hands. As the wag came closer, the scalies began to blast off shots at them. The bullets pinged off the metal plates that lined the vehicle, and Ryan felt one rush past his ear.

"Jak?" Ryan growled.

"On," Jak replied, standing up in his seat and pumping the trigger of his Magnum blaster.

Jak's shots spun off in the darkness, but two of the scalies either fell or had leaped aside as the wag closed in. Suddenly, Ryan thumped at another lever, and the wag picked up speed, leaping over the hillocks of the field with a howl of straining metal. Another bullet zipped past Ryan, and he ducked as the wag barreled onward.

Then they were on top of the scalies, bumping over their bodies and mashing them into the ground. Two of the tenacious muties managed to time the approach, and they leaped onto the front of the wag as it hurtled onward.

Jak lunged forward, using the butt of his revolver to strike the scalie to the left in the jaw. The scalie struggled backward, and Jak's booted foot came up, kicking the thing in the jaw with a loud crack of bone. The scalie fell, sliding from the wag and under the wheels.

The second scalie had clambered up the side, and he was clinging there, reaching to snag Ryan's right leg.

With the Smith & Wesson in her right hand, Krysty reached her left behind her as she dived at the scalie. "Hold me, lover," she shouted, and Ryan's arm whipped out, grabbing her left wrist tightly.

Ryan took Krysty's weight as she lunged forward, shooting the scalie between the eyes at almost point-blank range. Its face covered in blood, the mutie tumbled away, rolling over and over as it fell through the long grass of the field.

Ryan yanked Krysty back, and she stumbled to stand upright, falling against him for a moment where he sat in the high driving seat of the wag.

"It's not safe out here," Krysty said, concern furrowing her brow.

Ryan was thinking as he drove the wag through a hedge that divided the rotten fields. "We'll go back to Mitch's place," he decided. "It's well-protected, and we can at least spend a night there."

"What about Mitch and the woman?" Krysty asked.

"Chilled," Ryan told her, scanning the horizon until he spotted the silhouette of the farmhouse against the inky, moonlit sky. He spun the wheel, turning the wag toward it, and the train of mismatched wags behind him turned to follow.

"Goodbye Tazewell," Krysty muttered, clinging to the side of the stolen wag.

Chapter Nine

The wags rushed over the land, weaving through the trees that surrounded the outskirts of Mitch's property. With effort, Ryan had got the converted harvester up to almost twenty miles per hour, but it shook as if it was in an earthquake. The only lighting came from the glowing stovelike engine of Ryan's wag, but the other vehicles had lights that they used sparingly to check where they were headed and to ensure they didn't slam into anything solid.

They seemed to have lost the scalies, or whatever those nocturnal creatures were, in the panicked withdrawal, and Ryan counted his blessings for that.

Slowing the engine, he pulled the wag around the main house until he was at the rear of the barnlike outbuilding, close to the wrecked remains of the stripped-down wags in the yard. He drew the wag to a stop, the joints of the rusting metal squealing in protest as the brakes were applied. Behind them, the other four wags slowed to a stop, pulling close to the unlit buildings.

Jak leaped from the wag, and, needing no instructions to know what was expected of him, rushed to the broken doors of the barn to check inside. Ryan followed him, pulling the SIG-Sauer P-226 blaster from its holster as he ran after the albino youth.

Watching them depart, Krysty turned back to the idling wags and began passing on Ryan's orders. They were to wait until he and Jak had checked out some possible static. If everything was okay, they'd use the farmhouse as a safe haven for the night, a secure place to bed down. Some of the wag personnel complained, but they were all tired, and the encounter with the scalie mob had left them frightened.

Ryan found an oil lamp, a twin to the one he had shot earlier, resting on a tree stump just outside the barn. Using his butane lighter, he put a flame to the lamp and lit the oil. It cast a yellowish glow—pleasant, if weak—illuminating the area as he followed Jak into the outbuilding.

Jak stood inside, taking in the scene through narrowed eyes. Mitch's body lay in a puddle of congealing blood, the gunshot wound visible in his torso. His chest was still, and no breath escaped his lips. Part of his face had been torn away, and there were bite marks visible all over his body, rents in his clothes. Beside him lay the body of Annie. She had been gored through by a tusk, and the whole of her left arm and her right leg below the knee were missing. Sensing Ryan's approach, Jak pointed to a corner of the barn, and Ryan saw Annie's missing arm lying there amid the pig swill, feces and old, discarded bones; the fingers had been chewed to ragged bits, sharp bones sticking through the flesh. The mutie boars were nowhere to be seen. Even the one that had been chained up, the mother, was missing, just the metal ring remaining in the wall where she had been tethered.

"They got what was coming to them," Ryan stated, his voice emotionless.

Ryan turned, and Jak followed the one-eyed man back to the parked wags. J.B. stood at the front of the wags alongside Krysty, his M-4000 scattergun cradled in his hands once more.

"We staying?" J.B. asked, fixing Ryan with his stare.

The one-eyed man nodded. "Let's get everyone out of the wags, tell them to bring whatever they have to keep 'em warm. The four of us will go see if we can find a safe way inside."

Nodding his agreement, J.B. made his way back through the wags to get everyone ready.

Once they had left the vehicles, Ryan led the ramshackle group of travelers and his companions toward the farmhouse. It was difficult to discern much in the subtle moonlight, but the structure looked to be in a state of disrepair despite its metal cladding.

"Let's try the front, see if there's a way in," Ryan suggested, confirming his decision with J.B. and the other companions.

While Doc and Mildred shepherded Jeremiah Croxton and his band of travelers, making them wait in the shadows at the side of the old structure, Ryan, J.B., Krysty and Jak made their approach to the front door at a fast trot. Ryan checked over his shoulder as they rushed through the overgrown grass, wondering if there were any more scalies chasing them. There would be, sooner or later—it was inevitable. But if Ryan could get everyone inside, use the house as a fortress the way Mitch and Annie presumably had, they could either hide from or repel any further attacks by the nocturnal muties.

Ideally, the companions needed more light to see the path. Instead, they had Jak, who narrowed his eyes and made sense of the darkness. "Trap," he murmured, pointing to something in the grass.

Ryan and the others followed where Jak pointed, noticing the glint of metal in the long, overgrown grass—a man trap.

"'Nother," Jak stated, stepping off the path and moving through the long grass, his feet making an almost pleasant swishing noise as he did so. The companions said nothing, they merely followed his footsteps.

Then they were standing before the front door, a wide, heavy slab of wood with a scarring of old, cracked paint. The paint looked a dark color to Ryan—maybe brown or indigo—but it was hard to make out by the indifferent light of the stars. The door was preceded by a small porch, three wooden stairs leading up to it.

Pulling one of his leaf-shaped blades from a pocket of his camo jacket, Jak leaned forward in a half crouch and, very gently, touched the first stair with the butt of the blade. Then he waited, listening carefully. After a moment's pause, Jak leaned forward to full stretch and touched the butt of the blade to the porch floor, listening intently once more.

"Skip steps," Jak decided, glancing over his shoulder at the other companions. A moment later, the albino had leaped over the small flight of stairs and onto the balcony.

Following their alabaster companion's lead, Ryan, J.B. and Krysty jumped up onto the porch.

By the time the others had joined him, Jak was leaning against the door, pressing his ear to it, close to the lock. After a moment, he turned his head toward Ryan, his sinister red eyes twinkling in the moonlight. "Empty?" he said, the word a question.

"You think so or are you sure?" Ryan asked, his voice low.

In response, Jak simply shrugged. He couldn't say for certain.

The door was locked when Jak tried it and he stepped away from it. "Maybe window?" Jak suggested, peering left and right.

They could probably find a window they could either force or break, Ryan knew, but they were eating into valuable time. The majority of the house was clad in some kind of metal plating, like armor, that stretched around most of the first floor, reaching down to the ground. It was a homemade effort, pulled together from scraps. Ryan recognized parts of old automobiles and the corrugated cladding that would have once been used for roofing farm buildings. There was even an old advertising board showing a smiling woman with a drink, her bright smile matched by a single instruction in stylized white lettering on red: *Enjoy.*

"No," the one-eyed man decided. "We're too vulnerable out here. Let's just get it open. J.B.?"

Without a word, the Armorer turned and eyed the upright struts of the wooden balcony that ran around the house. He pushed firmly against one, feeling the give in the strut. Then, with a swift movement, J.B. stepped back and thrust his right leg forward, kicking at the join of the strut with his heel three times in quick succession, until it snapped away, falling to the ground with a clatter.

A moment later, J.B. returned to the front door, grasping the length of broken strut in both hands. He examined the door for an instant before slotting the jagged end of the strut into the frame, just above the rusting lock. He grunted, twisting his shoulders, pulling and pushing at the strut at the same time, force and counterforce, until the frame split with a crack.

J.B. took a single step back and looked at the door, running his eyes over the frame. The door seemed to still stand solidly in place.

"Step back," J.B. advised the others without taking his eyes from the door.

Jak crouched, pulling his Colt Python from its holster and waiting at the very edge of the porch, at the lip of the highest step. Having drawn their own blasters, Ryan and Krysty stepped across the porch, waiting to one side of the door, watching J.B. for any signal or reaction as he stepped warily back toward the door. J.B. swung the broken hunk of balcony banister around, as though some mythical vampire hunter wielding a stake. Then, using the rough, sharp end, he shoved against the lock of the door—hard—until the lock gave and the door swung slowly open on creaking hinges.

Even as the door retreated and the shadow-black hallway came into view, J.B. ducked to the side. Above him, about where his shoulders and breastbone had been just a fraction of a second before, a woodcutting ax swung on a pendulum arrangement, slicing through the air with an audible whoosh. Reaching its farthest point, the ax swung back and up, into the doorway, then sprang back again, swinging this way and that as its momentum ran down.

J.B. stood up from where he had dived, unconsciously adjusting the hat atop his head as he eyed the lethal ax. "Automatic haircutter," he growled dismissively, raising his hand to halt the swaying ax. Crossing the threshold, he led the way into the darkened house, his senses on high alert.

Beside J.B., Jak's nose twitched as he sniffed at the air.

"This place smells stale," Krysty said in a hushed voice, her .38 Smith & Wesson held before her in readiness, "like a dusty museum."

Ryan was at her side, the SIG-Sauer twitching this way and that as he scanned the hallway before them. Having left the oil lamp with Doc, there was no light except what little starlight came through the open door behind the companions, and the hallway appeared almost totally black. Ryan didn't want to waste the precious butane in his lighter. He waited for his vision to adjust, trusting his own instincts as well as Jak's heightened senses to alert them to any immediate dangers.

Gradually, their eyes adjusted and Ryan saw that they stood in an impressive, high-ceilinged hallway, wide enough to hold five men shoulder-to-shoulder. To one side of the hallway, set halfway along the passage, a straight staircase stretched to the second floor of the ancient house. Off to the left, an open doorway led into a vast room, its details lost to darkness, while to the right, a closed door hid its own secrets. Ryan stepped across to it, resting his hand on the doorknob and turning it. The door was locked—perhaps even nailed—shut. That didn't surprise him. Ryan had seen the building earlier, in the final dying light of dusk, seen how one side had crumbled, the roof caved in. That damage would likely account for the loss of most of the living space to the right of the front door, a full half of the impressive house. "Locked," Ryan informed the others in a whisper. His hushed voice sounded loud in the stillness of the hallway.

The rising sounds of winds picking up came from the open front door, where it stood like a gaping mouth at the companions' backs. Ryan looked back through it, watching the sliver of moonlight playing on the clouds as he considered their options. Finally he turned to Krysty, keeping his voice low. "Tell Mildred and Doc to bring the others inside," he instructed, "and tell them to watch those steps. We've come this far without getting caught in a booby trap. Let's make sure we keep a clean scorecard."

Krysty leaned forward, bringing her face close to Ryan's in the darkness. "Okay, lover," she breathed close to his ear, kissing him gently on the cheek before exiting through the open door.

Once Krysty had left, J.B. addressed Ryan. "You want to check the house?" he asked.

"I want to," Ryan pondered, "but I also want to get everyone inside. Plus, I don't want to get too spread out. Mitch and his scrawny bitch were psychopathic. I'm wondering just what surprises they might have cooked up here."

Jak scented the air with his finely tuned nose. "Not cookin'," he stated. It was probably Jak's idea of a joke, but neither J.B. nor Ryan cared to laugh.

KRYSTY LEAPED FROM THE porch and dashed back through the thick, overgrown grass, weaving around the man traps that were hidden in the yard. The wind was rising now, blowing her flame-red hair about her head and chilling the exposed skin of her face. Clutching the Smith & Wesson tightly, she reached around and cinched her shaggy fur coat closer, pulling its collar up close to her neck.

Ahead, lit by the twinkling starlight, Krysty saw the streaks of hip-high wire that made up the fence around the old farmhouse, held in place by rotting wooden posts that had been roughly staked into the ground at an approximation of vertical. She leaped over the wire at a run, never decreasing her speed, and made her way toward the side of the house and the outbuilding in long-legged strides. A moment later, the space between house and outbuilding came into view and, with it, the huddled group of travelers who waited in the company of Doc and Mildred, the oil lamp held in the former's hand.

"We're in," Krysty explained, her breath steady despite her recent exertion. "Ryan wants everyone inside, right now."

Mildred nodded, turning to the group in her care. "Wake up. Time to move, people," she said.

"Everyone is to follow me," Krysty said once she had everyone's attention, raising her voice to be heard. "This area is laced with booby traps so nobody is to stray. Got it?"

There was a grumble of mutual assent from the travelers.

Then the large form of Jeremiah Croxton spoke from the shadows by the wall in his stentorian voice. "I'll bring up the rear, make sure everyone gets inside as quick as possible," he said.

Doc added that he would follow them, covering their rear with his mighty LeMat percussion pistol as they moved into the house.

There was rustling from the undergrowth all around them as the party made their way swiftly through the field around the house, each of them carefully mimicking Krysty's steps. Suddenly, a hideous squealing came from the bushes opposite the rotten gate, held to the post by one hinge, and a dark form rushed toward the retreating group through the long grass.

"Move," Mildred instructed in a loud bark, keeping pace with the midsection of the group. "Keep moving." Even as she spoke, the ZKR 551 target revolver had appeared in her grasp.

Mildred saw Doc's tall, gangly form silhouetted against the silvery light of the clouds, standing his ground and readying his shot with a double-handed grip on his LeMat. A fraction of a second later, the mighty weapon blasted, a loud detonation and blinding explosion crashing from the barrel of its shotgun.

Mildred blinked as spots rushed over her eyes, the muzzle-flash casting a greenish splotch on her vision, momentarily blinding her in the darkness.

"A pig!" Doc's voice came back, incredulous. "We're being attacked by a hog."

From farther away, close to the door of the farmhouse, Krysty's voice drifted back, urging the others to jump over the steps there and get onto the porch. Ryan, J.B. and Jak were stood at the door, blasting shots out into the undergrowth as the animals charged.

Mildred heard the noise of something rushing at her and she blasted off a shot without spotting the target, certain she wouldn't hit her companions but still annoyed at her lack of finesse.

There, in the bright, half second of blasterfire, she saw the boar, a heavy, waddling creature with a dark, leathery hide, its round nose punctured by two enormous nostrils. It was mostly afterimage, her brain still making sense of what she had seen, but even as her subconscious fitted it together, Mildred's finger was working the trigger again, pumping another shot at the grass, determined to snag the monstrous creature.

Across from her, out by the gate, Doc tossed aside the oil lamp and fired another shot from his LeMat, aiming the barrel downward so as not to clip any of the people he had vowed to protect. In the sudden flash of blasterfire, they saw the mutie boar again, rushing toward Jeremiah Croxton as he urged the group forward, watching where he stepped.

The boar charged and Mildred pushed Croxton away, firing three shots—one-handed—at the creature. Suddenly, the dark shape fell, crashing to the ground with an agonized squeal. Almost as though in response, something in the far bushes, off toward the rotten farmland, squealed back—another mutie boar, Mildred assumed.

"Keep going," Doc urged, leaping over the fence and running through the garden. His free hand grabbed Mildred by the arm, waking her from her trance as she stood listening to the eerie, squealing chorus that seemed to be building all around them. "Get into the house," Doc instructed, deftly leaping over man traps and razor wire that had been left among the clumps of long grass.

Together, Doc and Mildred leaped over the wooden stairs, careful not to touch them with the soles of their boots. Doc shoved Mildred through the open doorway where the others had already disappeared, now lost in the darkness. Doc himself remained on the stoop, brandishing his lethal LeMat, scanning the grass as it swayed in the breeze. Something was still moving out there, he was sure of it.

Doc held his breath and tried to shut out the sounds coming from behind him as the travelers and his ever-present companions made their way into the shelter of the metal-clad building. The sliver of moon and the smattering of stars shed little light on the scene, and Doc's eyes widened as he tried to make sense of the eerie vista before him.

Mildred was back at his side, her breath coming fast. "Did I hit it?" she asked, urgency and desperation in her tone.

Doc remained still, watching the black horizon against the deep indigo sky, waiting for movement. "I don't think so," he whispered back.

"Where are they?" Mildred asked. "Do you see them?"

Doc continued watching the ragged garden ahead, straining his senses to detect any movement out there. There was the sound of the wind picking up, rustling the leaves as it raced through the trees. Other noises then, too, sounds of movements, of animal grunting, running feet slamming heavily against the ground. Then Doc saw something move, over by a copse of trees whose dark branches clawed at the gloom of the sky.

"Scalies," Doc said, the word barely a breath. He was already turning, urging Mildred back into the house.

Once they were inside, he slammed the door closed behind him, shaking it with such force that it rattled in its frame.

A second later, J.B. emerged from the darkness of the hall, shoving past the crowd waiting there for instructions. "Careful with that," he ordered. "Had to bust the rad-blasted thing out of its socket to get in here. We need to board it up."

As he spoke, Ryan and Jak appeared from the shadows, the younger man's pale visage like a ghost in the darkened hallway. Doc could see that both of them carried planks of wood, roughly the width of the door. Floorboards, he realized. Julius Dougal, the old farmer, was following them carrying a claw hammer he'd either brought with him among his bundled possessions or had found in the house, Doc couldn't tell.

"You might use this," Julius stated, offering the handle of the hammer to the Armorer, who was examining the door.

J.B. grabbed the proffered hammer from the man, pulling a small canvas bag from an inside pocket. The tiny bag was cinched together with a drawstring, and J.B. opened it up and dropped the contents on his hand. For a moment, Doc watched, mystified, until he realized that the ever-resourceful Armorer had poured a half-dozen nails from the bag.

"You never cease to amaze me, John Barrymore," Doc spluttered as the man got to work, hammering the boards in place where the door met the busted frame.

Maude White, the fifty-something woman who had been traveling in the final wag of the caravan, glared at Doc and the others, shaking her finger in annoyance. "What the hell is going on?" she snarled. "What is that out there?"

Barry Adams, the driver of the second truck rig in the convoy, joined in, raising concerns his companions clearly shared. "We've lost one wag," he spat, "left the others out there with who knows what. I thought you people were protecting us."

Ryan stepped across the hall, and his trim, muscular figure seemed to tower over the older man. "You're not chilled yet, are you?" he stated, sarcasm dripping in his challenging tone.

"Hell," Barry growled, "we very nearly—"

"'Very nearly' only counts in blackjack," Ryan interrupted, before turning away and issuing instructions to his people.

"Let's get everyone in the main room here," Ryan said, pointing to the open doorway to the left as J.B. and Jak boarded up the front entrance. "We checked it out while you were coming over, Croxton, and it's clean. There's a fireplace in there with an open chimney and plenty of firewood that the previous occupiers must have gathered. Get your people in there and get warmed up."

"What about the rest of this fine property?" Croxton asked, his watery eyes glinting in the darkness.

"We'll check it out," Ryan assured him. "Make sure there are no surprises lurking in the corners. Half the house is falling down so it's mostly just two or three rooms on the second floor and there's a door I figure leads to the basement."

"I'll come with you," Croxton announced as his people were herded into the main room.

Ryan shook his head. "Might not be safe," he said. "Let my people work and—"

"I'm sorry," Croxton said, "but I have to insist. If anything's in here that we need to know about I want to be the first to find out, not the last. You signed on as our sec team, but I'm still responsible for these good folks."

Ryan nodded, admiring the man's courage. "Just stay behind us and try not to get shot if anything goes down."

"I'll try that," Croxton assured him.

J.B. had finished his work on the door, and he and Jak walked across the hallway to discuss the plan of action with Ryan.

"I want two men to remain with the travelers," Ryan stated, and Mildred raised her finger to volunteer, closely followed by Doc, nodding once. "Fine. Jak, I want you and J.B. to secure the back of the house. Might not need it, mind you, but be sure. Real sure. Krysty? You're on point with me. We'll check upstairs first."

Krysty nodded, the Smith & Wesson blaster glinting in her hand.

As the other travelers made up beds in the main room or helped with the firewood, Daisy, the young-again girl, stepped out into the hallway and clung to Croxton's arm for a moment, whispering something in his ear.

"The girl needs to come to," Croxton stated. "Call of nature."

"We'll find a room we can set up as a latrine," Ryan said, annoyed with the necessity to mollycoddle these travelers.

J.B. AND JAK MADE their way swiftly through the house, checking the security of the windows and the doors. The whole place seemed secure as a fortress, boards over the windows with just the slightest gaps here and there.

As the pair stood in the darkened kitchen at the rear of the house they heard scratching sounds. With his Colt Python in one hand, Jak moved silently across the wide room, his tread as light as a cat's, until he reached the back door. Once there, the albino teen placed his free hand against the door, pushing lightly; it held, offering no give whatsoever. The scratching noises in the room continued.

As silently as he could, Jak grasped the door handle and inched it slowly counterclockwise until he heard the light click of the catch. Then he tried the door again, pushing with the turned door handle. Nothing. The door was still locked. Jak peered at the door in the darkness, trying to discern where it was bolted.

"It locked, Jak?" J.B. asked quietly.

"Yeah," Jak replied, his voice a whisper.

J.B. pulled his flint lighter from his pocket and lit the flame, bringing a dull, flickering pool of illumination into the room. They were in a typical farmhouse kitchen, a room of large proportions with a wide iron hob crouching on stubby feet, a chimney bent to take fumes from the room through an open-grilled ventilation space. There was a family-size table close to the left-hand wall with five empty chairs arrayed around it, space for a sixth that was no longer in evidence. Like the other rooms they had examined, this one featured thick boards over the windows, and an old manhole cover had been riveted to the large windowpane that dominated the back door. The room, like the rest of the house, seemed secure. Someone—presumably Mitch and Annie—had gone to great lengths to ensure they would be safe from attack. That made sense—they were haves in a world of have-nots.

J.B. walked across the kitchen, the flame of the up-raised lighter still burning in his hand, joining Jak at the back door. His feet scrunched on the floor, and the Armorer peered down and saw the black shells of insects on the worn, vinyl tiles.

"Something's getting in here," J.B. told Jak, bending to cast his flame closer to the carpet of tiny creatures. A few spots of hard-shelled black were moving here and there, tiny beetles scrambling across the room, away from the light, but most of the carpet of insects was carcasses, long since dead. "Nothing that'll hurt us overmuch."

Jak nodded before turning his attention back to the door. In the light he could now see that a series of bolts had been added to the door, five in all, running the full height of the door in horizontal lines like runners at their starting blocks. Every one of the bolts was locked tight. J.B. joined him, examining the door.

"Nice work," J.B. said, admiring the locks. "Efficient anyway. Nothing ever came into this house without the owners' knowledge, huh?"

Jak shook his head, his mane of white hair sweeping against his shoulders. "Nothing," he agreed.

SHOULDER-TO-SHOULDER, Krysty and Ryan led the way up the wide staircase to the second story of the house, while Jeremiah Croxton and the teenage Daisy followed, keeping four steps below them as ordered. The staircase, like the rest of the house, was cold, and Ryan could feel the chill radiating from the wall beside him where the side of the house had caved in.

At the top of the stairs, Ryan swung his blaster in a slow arc, covering everything to his right, while Krysty did the same to the left. With no source of illumination in the house, it was incredibly dark, and Ryan and Krysty were forced to trust their other senses— hearing, smell, combat instinct—to scope out the immediate area.

"Seems clear," Krysty said, her voice a whisper.

Warily, Ryan rummaged in his coat pocket and lit a flame from an old tinderbox, holding a bit of candle before him to light the way. Then he stepped forward onto the landing. The floorboards creaked beneath his tread, and he hunkered down into himself, the top of his head barely higher than the level of the SIG-Sauer blaster pointing outward before him. The landing continued into a corridor that ran the full width of the farmhouse. Off to the right there were two doors, both of them closed, and the corridor ended abruptly in a pile of rubble where the roof had caved in. This was the side of the house that had collapsed, though the surviving parts stretched out over the locked area below. Ryan peered over his shoulder, checking to see that Krysty was still waiting at the top of the staircase. Behind her, along the corridor, Ryan made out the walls in the darkness. He did a slow count to ten in his head, waiting to see if anything moved there; it didn't.

Turning back to the wrecked corridor, Ryan peered into the oppressive gloom. "Cover me," he told Krysty as he inched forward.

Moving slowly, his movements light and silent, Ryan stepped toward the door to the left. Hand on the door-knob, he opened the door swiftly, ducking back as it swung open. The flickering light from the candle cast an ever-changing illumination into the room, like look-ing at the pieces of a jigsaw puzzle, trying to sync up the parts in your head. It was a child's bedroom, small, with a cot pushed up against the corner, bright, friendly splashes of paint across the walls. The room appeared empty, but Ryan could hear something moving.

The SIG-Sauer held ahead of him, the candle waver-ing in his hand, Ryan walked forward, looking this way and that until he reached the cot. The flame danced at the end of the taper, caught in a strong breeze coming from a gap in the wall through which the deep indigo of the star-speckled sky could be seen. Ryan looked within the cot and felt his stomach begin to churn, a wave of revulsion threatening to overcome him for just a moment. There was a child there, lying in the cot, tucked into an old blue blanket. The child was tiny, little bigger than one of Ryan's hands. It lay there, its head against the pillow, thumb in its mouth as though asleep. The blanket was daubed with brown, the darkening color of spilled blood long-since dried, a darker stain where the child's legs had been. The legs were gone; Ryan could tell that even where the blanket had been used to try to hide their loss.

The child was dead but there was something moving in the cot. A small creature, two or three inches in all, at first Ryan took it to be a field mouse feeding on the dead babe's flesh. As he pulled the flame closer, the creature's head twitched, and Ryan saw then that it was a bird, a tiny finch or a sparrow with feathers the color of mud, its dark, alien eyes glistening like water in the light of the flame.

The bird watched Ryan for a moment as he stood still, its head twitching this way and that, sharp beak closed around a string of the baby's flesh, like a worm.

Slowly, ever so slowly, Ryan placed the blaster on the crossbar of the cot, letting it rest there so that he could free up his hand. The bird's head twitched, blurring with motion as anxiousness rose in its breast. Even in the flickering light of the flame, Ryan could see its tiny heart thumping against the wall of its chest, drumming so fast that he couldn't keep count of the beats.

Then, Krysty's voice came from the door, a low whisper. "Ryan? You okay?" She had followed him, worried for his safety.

In silence, Ryan held up his now-empty hand, instructing her to stay where she was, straddling the doorway. Then he brought his hand down again until it hovered just above the lip of the cot.

Suddenly, Ryan's hand darted forward, and Krysty saw something fluttering about within the illuminated circle of the cot. There was a chirrup as the bird jumped aside and took flight, wings flapping as it tried to escape the barred walls of the crib.

"Fireblast!" Ryan cursed as his fingers closed around empty air, the bird fluttering past his shoulder and up to the ceiling. Ryan swung the flaming candle around, keeping track of the little bird.

"What is it?" Krysty asked, and then she saw. "A bird?"

"Carnivorous or hungry," Ryan said, walking to stand beneath the fluttering bird as its wings brushed repeatedly against the ceiling. "Doesn't matter much which."

The bird flew this way and that as Ryan and Krysty watched. Ryan stood very still and let the bird expend its energy until it flew back toward the cot, alighting on the crossbar beside Ryan's discarded blaster. Then, Ryan's hand snapped out and grabbed the bird. It chirruped excitedly for a moment, and then Ryan had crushed it, feeling its tiny bones snap in his hand.

"Was that necessary?" Krysty asked, an edge of irritation to her voice.

Ryan held her gaze with his single eye. "Don't look in the cot," was all he said, tossing the bird's carcass aside. Then he picked up his blaster and urged her from the room, pulling the door closed behind him.

Outside on the landing, Krysty looked at Ryan, a frown creasing her brow. "A baby?" she asked.

"Not anymore," Ryan told her, striding warily across the corridor toward the other closed door.

Krysty raised her Smith & Wesson, covering her partner once more.

THE OTHERS SAT THERE, in the wreckage of the old house, listening to the wind rushing through the eaves. Across the room, Mildred was helping Paul Witterson build a fire in the old fireplace, snapping off pieces from the pile of dilapidated furniture and thick branches that had been gathered by Annie and Mitch and stored here. In the flickering flames, the walls were a mottled charcoal-black. The room was large, running the full length of the house across one side, and several of the party of travelers had already bedded down here with blankets brought from the wags. While Ryan, Krysty, Jak and J.B. were checking the house, securing the boarded windows with the help of Croxton and the old-young Daisy, Doc had remained here with Mildred—safety in numbers.

The occupants of the room were mostly silent, just a few hushed snippets of conversation coming from across the way as Patrick and his wife, Sara, discussed the day's events with their son, Neil. Neil was raising concerns about the health of the horses, especially his favorite, Charlotte, and their conversation had an irritated, familial buzz. There was a howling from outside, the noise of the building winds as they raced across the moonlit fields. And then, another noise, too; the noise of howling from a human throat; cursing and howling and screaming, the sound of an enraged mob venting its anger. It was the scalies, of course. They had followed Ryan's band here, or perhaps they simply patrolled the area every night, looking for stragglers to do who knew what to.

Doc shivered. Despite the rising heat of the fire, he felt the cold hands of the grave running along his spine. After a moment, he stood and walked past the fire, past Mildred and Paul, until he was at the windows at the front of the house. He stood there, examining the window frames that had been reinforced with metal, dull crisscross lines riveted to the sides, and, between the metal, heavy wooden boards, oak and ash and beech, stippled here and there with the trace of woodworm.

Doc reached forward and ran his hand across the boarded window, putting pressure there as he tried to force the thing open to see what it could take. It seemed solid enough. There was a draft, a needle-thin breeze that whistled through the tiny gap where two boards met, blowing against Doc's tired face like a fan. He ran his index finger along the line, feeling the freezing cold bite of the air, stopping as he reached the hardened putty mixture that had been used by the previous owners to presumably block the draft.

From outside, seemingly just beyond the window, the sounds of movement, of running feet and snarled cries, came.

"You okay?" The voice came from over Doc's shoulder, low and quiet.

Doc turned to see Mildred peering up at him quizzically, her face a picture of concern.

"Mildred," he said, hearing his own voice so loud in the quiet room. "It is nothing, just an old fool worrying about sleeping in a draft."

Mildred's expression didn't change. She turned to the boarded window, as though looking through the glass pane that had once been there, and waited a moment, listening. "They sound close," she said finally. "The scalies."

"At play in the fields of the Lord," Doc said with apparent good humor he evidently didn't feel.

Mildred reached her hand across, touching Doc gently on the upper arm, reassuring him. "I'd guess that the people who lived here," she said, "did so for a long time. It may look like a flea pit but this place is sturdy enough. They reinforced it all over."

"What about the wags?" Doc inquired. "What if they touch them? Burn them or break them apart?"

"What if, what if," Mildred said dismissively. "We'll deal with it, is 'what if.'"

Doc nodded sagely to himself, turning the thoughts over in his head. It wasn't the wags that he was thinking about, he knew; not really. Mildred turned, indicating the fire and Doc nodded once again. "You must forgive my restlessness," Doc said.

Mildred nodded, flashing him her broad smile. "Of course," she assured him.

Doc stood there for a few minutes, listening to the wind howling by, the abating sounds of scalies or maybe just wild animals, his eyes glued to the flickering shadows playing across the wooden boards over the windows. After a while, Doc became aware that someone else had walked across the room to stand beside him. Doc turned and saw Alec, the young man who had been in Croxton's original party with Daisy. Alec offered a thin smile as their eyes met. He was perhaps nineteen or twenty years old, still more a lad in Doc's eyes than a man. Thin, but wiry, with strong, weather-beaten hands poking from the ragged sleeves of the dark jacket he wore, the fingers jutting from the ends of his woollen gloves. In the half-light from the fire, Doc saw that Alec had pale blue eyes and light hair of a blond so pale as to appear silver. He had ruddy cheeks, too, the color showing there in his otherwise pale skin, just a hint of beard on his chin. His coloring was the same as Daisy, the young-again girl who had first convinced Doc to go on this strange quest. *Perhaps he's her son,* Doc pondered, before he remembered something that old man Croxton had said—that Alec was a miracle, just like the girl.

"Alec, isn't it?" Doc began, endeavoring to be sociable.

"Yeah." The young man nodded, his eyes fixed on Doc's.

After a few moments, Doc turned away and gestured to the boarded windows. "Do you think that they will hold?" he asked, really just to make conversation.

Alec frowned, then shrugged, dismissing the query.

They stood there once more in companionable silence, watching the flickering shadows on the boarded-up windows, feeling the drafts as they penetrated the tiniest gaps in the wood and metal shield.

Finally, Alec spoke again, his words interrupting Doc's thoughts. "You ever think about superpowers, Mr. Tanner?" he asked.

Doc turned to peer at the young man, his eyebrows raised in surprise. "I cannot say as I have," Doc admitted.

"That's what it's like," Alec told him, his voice low. "Being reborn like this."

"You were regenerated," Doc asked, "like Daisy?"

Alec nodded. "I was dipped in the waters by the spring out there in Babyville and I was reborn like you see me," he said. "Fifty years just fell from me, like it was nothing. Like dieting the years away."

"Incredible," Doc breathed. "Absolutely incredible."

"You say that," Alec said, "because you don't gone seen it yet. It's a miracle. And now everything is different. Everything."

With a few words, Doc led the young man out of the room and, so as not to wake the others, they continued the conversation in the hallway beyond the main lounge. In the light coming from the flickering fireplace in the room beyond, Doc saw now that the hallway was wide with peeling scars of wallpaper.

"Would you explain it to me," Doc requested, "this process? How it feels."

Alec nodded, his expression serious. "You get old," he said, "and you forget. That's the way I understand it, Mr. Tanner."

"My friends call me Doc," he told the young man, genuine affection in his voice.

"Doc then," Alec continued. "When you get old it's like something in you slows down and you don't even notice. Your eyesight—that's the one everyone always notices. That and hearing. They fade, like they have someplace better to go. Oh, you'll deny it at first, pretend it's just the same as it always was. 'Mebbe I couldn't read from this distance, right across the room,' you say, 'maybe faces were always kind of blurry and indistink-looking.'" The old-and-young-again man had said it like that instead of indistinct, but Doc didn't correct him now; he just waited for the old-and-young-again man to continue. "Or you miss words," Alec said, "like when your good miss calls you for grub and you don't hear her—you have a miss, Doc?"

Doc shook his head. "Not here," he said. "I did—once." He was thinking of Emily, of course, but, just for a second, another face flashed before him—flawless, inquisitive features framed by a swathe of blond hair. It was Lori Quint, he thought, but then he realized it wasn't. Somehow, in his imagining, Lori had become someone else: the girl, Daisy. Unconsciously, Doc shivered, recalling the strange dream he had had on the road, wondering at his fascination.

"She'll say something over dinner," Alec was saying, "and you'll miss it and you'll ask her to repeat it. Mebbe you wasn't listening properly, right? That's what you think, isn't it?"

Doc laughed knowingly before he encouraged the man to continue.

"You seem like a smart fella, Doc Tanner," Alec explained, "so you don't need me telling you that that ain't how listening works. Nobody ever missed nothing because they wasn't switching their ears on in time. You get old and these things stop working right, and mebbe you kid yourself they did like this always, or you forget enough that you think they did. But they didn't.

"That's what it is, Doc—being old."

Doc was captivated, and Alec could see that now in the old man's expression.

"You forget," Alec said quietly, "until it comes back. I dipped in that spring, out west in Babyville, day after day. And I wanted to disbelieve, Doc, just like you do, I think. But it worked, man, it worked. Look at me."

Doc looked at the man as though with fresh eyes, trying to imagine the changes that had been made to his body. He seemed young, strong. And yet, his words were the words of an old man, an old man who had shaken off the regrets of age like a dog shaking off raindrops from a storm.

"I was old," Alec told him. "Seventy-one. Couldn't always sleep a whole night, sometimes not even an hour. Needing to piss, to stretch out the cramps in my arms and legs, or just to lie there and feel all the aches that my muscles surely held in place. Wore eyeglasses, too, like your friend Mr. Dix. Didn't do much after a while, needed to get them changed I guess, but I never did.

You get old and you start to think it don't matter no more. You'll do it tomorrow or the day after. Or you'll be dead mebbe, the way things are, and then it won't matter anyhow."

"Life can be hard," Doc agreed, sensing the familiarity in this old-young man's burden.

"Used to run in the fields as kids," Alec continued. "Me and Daisy and some others. Don't know what happened to them. Mostly they died, I guess. But me and Daisy, we grew old and cantankerous and I guess we bickered enough to keep each other from just up and dying like most old folks."

"You're related?" Doc asked.

"Brother and sister," Alec said. "She used to be older than me, can you believe that? Now look at her. She's like some kid. Hurts the brain thinking like that."

"It surely does," Doc agreed, trying to fathom how their relationship had to have changed.

"We went to Baby because we had heard the stories. It wasn't far from the ville we come from, just a day's trek on foot," Alec explained. "Gave the people there their toll, their fee. You know about the fee?"

Doc shook his head. "Mr. Croxton said that it was high, everything a person owned. But that maybe, as sec men…"

Alec brushed a hand through his blond hair, shaking his head. "Yeah, sure," he said, "that could work. I mean, I couldn't say for certain."

Doc watched as the apparently old man stood there, peering up the wrecked staircase, glancing at the boarded-up front door. "Was it worth it?" he asked finally, already feeling the flush of embarrassment at asking such a foolish question.

"I stepped in that pool an old man," Alec said. "Older than you are now. I waited and I felt the waters washing over me, saw them washing over my sister. For days we did that, bathing there in these springs that smelled of fire and shit knows what else. But I could feel it, both of us could, even after that very first dip. A tingling. It was changing something, deep inside of us. Changing it, making it back the way it was. Making us alive again."

"Lazarus," Doc said, the word bursting from his lips no louder than a breath.

"What's that?" Alec inquired, eyeing the old man suspiciously.

"Lazarus, the reborn man," Doc explained. "His story is in the New Testament." At Alec's furrowed brow, Doc elaborated. "An old, old book, older than you or I. After his death, Lazarus is reborn. He needed only faith to do this. Only belief."

Alec looked stunned and, unable to mask his interest, a question tumbled from his mouth in a rush of words. "Died? You said this Lazarus guy died? And he came back? To life?"

"To life," Doc agreed wistfully. "But it's just a story, Alec. A legend. Whatever basis there is for it is lost to the passing of time. Though I wonder if, mayhap, this spring at Babyville is a similar proposition. All legends must begin somewhere, mustn't they?" he mused.

Alec was shaking his head in disbelief. "Bringing dead folks back to life," he muttered. "That sure as hell is some serious shit you read."

"Well," Doc said with a grin, "it does not compare, really, with the things you are telling me."

Alec's eyes rolled off to the left as he thought, as though he was trying to find his place in a script, before he picked up his train of thought once again. "At first," he told Doc, quietly, "I thought mebbe it was hurting. That tingling sensation, it stung, you know? Like the way rain can sting sometimes and you just have to keep out of its way until it's gone."

Doc nodded in response. The rains could be poisonous in the Deathlands.

"But even then," Alec continued, "I kind of knew. There was something going on, just under the skin. This feeling I'd not felt in a long, long time. A good burn, like when your skin tans too fast in the sun. And my breath was coming easier and I was, I don't know, more alive. I was still an old guy then, all wrinkles and aches, like you are."

Doc snorted, amused.

"Took, I don't know, three days," Alec said. "Then we started to really see the effects of this magic pond. The effects it was having on me and Daisy and the others that had come with us." Alec stopped, and his pale blue eyes locked with Doc's. "We were all getting younger, Doc. Really younger, the years just melting off. We felt like kids again. When we left Baby we were different people."

"Why did you leave?" Doc inquired.

"Ha!" Alec laughed. "No good getting a second chance at life if you don't go and live it, is there? First thing I did, first ville we got to, I got myself two gaudies and I screwed their brains out. I felt so damn alive."

Doc laughed once more, amused. "Then why are you going back now, Alec?" Doc asked.

Alec smiled. "I realized that I don't want it to fade, man," he said. "I want to go back and live there. Keep right where I am, nineteen years old, I guess. I don't want it to go away. I want it to stay just the way it is."

Leaning on his ebony cane, Doc nodded, appreciating the young man's honesty.

"We had to tell others," Alec continued after a moment. "We had to let others know about this, me and Daisy. Had to share the wonder we had found."

Doc turned suddenly, looking at the man with a penetrating gaze. "Did you find it?" he inquired. "Were you the first?"

"No," Alec said, "but I wish I was. The people that have it, they built a wall around it so no one could get in without paying their toll. In return they keep it clean, keep it pure, I guess. And they give you places to stay, lodgings while you're there. They were building them when we left."

Doc drew his eyes away from Alec, conflicting thoughts churning in his mind. Outside, the wind was picking up, howling across the fields with a low, spectral note. The front door shook in its frame, but it held solid. J.B. had nailed five heavy boards across it, and Doc knew the door wouldn't move until they had been removed from inside. Sounds were coming from up the darkened stairs, the noises of voices and of doors being opened where the others checked the house. In the vast lounge, Mildred was sitting on the floor beside the fireplace, playing a hand of cards with Paul and Mary by the light from the flames.

Having turned a full circle, Doc's eyes fell once more on the ash-blond young man. "Is it really worth it?" he asked. "Youth, I mean."

Alec smiled. "It's like a drug. You just keep going faster and faster. You never stop."

Doc looked at the man thoughtfully as he continued.

"My eyes are better," Alec said. "I'm stronger, I can do so much more. This world's a latrine of crap, and only the fittest survive. Me and Daisy, we're the fittest, Doc. We're the fittest by a long way. Ain't nothing going to take that from me now."

Alec turned and made his way back to his sleeping arrangement on the floor of the main room, a little way from the sparking fire. Alone in the hallway, Doc glanced down and a smile appeared on his face, as though seeing his walking cane for the first time. From behind him, Doc felt the icy draft coming through the slightest gap in the wood of the heavy front door, its touch like the skeletal fingers of the grave, clawing for him, reaching for one of their own.

"Oh, Emily," Doc muttered, "why did Chronos choose *me?*"

THE SECOND DOOR THAT Ryan tried turned out to be an upstairs bathroom, with a scarred bathtub and a toilet that had been nailed shut. There was evidence that a basin had once been here, too, plumbed into the wall, but all that remained now were the rusting water pipes, their outlets stuffed with rags. The room stank of human detritus, and Ryan coughed, as the stench assaulted his nostrils and the back of his throat. Beside him, Krysty held a hand over her mouth and nose and took shallow breaths, feeling her eyes sting with tears.

The candle sparking in his hand, Ryan stepped back into the corridor and nodded to Croxton where the grizzled, old farmer waited at the top of the stairs. "Tell Daisy we've found the latrine," he said, indicating the room with the muzzle of his pistol.

A moment later, Daisy appeared on the landing, pushing past Croxton, her eyes flickering with the flame of the taper. "Can I get some privacy?" she asked Ryan as she strode past him and Krysty and into the bathroom.

"I can stay with her," Krysty assured Ryan, but Daisy was already in the bathroom, shoving the door closed behind her.

And then Daisy shrieked. Krysty tapped at the door and pushed it open. Daisy stood in near-total darkness, glaring at the toilet.

"It stinks of shit in here and the fuckin' stool don't open," Daisy yelped. "How'm I s'posed to…?"

"Use the tub," Ryan instructed, standing in the doorway behind Krysty. Then he pulled Krysty out of the room. "Let's keep checking," he said, leading the way past the stairs toward the other end of the corridor. "Croxton, stay with Daisy, shout out loud if there's any sign of trouble. Okay?"

Scratching at his beard, Croxton stepped onto the landing, nodding at Ryan as he passed him. "Loud and proud, don't you worry," he assured the one-eyed man.

CONFIDENT THAT THE downstairs was secure, J.B. and Jak made their way back to the main corridor that led to the front door. In the flickering flame of his lighter, J.B. looked at the door that was set into the structure of the staircase, feeling certain that it had to lead to the basement.

Standing at J.B.'s elbow, Jak peered not at the door but toward the far end of the corridor. Intrigued, J.B. lifted the lighter in that direction and tried to penetrate the darkness with his gaze. There was a figure there, a tall man, standing beside the front door. J.B. automatically reached into his coat for his mini-Uzi, but he came up short when Jak breathed a single word. "Doc."

Cursing his tired eyes, J.B. followed as Jak strode forward, meeting with the older man standing alone in the darkness. It was Doc all right, but the man seemed to be oblivious to them.

"Doc?" J.B. began. "You okay?"

Doc seemed to take a moment to react. Then, he looked up and acknowledged his companions, the light of the flame playing across his fine white teeth. "I am well, John Barrymore," Doc said. "Just a little lost in my own thoughts."

"I hear you." J.B. nodded. The encounter with the scalies and the subsequent retreat to this old, ramshackle house had left them all a little spooked, himself included. "You should get yourself in there with the fire, warm up."

Agreeing, Doc made his way back to the main room where the majority of the travelers were now either sleeping or trying to.

J.B. turned, dismissing the old man from his mind as he made his way back to the door under the stairs. Jak followed.

"Doc okay?" Jak asked, his words abrupt and to the point as ever.

J.B. couldn't answer. "Let's just make sure we are," he said, pushing at the basement door.

DAISY SQUATTED OVER THE bath, relieving herself in the darkness. She could hear noises all about, the rustling and chirruping of insects hidden behind the wallboards and inside the pipes, the low thrumming of birds as they nested in the rafters of the house above her and in the broken rooms beside the bathroom. The bath itself stank, the combined smell of oil and vomit and feces and piss. Something dripped, the plip-plop sounds coming erratically, distracting Daisy as she forced herself to urinate into the tub. Beneath her feet she could feel a horrible slush, like standing in the stewed goat that she had eaten at the Traid n Post.

Once she was done, Daisy hitched up her pants and spit into the gunk in the bath, trying to get rid of the foul taste in her mouth that the almighty stench had brought in its wake. She pulled the door open and popped her head outside, spying Croxton standing there.

He tilted his head toward the far end of the corridor. "Our new friends are busy," he whispered. Then he pushed the door wider and stepped into the decaying bathroom with Daisy, pushing the door closed behind him and leaning with his back against it in near-total darkness.

Daisy retched, the awful stench irritating her throat. "They blowed up our wag," she said, an annoyed edge to her words.

Jeremiah harrumphed. "There will be other wags, Daisy," he said, his voice low. "Barry's got one, a nice-looking rig."

"Yeah, I seen it," Daisy drawled, but she didn't sound happy.

"Something will come along," Croxton assured her. "Just you wait."

"And these sec men." Daisy sounded incredulous. "You see them use their blasters? I don't like these people. They're scary trouble."

Standing in the darkness, the old farmer stroked Daisy's hair gently, pulling her close to him. She was shaking with the cold, and welcomed his comforting arms. "They're well-armed, but they won't be a problem," he whispered, his mouth close to the crown of her head. "Besides, they're what we need right now, if we're to get back to the ville."

Croxton felt the girl nod beneath him.

THE BASEMENT DOOR swung inwards at J.B.'s push, requiring no force at all to open. "Unlocked," he muttered, warily stepping forward. He ran the flame of his light right and left before him, trying to make out details. All he could see was the low ceiling and a flight of rotting, wooden stairs that ran down to the cellar of the old house. "Come on, Jak," he said, placing one foot on the first step, "and stay sharp."

Jak followed in a semicrouch as J.B. led the way down the decaying staircase, the wooden treads groaning at their weight. Jak held the Magnum Colt Python in one hand, a leaf-bladed knife in the other. His nose wrinkled, twitching as he scented the air. Jak could smell things down here. Dead things.

The last three stairs were missing, just broken splinters on the risers marking what had once been there. J.B. jumped ahead, ignoring the break in the stairs and landing solidly, his boots echoing on the stone floor beneath. He looked down and saw that the floor was part slabs of stone and part earth, and he was conscious that things were moving at the periphery of his vision, scampering to get out of the illumination that his cigarette lighter cast. Just bugs, he thought.

There had been a moment, back with the convoy, when he had become aware of the scalies surrounding them in the darkness, just like bugs. They had been there, creeping through the shadows, almost—but not quite—noiseless, assessing their prey. J.B. had wondered why he couldn't see them. He thought about this on his way to the farmhouse, sitting in the back of the canvas-covered wag, removing his spectacles and wiping them on his shirt. Before replacing them, he had run his free hand over the bridge of his nose, feeling suddenly old and tired.

Maybe this quest to Baby, to the Fountain of Youth or whatever the hell it was, maybe J.B. needed it more than he was ready to admit.

"J.B.?" Jak asked, his voice a penetrating whisper in the basement.

J.B. turned and saw the chalk-skinned young man crouching on the last remaining stair, staring at him. J.B. nodded, turning back to the task at hand, pushing the thoughts of his own mortality away.

Together, they made their way into the basement area, poised for attack.

WHILE DAISY TOOK CARE of her business, Ryan and Krysty checked the remaining rooms off the landing. There was a master bedroom with a grand four-poster in its center. The bed was old but serviceable, its coverings moth-eaten and stained. Krysty smiled as Ryan examined the bed, checking around and beneath it, even clambering up to check that nothing was hidden above the canopy.

"Mebbe we'll get a little sleep after all, lover," she said in a playful tone.

"Mebbe," Ryan grunted, preoccupied. After he had checked under the bed, he looked inside the cavernous wardrobe that lined one wall, but all he found were old clothes, rat droppings and the white splotches of bird feces.

Several pieces of old furniture had been used to barricade the windows, including an old sideboard and a cabinet, both of them piled with candles, books and firewood. One window had been left free, although it was boarded with thick slabs of wood up to two-thirds of its height. The top third remained unblocked, however, and the sliver of moon could be seen through the dirt-streaked glass.

Krysty watched as Ryan walked back around the bed, staring at it, his mouth a grim line in his face. "What are you thinking?" she asked.

"That mebbe they had the kid here," Ryan replied. "Made it here."

"What had happened to it, Ryan?" Krysty asked gently.

Ryan looked up, his single eye locking with Krysty's, a haunted expression on his face. "I think they probably starved it, mebbe they'd just forgotten about it."

Krysty gasped. "Who would 'just forget' about their own child? Their own flesh and blood?"

"Mebbe they had to forget," Ryan suggested. "You see the way this house is, the way they protected themselves. This isn't a ville with walls to protect its people, it's a single house in the middle of a war zone. Mebbe they were locked in for a while. Mebbe they had to decide who was going to eat."

"And a newborn child…" Krysty began, then stopped herself.

They remained in the room, in silence, for a minute or more, and when the candle in Ryan's hand burned down, he placed its flame against a candle that sat on a tray beside the bed, the fire starting anew.

Finally, Krysty spoke once more, her voice low, concerned. "I know you think about Dean," she told Ryan. Dean was Ryan's son, spirited away from his side by a once-upon-a-time lover, Dean's mother.

Ryan nodded. "Yeah," he said, "every day. Sometimes I think I hear him, but it's something else."

Standing before Ryan, Krysty placed her arms around him, pulling herself close. "If we had a child," she asked, "would it be like this? Would we have to decide if it was worth feeding?"

"Never," Ryan assured her, his arm reaching around to stroke her back. "They were psychopaths, Krysty. Brother and sister, hooped up on insanity. Not parents."

Krysty was shaking in Ryan's arms. "Life was good in Harmony. The Deathlands makes terrible people of everyone," she said sadly.

"Only if they let it," Ryan told her. "Only if they let it."

To HIS OWN EARS, J.B.'s footsteps seemed loud in the stillness of the basement, as he and Jak walked within the cone of light cast by the lighter in his hand. There were other noises, true, the little scritching of insects scuttling across the stones, burying themselves from the light, a dripping of water from somewhere, other low noises that would normally fade into insignificance. In the near-total darkness, these noises seemed loud, seemed ominous.

The basement was a cavernous space excavated from right under the house, mimicking its proportions almost exactly in what initially appeared to be one large, low-ceilinged room. The room was full of junk, stacks of wood and paper, several buckets of steeping mushrooms, stacked tins of food dating back to before the nukecaust, raided from who knew where. A large, coal-fired boiler occupied a position roughly below the kitchen.

They were looking around in an ever-widening circle when Jak hissed to get J.B.'s attention. Even in the darkness beyond the illumination of his lighter, J.B. could see Jak's ghost-white arm pointing to the far side of the cellar. The Armorer stepped closer, brushing past a tottering stack of old magazines that reached higher than his belt buckle.

There were three rooms over there, he saw now, small, cell-like spaces used for storage. They were on the side of the cave-in and the ceiling bowed above them where the house had crumbled in on itself. Together, J.B. and Jak made their way to that first door. Holding the flickering flame of the lighter high, J.B. peered through a small, square window at roughly head height on the door. The window was obscured by a simple grille covering, screwed to the outside. Inside, as he had surmised, was a small square storage room, not much bigger than a coffin, reminding J.B. of a prisoner's cell. It was empty.

The Armorer moved across to the next cell and, warily, peered through the grille in the window. There was a body in there, lying on the floor in a crumpled fetal position.

ON THE LANDING, the fourth door opened onto a small cupboard containing a water tank. When Ryan tapped his SIG-Sauer against the tank, a hollow metallic clang echoed back. "Empty," he muttered, closing the door and making his way to the final door in the corridor.

The last door opened onto a midsize bedroom that had been converted for storage. It contained ammunition for several different gauges of shotguns and handguns, along with a selection of blades arrayed in glass-fronted cabinets along the wall. Shelves lined the room, and almost fifty glass jars had been arrayed on them, each containing something sealed inside. Some contained preserves and jam, others bullets, nails and screws. One held what appeared to be a set of human teeth.

Krysty shrugged, replacing the jar of teeth on the shelf. "Collector types, I guess," she said.

"Not anymore," Ryan growled, exiting the room and pulling the door closed behind him. "J.B. might want to take a look-see, once it gets light."

J.B.'S HEART JUMPED when he saw the body, thudding beneath his rib cage, making him totter two pigeon steps backward before he even knew what he was doing, the lighter extinguishing in his hand. Standing to the side of the closed door, Jak raised his blaster and watched in the darkness.

"Okey?" the albino youth whispered.

J.B. had recovered himself and flicked at the warm ignition wheel of the lighter until the spark caught and a new flame appeared. "Someone's in there," he said, his voice low. "Mebbe asleep."

Without a word, Jak turned and peered into the cell window, standing on tiptoes to see inside. He assessed the contents of the claustrophobic room. "Dead," he concluded after a short while. There was no malice or judgment in the way he said it; it was simply a conclusion he had reached.

J.B. shook his head. "What the hell were these people doing?" he muttered, stepping forward and steeling himself to look in the third cell.

The third cell had a small, grilled window like the other two, and J.B. put his face up close to peer inside, the lighter held near to the opening. In the flickering firelight, he saw another figure, hunched in on itself where it had slumped on the floor. It looked human, about the size of a well-proportioned man.

And then it moved.

Chapter Ten

Moving in darkness, the thing in the cell powered forward, slamming a driving hand against the grille that J.B. was peering through. The grille shook in its frame, ringing with a metallic clang as the prisoner's arm crashed against it with bone-jarring force.

J.B. skipped back, moving away from the cell door, the flame swaying as the lighter shook in his hand. He stood there, Jak beside him in the insubstantial pool of light, as the occupant of the cell crashed against the door a second time, the knocking sounds that much louder in the closeness of the low-ceilinged basement.

In the flickering light, J.B. saw Jak look at him, a querulous expression on his chalk-white face.

"I don't know," J.B. answered. "Only got a glimpse before it moved."

With a firm nod of his head, Jak stalked forward, holding his blaster ready at his side, making his way to the cell door on silent tread. The thing inside, man or critter, continued pounding on the locked door, worrying at the handle, shoving bodily against the solid slab of wood.

At just five foot six, Jak had to stand on tiptoe to get a proper look through the window grille. J.B. stood beside the door, holding the flame for Jak to see better.

Inside the tiny cell, Jak saw the figure retreating from the door, head low, snuffling and grunting in a series of sharp, angry bursts. In the semidarkness, it looked to be a human male, stripped of clothing and very muscular. Jak's ruby eyes watched, emotionless, as the thing rushed at the door once more, spitting and cursing as it slammed it with a powerful shoulder, pumped its fists against the solid hunk of wood that barred its way.

Jak could smell it now, so close to him on the other side of the barricade. It stank of sweat and bodily waste, but there was something else beneath those scents, something familiar to Jak. "Scalie," he uttered, his lips pulling back in a snarl.

"You sure?" J.B. inquired.

Jak stepped away from the cell and raised his Colt Python blaster at the grilled window. His eyes flicked back and forth as he watched the shadow moving against the grille. Then, without a word, Jak pulled the trigger of his blaster, driving a single bullet through the small window, the flash of gunpowder illuminating the basement for a single, spectacular instant.

There was a thump as the bullet hit flesh, then the creature within the cell shrieked in pain, followed a second later by a crash as it fell to the floor.

J.B. stood before the window, holding the flame of his lighter at the grille and peering inside. The occupant was lying on the dirty floor of the cell now, its head dark with oozing blood, a pool of scarlet forming beneath it. It lay motionless, either dead or dying, and now that it was still J.B. could see the protrusions of callused skin all over its flesh, evidence of its mutie nature.

"That was one way of dealing with it," J.B. said gruffly. "I wonder what the family here were doing with it."

"Torment pet," Jak said, and his voice carried an edge. "No more."

When J.B. turned, he saw that Jak had walked away from the cell and, having placed his blaster beside him on a stack of old *Time* magazines, was sorting through the tins of food that had been piled in one corner of the basement. He had done the right thing, J.B. knew. The scalie had been held and most likely tortured by Mitch and Annie, the way a child will pull the wings off a fly, the legs off spiders. They couldn't let the mutie free without endangering themselves or the people they had been tasked to protect. Killing it, swiftly and without malice, was the most humane thing to do. A mercy killing, nothing more.

J.B. pushed the thoughts from his mind and made his way to where Jak was working. "What are we eating?" he asked, picking up a tin and peering at the water-stained label. It was old U.S. Army, with a use-by date that seemed meaningless. Didn't matter much, as long as it was food.

IN THE MAIN ROOM of the house, where Paul tended the fire, the majority of the travelers slept. Mildred was there, too, curled up inside her blanket, exhaustion making her head heavy. Doc rested with his back against a wall, his sword stick still clutched loosely in his hands as he dozed.

Mildred was thinking about the promise of Babyville, those late-night thoughts that wend their ways into half-awake dreams. She had realized that the attraction wasn't really youth at all. Well, perhaps in Doc's case, with his messed-up relationship to the aging process. But for most of them, it wasn't really youth. Being young was a state of mind. You couldn't really become younger. But physically, the opportunity to become stronger, to become fitter—that was something that Mildred understood. She had been a doctor, back before the nukecaust. Perhaps she still was, it was hard to tell when she had so little access to medicines, to facilities where she might truly heal people. Her whole life had been turned into an urgent rush, just field medicine, quick, patch-up repairs. Nothing in this environment was ever about building for the future, it was simply holding things together for the present, making them last another hour, another day.

In her early days as a resident doctor, Mildred had been touched by the cases she treated, especially the children and the elderly. For some reason, there was something about those two groups that made her feel somehow she had to do more. The "adults," the people like her, they would recover somehow anyway, right? But the elderly always seemed to have so much to give, and the kids hadn't even started to give yet.

There had been a patient, a man called Lester, who had been thirty-four and single, and he had been dying of cancer. Somehow, Mildred couldn't say quite why, he had seemed unreal to her.

His sallow face came back to her as she lay there in the darkness of the dilapidated living room, the bitter smell of his breath as he spoke, that faraway look he had in his eyes, as if he knew it was going to happen any day now.

As she lay there, thinking of Les, a man who would never see his thirty-fifth birthday, Mildred wondered if they all had that look that he had. Were they all just staving off the inevitable, trying to keep the game going until Death played his winning hand?

There was a sudden bark, loud and close, and Mildred snapped fully awake, her hand automatically reaching for the ZKR 551 under the bag she had used as a pillow. She sat up, looking around the vast room.

Baby Holly started snuffling as Mildred searched the room, and then burst into tears, bawling in loud, unforgiving screams at being woken.

The barking noise came again, and Mildred saw the figure across the far side of the room, sat doubled over, coughing into his hand. It was Charles Torino, hacking up whatever junk had settled into his besieged lungs.

Pushing herself up, Mildred walked across the room to where Charles sat, spluttering into his hand. She crouched beside him, bringing herself to his level, as the other occupants in the room rolled over, groping for sleep once more.

"Do you need anything?" Mildred asked.

Charles coughed, the noises throaty and strained, until he finally managed to snatch a breath. Mildred saw the way the man shook in the firelight, his shoulders bouncing up and down as he tried to stifle the next cough. Finally he cleared his throat, wiping at his mouth with a sour expression.

"Sweetheart," Torino said, his voice a hoarse whisper, "I need to not be in this body. That's what I really need."

"I'm a healer," Mildred told him. "I might have something in my bag to make you sleep easier."

"That's real kind of you," Charles said gratefully.

"Krysty's good with plants," Mildred added. "I'll see if she can brew you up a herbal tea or something like that tomorrow. It might at least ease the pain in your throat."

"Ye—" Torino began, then he stopped as his coughing started up again. There were grumbles from all around as he continued to hack gunk from his lungs in abrupt, pained barks. Once the fit has passed, he reached a hand to Mildred, waved and nodded. He didn't want to speak again for fear of starting up the coughing all over again.

Mildred nodded back in understanding. "Maybe we could find somewhere else for you to bed down for tonight?" she suggested and Charles agreed.

Mildred went back to her bedroll and rucksack, pulling them from the floor, as Charles did the same. Lighting a candle from the fire, the pair of them left the main room together.

Outside, in the hallway, Mildred saw the two figures guarding the main door—Jak and J.B. "Did you find anything interesting downstairs?" she asked.

J.B. nodded, the candle's glow playing on the lenses of his spectacles. "Some food, some trouble. Nothing we couldn't deal with."

Beside Mildred, Charles began to cough into his hand, trying his best to stifle the noise he made.

"The whole place is protected like a fort," J.B. said. "Suggests this isn't a great place to be living."

Mildred agreed, concern in her voice. "Any idea what those things were we saw out by the road?"

J.B. declined to mention the two—one living and one dead—that he and Jak had found in the basement cells. "Some strain of scalie," he said. "Nocturnal or just antisocial. Mebbe something else."

"You mean, something other than scalies?"

"Muties," J.B. said with a shrug. "All I know is we don't want to hang around these parts too long."

Charles spoke in a hoarse voice, his coughing fit having ended. "Agreed," he said.

NOISES FROM OUTSIDE drew Krysty to the window of the master bedroom. She peered through the section that hadn't been boarded over as Ryan snored on the worn, four-poster. Outside, she could see figures rushing about in the darkness, racing between the trees, illuminated now and then by the moonlight like old-time celebrities in the flashbulb glare of the paparazzi. The figures looked human, erect on two legs, running this way and that in search of prey. Nocturnal scalies, J.B. had called them. Another messed-up branch of the DNA tree that had started with man.

Feeling the cool air play on her naked skin, Krysty reached across to a stool by the window where she had left her fur coat. She took the shaggy coat, wrapping it over her shoulders, pulling it close, then turned back to the window as she heard the whooping and shouting of the monsters outside.

As Krysty watched, one of the scalies out in the far field stopped and, placing his hand to his mouth, hollered to his comrades, howling like a wild animal. Two lumbering scalies appeared from the shadows, then more, until a party of eight surrounded the shouting scalie, looking to it for instructions. The leader, the one who had begun the ululating call, pointed to something that Krysty couldn't see, a clump of bushes obscured by the shadows. They ran forward, spreading wide as they swarmed on the bushes.

Something ran from the darkness then, a mysterious shape, just a blocky square on short, stubby legs. It rushed at one of the scalies, charging the man-thing and knocking him off his feet. The scalie was tossed in the air and, as he fell to the ground, another boxy little shape came rushing out of its hiding place, following after the first.

Krysty watched, intrigued, as the scalies leaped at the second creature, while several of them chased after the first as it made its way across the field and toward the house. She could see it better now, illuminated by the sliver of moonlight that cast its pallid glow over the bleak terrain. It was a boar, with dark, coarse hair on its pudgy body and two tusks glinting with the moonlight.

"What are you watching?" Ryan asked, his voice coming from just behind her.

Krysty turned and saw her lover standing by her shoulder, naked. The strip of moonlight through the windowpane played off Ryan's taut muscles, and Krysty reached her hand forward, running it over his broad chest. "Monsters on the loose," she told him, "raising hell out there in the fields."

"Night things," Ryan said, his voice low. "Let them chill each other."

Krysty leaned her head back until it rested against Ryan's chest, and she felt his hot breath in her hair, the solidness of his body like a mighty oak tree as she leaned against it. "Will we be okay?" she asked. "Do you think?"

Ryan reached around and held Krysty close, kissing her high on the cheek. "Come back to bed," he whispered in her ear. "We can worry about all that tomorrow." With that, Ryan walked back to the bed, his large body moving with the grace and fluidity of a jungle cat as Krysty watched in the semidarkness.

Krysty shrugged the fur coat from her shoulders, tossing it aside as she climbed onto the bed beside Ryan, sinking against him, feeling the warmth of his body as he pulled her close.

DAISY AND CROXTON HAD returned to the main room of the house, and they lay down in a corner with Alec. Daisy and Alec shared a single blanket, conserving their body heat.

Awake, Daisy spoke in a whisper so quiet, it was if she was hardly speaking at all. "What if they turn on us?" she asked.

"They won't," Alec assured her. "I gave the full speech, word for word, to the old man—Tanner—just like you taught us. He'll keep them in check, make sure we get back to Babyville."

Daisy pulled the blanket about her. "I don't trust blastersmiths," she said. "What if they turn on us?"

Croxton shook, struggling to stifle his laughter lest it wake the other occupants of the room. Finally, his whispered voice came to Daisy's ears in the darkness. "Well, wouldn't that be something," he said.

WITH DAWN CAME RELIEF; the relief of surviving another night in hell.

In the master bedroom of the old farmhouse, Ryan stood by the window, scanning the field that backed onto the property. He had been mildly surprised to find that, in the daylight, the walls of the room were decorated with bright and cheery wallpaper that showed tiny flower petals arrayed in sun-faded shades of blue and pink and green. There was movement out there, through the window. A half-dozen birds with black feathers circled in the sky before they swooped down, landing in the branches of two anemic trees that lined the field. There was something down there, Ryan saw, but he was too far to make it out. A dark lump of something that lay unmoving in the center of the field.

"Morning, lover," Krysty said, pushing herself up in the bed. Ryan looked across to her and saw her face drop in mock disappointment. "Oh, you're already dressed."

Ryan knew that she didn't mean anything by it. "Let's just get moving," he confirmed. "Get out of this freak show and on the road again."

He watched then as Krysty stood, the supple curves of her flesh shining in the rays of the early-morning sun that lit the room. He smiled, marveling at her glorious beauty.

"I think we should do something before we leave," Krysty said as she put her legs in the pants of the black jeans she wore. "The thing we spoke about last night," she reminded him.

Ryan agreed. "I'll go," he said, plucking up the bed-side candle and making his way from the room, lighting it as he went ahead in the dim, old house.

THE OTHERS HAD awakened and were busy filing back through the garden and into their battered wags. J.B. had wrenched off the quick-fix barricade he had nailed to the front door, and he and Doc had checked the immediate area to ensure that it was safe before they let the people under their protection emerge. In the morning light, the man traps in the garden were easy to spot—the traumas of the preceding night seemed a hundred years distant, nothing more than a bad dream half remembered. As

Mildred and Jak led the way, blasters ready just in case, they saw a writhing form had been caught by one of the man traps. It was a mutie boar, roughly two feet in length—just a piglet—and it squealed shrilly as the people approached. Jak stopped to look at it, as Mildred kept everyone else moving.

While the travelers shuffled past, Jak went down on his haunches to get a closer look at the creature in the trap. It was an ugly thing, porcine but with a covering of matted hair the deepest shade of brown, a squashed, lop-sided face and two sharp, dirty tusks that curved from lower jaw to high above its head like a devil's horns. Its eyes glistened wetly, two dark pools of mystery that watched the albino youth with inscrutability. A cloud of tiny insects buzzed around the piglet's leg where the trap had cut into its flesh. Its breathing was loud and came faster and faster as Jak tentatively reached out with his free hand until, as he appeared close enough to touch the beast, it began squealing once more. The loudness of its cries scared the scavenger birds from the trees, and they took flight in a flock, swirling through the sky before alighting on a group of alders a little farther from the farmhouse.

Emotionless, J.B.'s voice intruded on Jak's thoughts as he studied the hog. "Move yourself, Jak. Time to get the hell out of Dodge."

Looking over his shoulder, Jak addressed the Armorer. "Hurt," he said, meaning the animal in the trap.

"Not our problem," the Armorer said. "Chill it and you just waste good ammunition."

Jak glanced back at the piglike, mutie creature, thoughts whirring through his head.

J.B. turned back to the house, making his way along the overgrown path toward the mined porch. As he reached the booby-trapped steps, he called back to Jak. "You coming?"

In a move so swift it was just a blur, something flashed in Jak's hand and the struggling beast suddenly slumped to the ground. As J.B. watched, a thin stream of red formed on the monster's neckline where Jak had cut its throat with his knife.

"Mebbe we can eat," Jak explained, pushing himself from the ground and following J.B. back to the house.

ELSEWHERE, MILDRED WAS encouraging everyone to the wags. There would need to be a redistribution of personnel in the wags, of course, now that Croxton's was nothing more than a burnt-out husk, but the travelers were amiable, enjoying a rare camaraderie in their shared quest. Ryan would take Mitch's converted harvester, but the beast of a machine accommodated only two people, including the driver, in its high seats, and wasn't practical for transporting more than that long-term. "It'll do for me and Croxton," Ryan had said. "We'll lead the way and the rest of the convoy can follow." Croxton had agreed.

As the travelers busied themselves, loading their possessions—and the useful things that the house had turned up—into the wags, Ryan and Krysty took the time to dig a hole in the backyard. The earth was muddy here, and the topmost layer had been hardened with ice where the morning dew had turned to frost. As Ryan worked at the ground with a small, handheld spade he had found in a kitchen cupboard, Doc emerged from the back door that led into the kitchen of the farmhouse. He had been helping J.B. ransack the property for the last of the food and ammo supplies, and had noticed them working in the yard.

"Everything is loaded up," Doc explained from the doorway to the house.

Krysty's head turned to look at Doc, and Ryan glanced up from his work, holding his hand up in the universal sign to yield. "Be with you in a few minutes, Doc," he said. "Just got to finish up here."

Doc stepped through the kitchen door and strode across the icy, muddy ground. "Might I inquire as to what it is that trammels you?" he asked.

Krysty turned then, and Doc saw that she held a tiny figure wrapped in a blanket. It appeared to be a child, a baby, and Doc suddenly felt that plummeting feeling in his stomach.

"We found her upstairs," Ryan explained as he continued digging the shallow grave in the soil. "Seems wrong, somehow, to just leave her for the birds to peck at."

Doc bowed his head respectfully, and stood in silence as they finished their funereal task. Loading a wag by the edge of the yard, Croxton spied the group and stood unnoticed, watching silently as they buried the child's body.

Once Ryan was done, Krysty laid the baby out in the soil as black feathered birds circled above, cawing back and forth in their ugly, discordant voices. As Ryan picked up the spade to begin piling soil on the child, Doc stopped him. Ryan and Krysty watched, and then the old man spoke the Lord's Prayer in his bold, stentorian voice and all three of them bowed their heads over the tiny grave. Once Doc had finished, Ryan set about burying the baby girl, aware that the corpse would likely be dug up again by wild animals in a matter of hours.

It didn't matter; they had done what they could.

WHEN THEY JOINED their companions, out by the wags at the side of the house, Krysty, Ryan and Doc found them eating. In the morning light, J.B. and Jak had raided the tinned supplies in the basement and were sharing cans with everyone in the group.

J.B. turned at their approach and handed an open tin to Krysty. The circular can was about an inch and a half deep and it sat snugly in the palm of her hand. "Have some breakfast 'fore we hit the road, why don't you?" J.B. suggested.

"Why, thank you," Krysty said, taking the proffered can. She looked at the contents, sniffing at it warily. The can contained a powder that J.B. had added boiled water to, creating a brown sludge. With no label on the can and its scent an indefinable mixture of chemicals, the contents could have been some kind of gravy, but may just as likely have been chocolate sauce. Krysty dipped her finger in the gunk and tasted it, before smiling. "Tastes good," she announced.

Beside Krysty, Doc and Ryan were tucking into their own cans, neither of them saying very much.

Twenty minutes later they were on the move.

Chapter Eleven

The five wags rolled over the shockscape, passing dead trees in their fields of dust, lumbering past forgotten spots on the map that had once been thriving communities before the nukes had fallen.

The old farmer and leader of the refugees, Jeremiah Croxton, was riding shotgun as Ryan drove the converted harvester that he had acquired from Mitch and Annie.

"I figure we're about a day away from Baby," Croxton said as they pulled away from the road sign that welcomed visitors to Tazewell. The scalies were nowhere to be seen, presumably they had gone back to whatever passed for a nest during the daytime. Ryan turned the wheels hard, guiding the peculiar wag off the road and over a flat expanse of field. Croxton looked at him. "Probably quicker by road, Ryan," he said, smirking.

Ryan shook his head. "Krysty told me all about those tenacious muties you bumped into on the road," he said. "I don't want to run into them again. No point tempting fate."

Croxton shrugged. "Can't say I blame you."

Maude White's canvas-covered tractor wag trundled along at the rear of the group, carrying Vincent and J.B. as before. They had been joined by another passenger, the seemingly young girl Daisy. Daisy seemed restless, and she kept pulling the heavy curtain back and peering down the way they had just come.

"You expecting someone, Daisy?" J.B. asked when he saw her peer out for a fourth time.

She turned back and graced him with her warm, friendly smile. "I fucking hope not, mister," she said. "What were those things we saw anyway? Back in that Tassel place."

"I don't know what they were."

"They seemed pretty pissed," Daisy drawled, shrugging.

J.B. agreed. "People out here, outside of the villes, can be kind of territorial sometimes," he explained.

Sitting close to the front flap of the tentlike wag, Vincent White shook his balding head. "Those things weren't people, friend."

"Mebbe they were once," J.B. told them both, "a long time ago. Now they're just territorial bastards with too much rad-blasted shit in their heads."

"Nothing like that in Babyville," Daisy said. "Wouldn't get past the gate."

"Have you seen them before?" Vincent asked Dix thoughtfully.

"I've seen similar things," J.B. assured him. "Muties of every stripe, things that you think might almost be human apart from one difference. Some of them are smart and some of them are triple stupe, but they all follow one basic rule—they protect themselves against outsiders."

"We all do that, Mr. Dix," Vincent remarked, turning back to watch the path ahead as his wife urged more power from the wag's chugging engine.

"I guess we do, at that," J.B. muttered.

OTHER THAN THE occasional refueling stop, the wags
didn't pull to a halt until midafternoon. The winter sun
was a distant white ball, low on the horizon. They had
joined onto something called Route 25, whose occasional, surviving signs promised it would lead them to
Newport, Morristown and Knoxville. Newport and Morristown had both turned out to be bombed-out wreckage.
They hadn't got as far as Knoxville.

But in the midafternoon, they hit a snag. Ryan pulled
the wide wag he drove to a shuddering halt, letting
the engine tick over as he stared at what lay ahead.
Where once there had been road, now there was just a
huge crater, over a half-mile wide and hundreds of feet
deep.

Croxton looked behind them, watching the other wags
dutifully pull to a halt. "What we going to do?" the old
farmer asked, assessing the crater ahead of them.

In his seat, Ryan was checking his lapel Geiger
counter. The area was hot. "We need to turn around,"
he decided, "and find another route. I'm not going in
there."

"The sides aren't that steep," Croxton argued. "The
wags can make it. Mebbe not this heap of crap, but the
others can. We'll double-up some."

Ryan looked at him, his blue eye holding Croxton's
gaze. "No, we won't," he said. "Some kind of missile
hit that place, and whatever it was the residual radiation
is still off the scale. We need to back up."

As Ryan began turning the wag, lurching toward
the side of the crumbling Route 25, Croxton waved
to the following wag train, indicating that they were
to follow.

"You know," Croxton said as the harvester bumped over the wreckage of the blacktop and onto the dusty plains that surrounded the crater, "I would have just driven in if you hadn't been here."

"Whatever Baby is offering," Ryan told him, his eye locked on the uneven ground ahead, "you wouldn't have survived two weeks after being in that heat. I don't even like being this close."

Croxton shrugged, dismissing Ryan's concerns. "Radiation is everywhere," he said.

"So are bullets," Ryan told him, "but I don't intend to stop long enough to catch one."

They continued trudging, bumping and crashing over the mess of wasteland that had once been lush fields and proud towns, feeling the wintry chill as the sun sank lower to the horizon.

DOC GAZED OUT of the windows of Charles's horse-drawn wag while Mildred sat in the back, squeezed between newcomer Alec and Mary and her baby. Alec's head kept lolling back until he finally drifted off to sleep; the night in Tazewell had been exhausting for him, and his time in Mitch's farmhouse had been restless, his sleep patchy. Alec gave a funny little snort-gurgle as the wag skipped over a bump in the field, and Mary and Mildred stifled laughter, looking at each other like guilty schoolchildren.

"Wish I could sleep like that," Mary said, keeping her voice low.

Mildred looked at the baby in Mary's arms. "At least Holly seems to be sleeping through it all," she said.

"Yeah," Mary agreed dispiritedly. "She's a well-behaved girl. Guess I should be thankful for that."

"Why are you here?" Mildred asked, admiring the baby in the woman's arms. It was a question that had been on her mind for a while, but she surprised herself with the way she just blurted it out.

"What?" Mary asked. "You mean, where's the daddy or why am I running away?"

"I didn't realize you were running away," Mildred said, her eyes meeting Mary's. "I didn't mean to pry."

In response, Mary smiled. "That's okay, Mildred. I don't mind. You've been good to me, and you have a right to ask."

"It's just that, you seem so young," Mildred began, "to be looking for this promised fountain of eternal youth, I mean."

"I'm thirty-eight," Mary told her. "Be thirty-nine soon, once spring rolls around."

After a moment's thought, Mary continued. "You see Alec there?" she asked, indicating the blond-haired young man with the bow. "I'd just had Holly when Alec came to our farmhouse out near 'Tucky border. I mean, she was just two weeks old. And my old man, Joe, he was so mad with her. I thought he was going to kill me and her both. We already had two lovely children, you see, and there was no room in his heart for Holly."

"Raising a child is hard work," Mildred said gently.

"Holly isn't his," Mary said. "She's mine, that's true, but… Well, he had an accident and so she ain't his. I tried to tell him about the man. I'd been at the nearest ville, an awful place—more blasters than brains inside those walls, I swear. I'd been there to trade some carrots and beets, try to get some better seeds, because the farm was doing well by then. And this man, he'd said he wasn't interested in carrots, he wanted something else."

Mary's words trailed off and Mildred looked at the baby in her arms once again. "And you…?" Mildred encouraged.

"No, I wouldn't," Mary said firmly. "I love my Joe. Wouldn't do nothing like that. But this man, he wouldn't take no for an answer. Holly's a rape-child, Mildred. That's what she is."

"I'm so sorry," Mildred said, her words barely a whisper.

"I don't mind," Mary said. "I love her and that's all that really matters, isn't it? But this pool, this magical pool in Babyville… I figure that can fix us, restore us to what we was. Repair me. So Joe can love me again. Love us both."

The wag hopped over another lump in the track, and Holly woke with a start, her blue eyes popping open. A moment later she began to wail, and Mary soothed her, cooing words of consolation.

The noise of the baby woke Alec then, and he groaned and swore as he looked around him. "Can you mebbe shut your brat up?" he asked, glaring at Mary, rubbing his hand over his tired face.

The wags trundled on.

TWO HOURS LATER, as they drove along another road, just a dirt track between the fallen ruins of civilization, Croxton told Ryan to turn off.

"You know where we are?" Ryan asked.

Croxton laughed. "I got me a fair idea," he said, pointing. "Look."

Ryan looked where the man pointed, and saw people bent over, working in a field. They were planting crops in long rows, a half-dozen people working the field together. As Ryan looked around, he saw that other fields showed evidence of farming, and each one a handful of people—young and fit, some just children—worked at sowing and plowing and picking. One field had been left fallow, just the churned-up soil showing in the afternoon sun. Several youngsters were playing in the field, throwing a ball to one another.

"Promised land, you reckon?" Croxton asked, unable to keep the joy from his tone.

"We'll see," Ryan replied, urging the shuddering wag along the dirt track, trundling over a small rise.

As they came over the rise, Croxton leaned forward in his seat, studying something in the far distance. Noticing, Ryan looked up from the road and off to the horizon. There, looming low on the skyline, were irregular, dark shapes, angling toward the cloudy, silver sky. It looked like the fingers of a dead man, reaching from the grave, grasping at the sky above.

"We're here," Croxton said, the hint of pride in his voice. "That there is Baby."

Struggling with the wheel as the old harvester bumped over the pockmarked ground, Ryan glanced at the old farmer sitting beside him. "You're sure?" he asked, turning his attention back to the dark shapes on the horizon.

"Oh, this is it all right," Croxton assured him. "Looks just like what Daisy described."

Ryan studied the structures of the ville as they drew closer, the other wags following in their wake. There was a wall, he saw now, a wide concrete structure almost ten feet in height. Its surface was smooth, reflecting the glint of the dwindling sun's rays, and it looked substantial. There was a gate, Ryan saw, a towering hunk of wood strengthened by metal, that had been set in place in the structure of the wall. The gate looked incongruous, out of place in the smooth lines of the wall.

Beyond the wall, towering above it, Ryan could see buildings now, the sunlight turning them into dark, brutal lines snatching at the sky. These were the dead man's fingers he had seen when they had first bumped over the incline and spied the ville. Three in all, they looked firm, solid.

Ryan was surprised. This didn't look like a ville, not the kind he had imagined at least. He had expected some broken-down settlement of splintering shacks and rusting wags. Instead, here was a ville from another era. It looked like something from the old days, before skydark—a city. Nothing about it was temporary; it had been planned and constructed with thought, with one eye on the future.

As Ryan led the convoy of wags toward the new ville called Baby, he wondered if what he was looking at was the future of humanity. Was this the kind of place that would finally replace the Deathlands? A place where people would be safe from the horrors of the outside world?

Unconsciously, Ryan worked the accelerator, urging more power from the beast of a wag, jolting over the rough ground toward the gates of Baby.

Chapter Twelve

Working the brake, Ryan pulled his wag up to the imposing, wooden gate that waited in the high, concrete walls surrounding Babyville. There was a huge clock face to the side of the gates, high up in the wall and angled to catch the sun. The clock hands were still, stuck at 10:10 for slow eternity. Two other wags waited before him, engines idling as their occupants spoke to the sec men waiting in a sentry post beside the tall gate. The wag's engine shuddered beneath him as Ryan scanned the top of the wall and the spaces around the gate, spotting more sec men.

Behind Ryan's wag, the four other vehicles in the convoy drew to a halt, waiting in line to see what would happen next. Out across from the ville, people were working in the fields, tilling at the land, turning it into something good again. The trace of a smile crossed Ryan's lips when he saw this. Young men and women were out there, some just kids, trying to reap some good from the poisoned land. Perhaps this was the future, he thought. Perhaps this was what was needed to make the world right again.

Beside him, Jeremiah Croxton was struggling to get up, clambering out of the bucket seat and working his way ungracefully down the short ladder that led down the side of the high wag.

"Need me to come with you?" Ryan asked him.

The old farmer nodded. "You're my sec man, aren't you?" he grunted.

Ryan slipped out of his seat and leaped down from the wag, landing on the soft earth that formed an erratic track to the proud gate of the ville. He reached up and pulled his Steyr rifle from its cubbyhole beneath the driver's seat, slung it over his shoulder by the carrying strap. It wouldn't be much use here, and if they ran into trouble Ryan would rely on the SIG-Sauer he wore at his hip, but he disliked leaving the powerful rifle untended in case it was lifted while his attention was elsewhere. As he pulled it from its storage place, Alec the young-again lad, came running up to them from his place in another wag, reminding them of what needed to be done. Krysty followed him, her hand held close to her holstered weapon.

"There's a procedure," Alec said. "They'll want to check you out before you can enter."

"You've done this before," Ryan stated. "Anything special we ought to know?"

Alec shrugged. "Just be honest with them."

Ryan thanked him and indicated that he was to stay in his wag for now. Alec ran back to Charles's four-wheel drive, kicking up the dirt as he went. Krysty followed, slamming the door behind him and standing ready at the front of the idling wag.

Croxton walked over to the main entrance, his gait evincing a slight limp to the left as he walked.

"You okay, Croxton?" Ryan asked as he caught up with the man.

"Leg's giving me trouble," Croxton grumbled. "Sitting in that bone-shaking pile of crap too long."

Agreeing, Ryan smiled. It was good to be on his feet once again.

Behind Ryan, in the line of wags, his companions were watching carefully to see what would happen next. In the rearmost wag, J.B. pushed through the canvas cover and dropped down to the ground, leaving Jak to cover the wag alone. As the Armorer walked past the next wag in the line, Daisy pushed forward and slipped from the back. J.B. gave her a fierce look. "I don't need any backup, girl," he said as he stalked past.

Mildred and Doc waited at the doors of the next wag, and Krysty the one after. J.B. gave them each the same instructions. "Wait, keep your eyes open, don't get trigger-happy unless you need to." It was just reassurance; the companions had worked together for long enough that they knew how to handle situations like this.

Up ahead, Ryan and Croxton made their way to the sentry booth and waited their turn. To Ryan's surprise, an orderly line had formed there, each visitor waiting his turn under the watchful eyes of the sec men. Four sec guards—three men and one woman—stood watching the visitors, their expressions grim. Each was dressed in an armored vest over their clothes, and each held an automatic rifle in the at-ease position. Two more sec men—a man and a woman—stood inside the sentry post itself, looking over the visitors, interrogating them with practiced ease.

Standing beside Croxton outside the sentry post, Ryan watched the proceedings warily. The sec men looked healthy, strong, and none of them looked to be over twenty-five. Two looked like teenagers, the girl in the booth couldn't have been much older than thirteen.

Babyville, Ryan thought, where the population keeps growing younger. For just a second, his hand tensed by the holster he wore at his hip.

The travelers in the booth were being ushered out by the sec men. They were an elderly couple, husband and wife most likely, and neither of them would see sixty again. Their old, wrinkled faces vividly showed their relief, and Ryan watched as the sec men gave their battered old wag the once-over before letting them drive through into the ville. The huge gate was winched open to let the wag through, and Ryan saw now that it had a portcullis shielding it as well as the sturdy gate itself. Both needed to be opened separately before anyone could gain entry into the ville, like an airlock.

That expression on the oldsters' faces haunted Ryan's thoughts. It said something. It said that they had found salvation, the promised land. Ryan wasn't so sure.

The line shuffled forward under the watchful eye of the sec men, and Ryan took everything in as he and Croxton waited their turn.

The old man looked at Ryan, seeing the grim expression on the one-eyed man's face. "You okay, son?" he asked.

Ryan nodded, saying nothing.

Croxton pressed the issue. "You look a little out of sorts, is all. If you don't mind my saying."

"I don't mind," Ryan said, his voice low. He didn't look at the old farmer. His single eye was scanning the top of the high wall, searching for other sec men. The operation seemed heavily fortified, and Ryan would bet his last clip of ammo that there were more guards watching them from hidden positions all around. The place was unnerving, disquieting. It was so well-fortified, in some ways it seemed like a prison.

"Lighten up," Croxton urged Ryan in his rich, friendly voice. "We're here now. The worst of it's over."

"The worst of it's never over," Ryan replied, still scanning the battlements above them. "You're old enough to know that better than me."

Croxton shook his head, laughing just a little, albeit uncomfortably. "Yeah, mebbe you're right at that," he admitted. "It's a mad world and we all do what we got to to survive. Those folks we met back in Tazewell—they mebbe were just trying to survive, too."

Ryan's eye fixed on Croxton, and it seemed to skewer the old farmer as he tried to meet it. "You sound like a man with something on his conscience," he said.

Croxton visibly flinched, swallowing hard and taking a half step back before he spoke. "They were nothing to do with me," he said. "You can't think for a moment…"

"I didn't say that," Ryan said. "But they were psychotic. They starved their kid, left her to die. There's no excuse for that."

Still uncomfortable, Croxton looked away, watching the people in the sentry booth as they discussed their needs and answered the sec men's questions. Ryan continued to watch the man, his single, piercing eye fixed on Croxton's shifting gaze.

A LITTLE WAY DOWN the dirt track road, Mildred leaned against the hood of Charles Torino's four-wheel drive, watching the proceedings up ahead at the main gate.

Beside her, leaning on his ebony cane with the silver lion's head, Doc watched the sentry booth with rapt attention.

"They're going inside now," the old man said, not turning from the scene.

Mildred peered across to him. He was a curious figure, strangely incongruous when placed beside the other companions in Ryan Cawdor's group. An old man with an inquisitive, scientific mind, who, if his true nature were ever allowed to surface, most probably abhorred the violence that he saw all about him every day of his life. "How are you doing, Doc?" Mildred asked.

After a moment, he turned to her, bemused. "I'm sorry, my dear Dr. Wyeth?" he inquired.

Mildred smiled. "I know this means a lot to you, coming here," she said. "I mean, I'm interested in the sense that I'm a medical professional—a scientist, like yourself. But you...you *need* this to happen, don't you?"

"*Need* is a very strong word," Doc responded. "What I need is in the hands of a higher power than you or I or the people of Babyville. What I want, on the other hand—well, that is still open to interpretation." With that, he turned back and continued to watch the proceedings at the sentry booth.

"I hope it's true, Doc," Mildred told him. "I hope that you find what you're looking for here."

"And if I do find it," Doc said, his eyes still on the sentry booth by the ville's main gate, "do you suspect that would be the end of my quest? Or would it be just another step on the long road we all travel?"

Despite herself, Mildred felt her lips rise into a smile. "You sound like a fortune cookie," she said.

Doc shook his head. "If I knew what that was," he said, "I'm sure I'd be insulted."

But Mildred could see that the old man was smiling, too.

FINALLY, RYAN AND Jeremiah were encouraged to enter the sentry booth. Within, the two sec men looked them over with open disdain.

The male was perhaps twenty years old, with dirty blond hair cropped close to his scalp. There were scabs in his hair, and his face showed acne scars. He stepped out from behind his desk and strode across the little booth, making it clear this was his domain, stopping before Ryan and the old farmer and looking from one to the other. Behind him, the female sec officer chewed on something as she watched, her hand resting on the butt of a blaster that was clipped to her belt. Her hair, like the young man's, was a dirty blond color, but she wore it longer, so that it brushed her shoulders.

"Let's hear it then," the man said, sounding bored. "What have you heard and what do you want?"

Taller than either sec man, Ryan looked down at the lad before him, his face betraying no emotion.

"Well?" the young man prompted, looking from Ryan to Croxton.

"We're here for the spring," the old farmer finally said, a tremor in his voice. "The miracle spring we heard so much about."

"This true?" the youth asked, placing his pointed index finger on Ryan's chest.

Ryan nodded. "I'm just the sec man," he explained.

The pumped-up, light-haired man turned to Croxton, waiting for confirmation.

Croxton nodded. "This man and his crew brought us here," he said. "Kept us all alive."

The young woman spoke up then, stepping out from behind the desk. "How many in your party?" she asked. To Ryan's ears, her voice still sounded like that of a little girl.

"We have, um…" Croxton stuttered, trying to count the people in his head.

"Twenty-two," Ryan said, "including six sec men and one baby."

"Fifteen then," the young woman said after a long pause of thought, clearly struggling to calculate the numbers in her head.

"Two of them have been here before," Croxton stated.

The young woman nodded, smiling. "You have to hand over any weapons you're carrying," she explained. "We don't allow blasters in Babyville." Then she called to the sec men outside. "Check over their wags and let these fine people through the gate," she instructed.

Ryan glanced back at the pair in the sentry booth before following Croxton to the wags, where the sec team was beginning their inspection. "What happens if we'd answered their questions wrong?" he asked.

"I guess it's a screening process," Croxton admitted. "Keep the bad folks out."

Ryan wasn't convinced. "Seems pointless," he said. "I could have broken that little twerp's hand in a second when he shoved it at me like that."

Croxton smiled. "That mightn't have endeared us to them."

"Mebbe not," Ryan agreed.

They walked past a waiting wag and to the converted harvester that Ryan had driven here from the Tazewell farmhouse, the three sec men keeping pace with them. Croxton took charge, showing the sec men the battered wag and pointing to the other wags in their convoy, leading them to the next in line.

As Croxton led the sec men to the moonshine-powered truck rig, Ryan's attention was distracted by a noise coming from the wag waiting by the gates. He watched as a mean-faced sec man grabbed the driver—a gray-haired man in his fifties—from behind the steering column of a patched-together VW Bug and tossed him to the ground. Up ahead, the main gate had been raised, but the portcullis that covered it was still in place. As Ryan watched, another sec man, this one a young woman, maybe eighteen years old, rushed over and, to Ryan's surprise, kicked the driver in the ribs as he lay in the dirt. She leaned down and punched the man in the face with a gloved hand, knocking his head hard into the ground as he struggled to get away. Then, the male sec officer reached down and pulled a stub-nosed revolver, a Brazilian rip-off of a Smith & Wesson, from the man's belt.

The woman stopped pounding on the gray-haired man then, standing back as he lay before her. Then, the sec man turned the blaster on the man, pulling the trigger twice, firing two successive bullets close to the man's head. The gray-haired man rolled this way and that in the dirt, trying to fend off the shots as they tore up the soil beside him. From the back of the VW Bug came screaming, two voices howling to make it stop. Emotionless, the sec man ignored them, holding the blaster on the man in the dirt, barking instructions.

"You were told to hand over all blasters," the sec man growled angrily.

The gray-haired man held up his hands in defense, and the sec team stood there, listening to his pleas. There was a brief negotiation, and the man pulled off his wristwatch and handed it to the first man. The sec man shoved the shining watch in his pocket along with the blaster. After that, they shot him in the head, leaving him to die where he lay. Terrified, one of the passengers took over the driving, starting the rumbling, shuddering engine and drove the Bug through the gate as the portcullis was raised. In the back, Ryan saw a child of perhaps ten years old along with an elderly woman. Heck of a family outing, he thought with grim humor.

Ryan took that moment to study what lay beyond the gates. There were buildings in there, solid structures that had lent their fingerlike towers to the sky. There were people, too—not many, but a few, scurrying back and forth, going about their tasks, as well as chickens and geese and other farmyard animals roaming wild in the main thoroughfare. In the farther distance, Ryan spotted a squarish structure sitting on the banks of a stream—a water mill.

As the gate came down and settled back in place, Ryan turned away.

The sec men walked with Croxton as he showed them the other wags. The passengers were checked over for any obvious diseases, and their vehicles were appraised.

After a few minutes, Croxton came waddling back to where Ryan waited between the lead two wags, the three sec men following. "They've asked that you hand over your blasters," the old farmer explained.

"That's an interesting request," Ryan said noncommittally. He didn't cherish the idea of him and his team being disarmed, but at the same time he could understand the reasoning behind it.

"Well?" one of the sec men prompted, his eyes locking with Ryan's. The man looked to be about sixteen, a downy blond mustache on his top lip.

"We're here in the role of sec men," Ryan said. "Which means we're here to protect Mr. Croxton and his people."

The sec officer smiled and his smile was a hideous thing, like something rabid. "You won't need your blasters inside," he said. "No one's shooting no one in Baby."

Ryan considered this for a moment, his lone eye flicking to Croxton, then along the line of wags that waited to gain access to Baby. Behind the five wags in their train, another two were pulling up, one of them piled high with belongings. Ryan had been tasked to bring Croxton here safely, that was the deal, but there had been no mention that his people would have to hand over their weapons. But then, there had been no guarantee from Croxton that they would gain admittance, only that he would ask and pay their fees if the locals proved agreeable.

Ryan's gut instinct was to walk away. The assignment was completed, the contract fulfilled. But he thought of Doc, who wanted this piece of mumbo jumbo to be true so much.

"If my people are agreeable," Ryan told the sec man, "then we'll disarm here, on promise of the return of our weapons when we depart. Otherwise…"

The sec man's harsh laugh cut across Ryan's words. "There's no 'otherwise,' you dimmie," he said through smiling teeth. "This is the only way inside."

Ryan nodded. "Let me speak with my people," he said. "Tell them to stand down."

Croxton gave him a single nod of affirmation as Ryan made his way back along the wags to explain the situation to his team. The sec men followed at a leisurely distance.

Ryan passed the other wags until he reached J.B. Ryan had known the Armorer longer than any of the other companions, and he trusted the man's judgment implicitly. Plus, he knew that, of all of them, J.B. was the most likely to rebel against the notion of trusting their weapons to these strangers and entering the unknown ville unarmed.

"They want us to hand over our blasters, J.B.," Ryan explained. "They say Baby is a peaceful place and they don't want any trouble. I can see where they're coming from, at that."

A sly grin appeared on J.B.'s lips, as he saw the sec men walking steadily toward Ryan. "You think this is a good idea?" he said, sotto voce.

Beside the leather eye patch, Ryan's single eye closed in a slow blink. "I think we don't have any choice."

J.B. unslung the M-4000, then reached into his coat, producing his Uzi, removing the clip and stashing the ammo back in his pocket. "Doc really dropped us in something this time," he muttered.

At that point, the sec men joined J.B. and Ryan, producing a carryall in which they encouraged the men to stash their weapons. "You have anything else?" the lead sec man asked.

J.B. looked the man up and down. "Nothing I don't need," he said. "You allow people to use knives in your peaceful ville?"

The sec man nodded. "Not on each other," he said with a laugh.

"I'll try to restrain myself then," J.B. assured him.

With J.B. watching carefully, Ryan led the sec men to the other members of his crew. Krysty and Doc did as they were asked without complaint; Doc even tried to place his walking cane with the hidden sword blade into the carryall until Ryan held out his hand to stop him.

"You may still need to walk, Doc," Ryan said, holding the old man's confused stare. "You keep hold of that in case you need it."

"Caught up in the moment." He laughed, realization dawning on him as he withdrew his sword stick. "Like some old fool who forgets his hat when it is raining out."

Besides the weapons that the companions handed over, Charles Torino produced his blaster from the glove box of his 4WD. It was a handy little Taurus, a little scratched but Charles had obviously kept it in very good shape. He seemed reluctant to part with it.

"You'll get it back when you leave the ville," a sec man assured him.

"Hope I don't need it before then," Charles muttered.

Alec was allowed to keep his bow, although the quiver of arrows was taken and slung over the shoulder of one of the sec men. Mildred was made to hand over her medical supplies however.

"What happens if one of us gets sick?" she protested.

"Nobody gets sick in Babyville," a sec officer told her, a mean-spirited grin on his face. "Unless you're the sort that likes to play rough."

Mildred glared at him. "Put it back in your pants, soldier boy, you couldn't handle me."

Ryan stifled a chuckle as the young sec man blushed and moved to the next wag.

Finally, the party came to Jak, at the rearmost wag of the convoy. Jak sat cross-legged on the crossbar of the tractor carriage, with Maude and Vince watching the sec men from their perches by the steering column.

"They need your blaster," Ryan explained, "for safe-keeping. It's standard procedure."

Jak nodded and began unclipping the holster that was attached to his leg, pulling the whole piece away, including the sheathed Colt Python, and dropping it in the carryall that the sec man held out ready. Ryan's comment was clear enough. Jak carried more than a half-dozen throwing blades about his person, and it was a weapon he much preferred to the brutal barbarity of the blaster. While the other companions were going in compromised, their main weapons lost to them, Jak was armed enough for any eventuality. Ryan knew that, and was trusting the albino youth to provide any backup that might be required.

Once everyone had handed over their blasters, the sec men waved the five wags on toward the gate. Ryan sat in the driving seat of the harvester, urging it slowly forward as the gate rose before him, then the portcullis. A moment later, the wags were lumbering through the gateway.

The ville was huge. A vast tract of land that had been walled in, hidden from view, protected from the outside world. There were buildings here, solid constructs made of brick and wood. These were not the scrappy remnants of preskydark dwellings, nor were they the ramshackle structures that had begun to spring up all over the Deathlands, the humble abodes that had been forged from the leftovers of civilization. No, here was something new. Here was something that Ryan knew just one name for: the future. A whole ville had been built—was still being built—where people could live and do more than simply survive. Like the walled cities of Ancient China, here was a place where people could grow, a place where they could expand their knowledge, increase their learning. Here was the new society.

As the wags trundled forward along a shining, cobbled road paved with shells and stones, a sec man— maybe twenty or twenty-five—directed Ryan to a spot off to the right. The sec man smiled happily, a proud member of the new world.

Chickens and geese ran across the road as Ryan turned, and a yapping, black-and-white dog came hurrying after them a moment later, his salivating tongue hanging from his mouth.

As he drove closer, Ryan saw the buildings were still being constructed, big wooden beams and struts sticking out here and there where they were being slotted slowly together. There were other places, too, where foundations had been laid but nothing else yet, just a grid, a square where a building would be placed. Some squares were even being laid as Ryan watched, crews of young workers, some just children, working hard to get the pieces in place, to dig holes in the ground. It looked labor-intensive.

Everyone in the ville was young. Everyone. Ryan looked this way and that, trying to find anyone over thirty, and could see no one. Baby was a young ville full of healthy, hard-working young bodies, because, of course, it had the secret right there—the secret to eternal youth. Maybe it shouldn't surprise Ryan that the place was so spectacular, that the people here had actual plans, real ambitions. If this fabled spring worked then these people would never grow old, never become tired or suffer rheumatism or arthritis or just that feeling of weariness that old muscles get from too much stress where young muscles simply yearn for more.

Far down the road, snuggled against a glistening stream that sparkled as it caught the sun's rays, Ryan observed a watermill, its huge, wooden wheel turning over and over as the water splashed through it. The stream looked thin, a weedy little nothing of a water source compared to the vast rivers that crisscrossed the continent, but it sloshed along on its path, making its way to whatever sea or lake it finally fed, miles from here. The stream was why they were all here, Ryan realized. Its healing properties were what the whole of Babyville had been built up around, why the place was now guarded so firmly. And yet, the stream continued on, past the towering walls of the ville, through the Tennessee countryside. What was there to stop a bather dipping himself in there? Ryan wondered. Were the miraculous effects unique to this one spot?

Ahead of him, Ryan saw a number of parked wags, more than thirty in all, from the various visitors who had come to sample the rejuvenating wonders of the bathing pools. There was the VW Bug that he had seen drive through the gate, now unoccupied and parked beside a rusting military transport that was coated with sand. Some of the wags had been here a long time, Ryan could tell; they had been stripped down, broken up for their component parts.

When people left Baby did they just walk? Was it so incredible to feel that first flush of youth all over again that the converts walked, ran—hell, mebbe they even skipped—through the gates, not caring what they left behind? The people who ran the ville insisted on a high price for entry, Ryan knew, a great big chunk of everything a person owned, but leaving your wag behind, trekking out there into the wilderness on foot? That seemed incredible to Ryan's way of thinking. It hadn't been so far down the road that they had met Mitch and Annie and the nocturnal hordes of scalies. That had been rough, and they had had wags for protection. Would people really leave here with nothing?

Or mebbe they stayed, he thought. Mebbe that was the secret of Babyville—people grew young and then they stayed on to build the perfect world. It was only the few like Alec and Daisy who left to spread the gospel, share news of the miracle.

"You look troubled, Ryan," Croxton said from the passenger seat of the wag, snapping Ryan from his thoughts. "Nervous?"

"New places," Ryan said after a moment's pause. "Don't always know what you're getting into."

"I quite agree," Croxton said, smiling amiably at Ryan as they pulled into the parking lot. "But I'm sure we'll be quite safe. After all, you and your people have done a good job of keeping us all alive so far. And soon, friend, we'll all be young and fit and healthy, even your man Doc back there."

Ryan nodded, pulling the heavy, grumbling wag to a shuddering halt.

"You still doubt, don't you?" Croxton said, gesturing all around him at the towering buildings and the construction work that was going on. "Even after seeing all of this."

"I like miracles that I can touch and hold, Croxton," Ryan told the old farmer as he climbed down the side of the wag, "not ones I have to be frisked and disarmed to witness."

Croxton laughed, a booming, hearty sound. "I didn't always believe, either, you know," he admitted. "I wondered if Daisy had been entirely honest when she told me the story of her and her brother. But now we're here, now I can see all this with my own eyes…? Well, it's really something."

Ryan sneered. "It's something all right. Just keep your eyes open as to what."

Chapter Thirteen

They were given simple accommodations in one of
the blocky buildings of the ville, four to a room. The
building was constructed of bricks and mortar, and,
inside, the poorly plastered walls had been enlivened
with bright stripes running to halfway up their sides,
sunshine yellows and pomegranate reds. It all seemed
a little overpowering.

There was negligible security here in the sleeping
quarters, clearly the hope was that by disarming all
visitors the capacity for trouble had been sufficiently
diminished. The fact that most of the ville's visitors
were likely old folks probably helped reassure the locals,
too. The group, along with similar visitors to the ville,
mostly arriving in twos and threes, or sometimes elderly
couples with grandchildren, were instructed that they
were here for the use of the spring and that this would
begin in the morning.

"How long will treatment last?" Charles had asked,
his voice sounding gruff and his breathing strained.

"Just a few days," explained the guide who showed
them to their rooms. She was a perky blonde girl, with
tanned limbs and a charming smile.

The rooms were small and their amenities nonexis-
tent. Each had a small window with wooden shutters,

and the one that Ryan shared looked out over the main thoroughfare of the ville. Each room featured two small bunks; the occupants were expected to double up.

"Huh. Guess this place proved more popular than they'd thought," J.B. said when he learned of the sleeping arrangements.

"They seem to be doing a lot of construction work," Paul pointed out. "I'm sure it's just temporary."

While the travelers settled into their quarters, Ryan and the companions huddled together in one of the cell-like rooms to discuss tactics. Ryan sat on a bunk beside Doc, while Mildred and Krysty took the other bunk. J.B. peered through the small, open window, watching proceedings outside as the sun sank, and Jak remained by the open doorway to the room, crouched on his haunches, listening for trouble. There was no door on the room, nor on any of the others—that was a luxury that visitors weren't to expect.

"So?" Ryan said, opening the debate. "First impressions?"

The room was silent, no one speaking until finally Mildred piped up. "We need to look around. It seems to be what Daisy and Alec promised, but I hadn't expected it to be quite so large."

Doc agreed. "It is an impressive place," he said. "This feels like that wondrous thing that people have been waiting for. A real town with real buildings, not just shacks. People helping one another with the miracle spring as the catalyst."

"People helping one another?" Krysty repeated. "Did you see what they did to that man in the wag in front of us?"

"He tried to smuggle a blaster inside," Ryan pointed out reasonably.

Almost before Ryan had finished, J.B. spoke, not turning his attention from the window. "You think this place is on the up-and-up?" he asked. "No. There's something not right here."

"And what would that be, John Barrymore?" Doc asked, ruffled.

J.B. just shook his head. "I can't put my finger on it, not yet. But it's there."

"You have doubted this from the beginning," Doc reminded him.

"And I ain't seen anything to alter my opinion, Doc," J.B. stated.

Doc looked as though he was about to say something more, but Ryan stopped him with a look. "Let's play along for now," Ryan proposed, "see what's what. Keep an open mind."

J.B. turned to the group, responding to Ryan's words but clearly directing his reply to Doc. "My mind is open. Are your eyes?"

Mildred spoke then, trying to break the tension in the room. "I want to check out the spring, find out what I can about what's going on here. That's why we're here, isn't it?"

As the companions sat there, mulling Mildred's suggestion, Jak cocked his head. "Woman coming," he said, indicating the corridor outside.

A moment after, the perky blonde strode past the open doorway, peering inside as she passed. She wore a loose summer dress that left her tanned arms bare. She was tall, but beneath the dress she still had a girl's figure, the hints of womanly curves only beginning to take shape. Seeing people within the room, she stopped. "Cheer up, friends," she said. "You're here. You made it. This is your salvation."

"We came a long way," Krysty said, standing up from the bunk and approaching the blonde.

"My name's Michelle. Your dreams are about to come true," the woman assured her. "Life out there takes its toll, but we'll fix that. The spring—you've never felt anything like it."

"How old are you?" Krysty asked, watching the woman closely.

Michelle smiled. "How old am I *now,* you mean?"

Doc stood then, his eyes wide. "You've tried it then? You've tried this…treatment?"

"We all have," the apparently teenage girl assured him. "Everyone you see here. It's a miracle."

"We need to see it for ourselves," Doc insisted.

"Tomorrow," the girl told him, casting her glance across the whole group to take them all in. "There's room for everyone."

Doc peered closely at the girl, as though examining a slide under a microscope. "You are…?" he began, and stopped himself, a blush rising to his cheeks and up into his white hair. "I am sorry," he said. "I am forgetting my manners. It is simply that I am—"

The girl placed her hand on Doc's arm, squeezing it with mock flirtatiousness. "I don't mind," she told him. "I used to be just like you."

Doc met her eyes. "Yet, you look so…beautiful," he said, clearly at a loss for words—a rare event for the typically verbose Theophilus Tanner.

"What I have now is what the water gave me," Michelle told him. "You'll be the same, soon. Be patient and have faith. You're among friends here."

Still holding Doc's arm, the blonde woman led him from the room and down the corridor. The companions followed, all except Ryan and J.B., who remained in the cell-like room for a few seconds.

"It's not good," J.B. said quietly. "Not good at all."

Ryan looked at his oldest friend, his face racked with turmoil. "Do you ever wonder, J.B., if we have been running for so long that we wouldn't know when to stop?"

"You think this is it?" J.B. asked, a hint of annoyance in his sharp tone.

Ryan inclined his head noncommittally. "I think we need to remember that one day we might just find something worth stopping for," he said, and strode through the open doorway after Doc and the others.

The Armorer watched the open doorway for a moment before pushing himself up from the windowsill and following. "I just hope you have a plan, Ryan," he muttered.

They followed Michelle down into a large, communal room on the first floor, where their travelers and a few other newcomers were milling about. Michelle pointed to the tables scattered around the room, and promised that a meal would be served shortly.

"What eat?" Jak asked.

"I'm starving," Mildred added.

"We make our own bread here," Michelle explained proudly. "And we have fresh and cured meats. Not much, but we're always pleased to share with our new friends."

Along with the other newcomers to the ville, the companions sat down to eat.

AFTER THEIR MEAL, the visitors chatted a little with one another before retiring to their rooms. They had all suffered long journeys to get here, each of them drawn by the story of a spring of eternal youth. There was a curious, shared sense of relief among the visitors. It was as if, now that they had reached Babyville, one more night wasn't going to hurt them.

THE NEXT MORNING, Ryan and his companions were awakened with the other visitors and given a brief but enjoyable breakfast of toasted bread and a choice of goat's cheese or fruit preserve. After they had eaten, Michelle encouraged everyone to follow her into an open-air courtyard that sat between the accommodations buildings. Ryan's group of travelers, along with a number of other folks—most of them elderly, and including the people from the VW Bug—waited eagerly in the warm, morning sun. Alert, Ryan and his companions noticed that several armed sec men were wandering nearby, giving the appearance of acting casually, but doubtless keeping an eye on proceedings.

Encouraging everyone to form a circle, Michelle took center stage and introduced herself. "Hi, everyone," she said, "and welcome to Babyville. I'm Michelle, and I'll be your friend while you're here."

Michelle gestured with a fluid sweep of her tanned arm, and a young man politely made his way through the crowd from the back of the group. He was six feet tall, broad-shouldered and he wore his thick blond hair like a lion's mane, its curls brushing against his shoulders.

He looked to be in his mid-twenties, with well-defined arm muscles and he sported a healthy tan. A sliver of white, like a hairline fracture, ran down the right-hand side of his forehead, evidence of an old scar.

"New friends," Michelle trilled as the man joined her, "I would like you to say hello to Eddie."

Self-conscious, the crowd mumbled a hello.

"Hi," Eddie began, presenting the crowd with a friendly wave and a bright smile of white teeth. "I'm going to be your friend, too, for the duration of your stay in our wonderful ville." He gazed around the crowd, nodding when he saw Alec and Daisy as well as several other younger people that had traveled with other groups. "I see we have a few returning friends here, and to them I say 'welcome back.'

"You have all heard stories about this place, about what we do here," Eddie continued, his presentation smooth. "Perhaps you came because you couldn't resist trying the miracle we have. Then again, perhaps you thought that it sounded incredible, mebbe even unbelievable, so you just wanted to take a look-see yourself before you dismissed it out of hand." He pointed to one of the crowd at random, an elderly woman, stooped over a walking cane, with no front teeth in her mouth. "You, ma'am, why did you come here?"

The elderly woman looked uncomfortably about her before she spoke in a frail voice. "I been hoarding all my life, and when I heard of this place I figured that mebbe you had something here what would be worth all my hoarding."

Eddie put his hands together in sincerity, offering her a genuine smile before moving on to another member of the group. It was Julius Dougal, one of Croxton's party. "And what about you, sir? What brung you here?"

"Well, I'm not getting any younger on my own." Dougal chuckled. "So I figured I'd give this a shot."

"And you, sir?" Eddie moved on, working the crowd, pointing at Jeremiah Croxton.

"The bright young Miss Daisy here came to my ville," Croxton said, "and told us all about the miracle she had found here. That you could make me young again."

Eddie swept his arm to encompass the whole crowd. "Is that what you all heard?" he asked, raising his voice.

As one, the crowd nodded or spoke their agreement.

Eddie chuckled, and beside him, Michelle broke into a broad smile.

"You know what?" Eddie said, once he had finished laughing. "It's all true. Whatever story you heard, about the pool, the spring, the rejuvenating waters—all true.

"Six months ago, when I submerged myself into the pool, I was a man of forty-seven years of age. I had moved from farm to farm doing what chores I could for whatever jack the owners would pay me. I slept in warm houses and I slept in cold stables and sometimes I slept right there under the stars. I had such cramp in my hands that they looked like claws, the muscles so fucked I could never straighten my fingers." Eddie flexed his digits theatrically before the crowd. "I took a dip in the pool. That was all it was, just a dip. I'd been working these lands, the very fields you passed on your way in here, and I was all messed up so I stripped off my clothes and I took a dip in this pool what I found. Water looked clean, tasted fresh. What harm could it do? Right?"

The crowd was quiet, listening in awe to the man's story.

"I didn't even notice at first," Eddie continued, and he indicated Michelle. "It took my lady here to see what had happened. 'Eddie,' she said, 'you look real fine today.' That's the words she used—*real fine*."

Michelle smiled, pointing to Eddie. "His hands weren't bent up anymore," she said. "A woman notices that in her fella."

"I went back to the stream, the pool—" Eddie picked up the story "—and I washed there every day for a week. And every day I got a little better, a little bit younger. Didn't even realize it at first, not till the third day, in fact, when I looked in the mirror to shave and I saw this familiar face looking back at me. It was me, only the me I hadn't seen since I had turned forty. Freaked me the hell out, it did." He laughed again at that.

A middle-aged man standing in the crowd raised his hand to get Eddie's attention. He had his arm around the waist of an attractive woman; slender with dark hair showing streaks of gray, crow's feet at her eyes. "Why do we have to pay so much to use the pool?" he asked. "Isn't it there for everyone?"

Eddie nodded as though he agreed. "That's a darn fine question, sir, and I will answer that because I figure it's one that's crossed a lot of folks' minds.

"The world's a pretty nasty place just now, what with the muties and the chem rains and everything else that's floating about out there, waiting to kill us. I heard it wasn't always like that, but that's neither here nor there.

Imagine you take a dip in that pool, you and your good lady wife there, and just then some mutie son of a bitch comes along and steals your clothes, takes your woman. Mebbe that mutie pulls a knife on you, mebbe even a blaster. What do you do?"

"I don't know," the man admitted. "Shoot him, I guess."

"What if it's not one mutant but a dozen of the mad fuckers?" Eddie asked. "What if it's a hundred and each one of 'em is gonna have his wicked mutie fun-time with your woman before they chill you and her both. Mebbe even have his fun-time with you. What do you do then?"

"I don't know," the man admitted, clearly uncomfortable.

"Yeah, you do," Eddie told him. "Everyone here knows the answer to that question. You build a great big wall around the pool so no more muties can come along and surprise you ever again. So, that's what I did. I built a wall and the wall became a ville and I called it Baby, because I figured that if everything around here was going to keep becoming younger then the place would never grow up." He looked around, taking in the construction work within the ville's walls. "Boy, was I wrong." He laughed.

Doc stepped forward then, his ebony cane in his hand. "How does it work?" he asked.

Eddie met Doc's gaze, considering his question. "How does it work, friend?" he repeated. "What am I, a whitecoat? It works."

"But there must be a reason," Doc insisted.

Michelle stepped forward, smiling at Doc. "Could I ask your name, friend?"

"Of course," Doc replied. "It's Theophilus Algernon Tanner."

"Theoph—" she began and stopped as she struggled over the syllables of Doc's name. "Mr. Tanner, not many people remember, but do you believe in God?"

Doc nodded. "I would say that I do, to an extent."

"The pool works," Michelle assured him. "It's magical. It's the work of God. That's how it works."

Doc was about to challenge this, for it was no explanation at all, just circular nonsense, but he checked himself. "Maybe it is," he said agreeably. He realized that he would need to see it in action to get to the bottom of this mystery.

Standing together at the back of the group, Ryan and J.B. watched Eddie and Michelle's performance dispassionately. Both of them were also watching for the sec men all around, wary of what could happen in this enclosed space. The other companions remained on guard as well, observant to everything around them.

Finally, questions from the crowd finished and Michelle and Eddie led the way to the magical pool of which they had spoken. The forty-strong group made its way out of the courtyard, down a wide alley between two accommodation buildings, one of which was still being constructed. Six young workers toiled at the building, hammering floorboards in place, laying guttering from the flat roof down to the ground.

The group didn't rush, moving, Eddie assured them, as slow as the slowest member of the party. There were several very elderly people there, old and frail, who seemed permanently out of breath and with barely the energy to stand. Mildred watched them, amazed. How had these people survived in the Deathlands at all? How, with no organized medicine, no proper community to shelter them, could people possibly get like this and still live? She remembered television news reports from her day, showing the wise men of tribes who seemed a million years away from civilization and yet still lived into their nineties and beyond, surviving on a diet of leaves and whatever the tribes' hunters found. What she saw now was a stark reminder that civilization, whatever that meant, wasn't the only way to survive.

Walking beside Ryan, J.B. jabbed his thumb in the direction of the building and offered a cynical smile. "Lot of work going on around here," he said.

Ryan nodded agreement. "I guess this place is becoming something," he suggested. "A community mebbe, like the old days before it all fell down."

J.B. pulled the spectacles from his nose and wiped the lenses. "You really believe that?"

Ryan shrugged. "One day somebody's got to build something permanent again. Something new that offers a real future."

"Mebbe so," J.B. grunted as he replaced his glasses, "but you really think it'll be built around a magical fish pond?"

Ryan's lone blue eye searched all around, taking in the construction work inside the ville's colossal walls. "I guess it'll be built wherever people end up," he said. "Here's as good as anywhere else."

As the bulk of the group continued past the living quarters, Daisy, Alec and another young man who had come with a different group of travelers, peeled off and headed toward the main buildings of the compound.

They didn't require proof of the magical pool, nor to dip themselves in the water with its magnificent restorative powers.

Jak slowed his pace and knelt on the cobblestones, as though to adjust his boot. He fidgeted with the boot, watching the trio of young people depart, aware of the crowd moving ahead of him. As he pulled at the top of his boot, a youthful sec man in a hard helmet sauntered over, acting casually but clearly watching what Jak was up to. "You had better get moving, friend," the sec man prompted. "You don't want to miss the show."

Jak smiled, standing up and brushing at his pants' leg. "Right," he agreed, trotting forward in a little five-step run before he reached the very rear of the group once more.

At the back of the tour group, Jak could feel the sec officer's eyes on him, and he relaxed, walking normally, resisting the urge to look behind him, trying not to draw any further attention.

Following Eddie and Michelle, the party moved onward, a hubbub of interested conversation coming from them. As they passed another building, still only partly constructed, Jak slowed his pace again and slipped into the shadows beneath an awning, letting the group carry on without him. He wanted to find out where Daisy and the others were going. Most likely they had old friends here, people they had seen when they had last used the pool. Even so, Jak's instincts told him it was worthy of investigation.

Michelle and Eddie led the party through the compound in the direction of the watermill. The mill had two stories aboveground, with a further, lower story abutting the narrow but fast-flowing stream that ran beside it. A huge wheel was at the side of the mill, eleven feet in diameter with a shaft disappearing into the structure of the building itself just below a little stairwell that led to a door on the second story. The wheel spun as the clear stream rushed through it, and the constant shushing-and-crashing noise of the water disguised the sound of the gears turning inside the mill, grinding wheat into flour.

"This is where we make our bread," Michelle told the visitors. "You've already been allowed to partake in eating it, now that you are our friends."

Amid the crowd, Mildred gave Krysty a suspicious look. "Hand over everything and in return you get bread and water," she said, her voice low. "What is this place? A monastery?"

The group passed the mill and continued onward, following the course of the stream for another fifty yards. There were several trees along the riverbanks, and one grew in the stream itself, its branches drooping down so low that they brushed the water when it caught the breeze. Then Eddie, leading the party, signaled for them to stop. "If anyone is thinking of turning back, now would be the time to do so," he said, raising his voice to be heard over the sound of the rushing water.

"Once you see this," Michelle added, "that's it."

The couple waited for a half minute, to see if anyone would turn away. It was all for show, of course, just to bring the tension to the boil. Doc admired their showmanship skills.

Abruptly, Eddie turned and started striding onward, with Michelle herding the anxious party along. He led the way over a small wooden bridge that crossed the stream, just wide enough for two people or a single cart.

Beyond the bridge, there was an inlet off the stream, naturally hidden from casual glances by the rocky terrain and the trees all around, while, off in the other direction, there were fallow fields and the beginnings of a further exterior wall being constructed for safety. Eddie strode along the curving edge of the inlet, and they saw that the current of the water here was slower, the inlet almost still. Unlike the main stem of the stream, the water in the inlet was slower, silty and it smelled of sulfur.

As they walked farther along the course of the narrow inlet, it became its own little river, bending in a U-shape off the main stream before rejoining it thirty yards distant. Trees were dotted here and there, autumnal leaves clinging to their branches in shades of red and brown. In the stream's inlet there were rocks beside which came a steady flow of bubbles that sat on the surface of the water in fat, wide blobs until they finally popped or flowed away with the current. There was something else in the water as well: five people, ducked down so that only their heads bobbed above the surface, men and women. As the visitor party stopped at the edge of the water, the group in the pool began pulling themselves out and drying themselves off on towels and blankets that they had left on the rocks. They were young and each was blessed with a beautiful, flawless body.

Paul's easy humor broke the silence. "I do believe we have died and gone to heaven. And no one has told us that the angels would be so beautiful."

The crowd laughed, and one of the girls from the water looked up, smiling at him. Eddie called her over.

"Why don't you tell our new friends how you came to be here, Tress," Eddie said.

Her damp, strawberry-blond hair clinging to her pert, naked breasts, Tress wound a blanket around her and strode over to the group. "My name's Tress O'Dowd," she said, "and I am fifty-three years old."

A gasp came from the gathered crowd; Tress looked no older than nineteen or twenty, her hair and skin was vibrant, her eyes bright.

"I been here for four days," Tress continued. "Dipping in the pool every daylight hour of every day. And, I have got to tell you, I am starting to think there may just be something in this."

The group laughed.

WHILE THE GROUP he had traveled with were admiring the fabulous pool, Jak was making his way around the half-built building, alone and sticking to the shadows. His chalk-white skin and hair made hiding difficult, but his clothes were dark and he made sure to keep out of people's line of sight as the four-man construction team continued its work around the area.

There was an open wall to the side of the building, where a window or door was presumably to be placed, and Jak ducked through it as two of the construction workers walked toward him carrying a long wood beam on their shoulders. Within, the building was warm, its brick walls retaining the heat of the morning sun. Jak was in a corridor that ran the length of the building, with a slight kink in its route at the midpoint. Swiftly, he silently moved along the corridor, making his way to the far side of the building.

At the end of the corridor, Jak stepped past a stack
of wooden planks and out into the main area of the
ville. He was close to where the sec man had hurried
him along a few minutes before, and he looked around,
scanning for Daisy, Alec or the other young man. He
couldn't see them. Just two dogs chasing one another,
barking happily at their game, a goat mewling as the
hounds ran past it.

Looking this way and that, Jak walked past a wooden
cart stacked high with blankets. A mule was reined to
the front of the cart, and it snorted as Jak peered at it.

The albino youth walked aimlessly around the ville,
the thoughts turning over in his head, the sun rising
slowly in the sky. There was a lot of construction work
going on here, buildings being set out and foundations
being laid. Right now there were just five buildings,
several still in midconstruction, but Jak could see plots
marked out for at least another six, and there was space
for more. The unattended wag park over near the main
gate held plenty of vehicles and Jak walked through
it, examining the condition of the wags. Some looked
solid enough, old and worn maybe, like the ones he
and his companions had traveled here in. Others were
falling apart, wrecks that were now only useful for
spares.

When he looked up, the tall main gate to the ville
filled Jak's vision, a solid barrier within the high wall
surrounding the ville. He hadn't realized that he had got
so close. He wandered up to the gate, considering what
he had seen on the dirt approach to the ville. Just fields,
cereal grain being coaxed to life, some vegetables, including a field with rows of leafy cabbages.

As Jak neared the gate, two sec men stepped forward to bar his way.

"Where do you think you're going, mutie-boy?" one challenged.

"No," Jak said, realizing they had mistaken his peculiar appearance for mutation. "Not mutie."

Another sec man spoke up, his eyes fierce as he glared at Jak. "Get away from the gate," he said. "No visitors are allowed beyond this point."

"Not outside?" Jak asked.

"Not outside, mutie-freak," the man told him.

Jak turned and walked away, his ears sharp as he listened to the men's comments.

"We shouldn't be letting muties like that inside," one of the sec men grunted. "Is Monica on the gate? Did she vet these people?"

"They brought a lot of stuff," his companion replied.

Their body language alone had made it clear to Jak that they wouldn't allow him past. Could it be that once you were in Babyville you were never allowed to leave? What gain could there possibly be in that?

Something was going on here, but he would have to keep his wits about him if he was to find out what it was without getting himself hurt.

Jak nodded when he saw the same cart he had passed just a few minutes ago, the one piled with blankets and pulled by the mule.

The handler tugged on the hide reins, encouraging the mule toward the mill, where the great waterwheel turned in the stream. The cart bumped away along the cobblestones and onto the track that led to the wooden footbridge, and, as it did so, something caught Jak's keen eye. It was a hand. A hand in the back of the cart, dropping out between the pile of blankets. Just two fingertips and the thumb with its ball-like joint, in fact, but enough that Jak recognized what it was. Someone was under those blankets. Perhaps they had become trapped?

Jak picked up his pace, following the cart as it bumped along the path toward the bridge.

MICHELLE SPOKE UP from the rear of the group standing by the stream inlet. "There's room for twenty people in the pools," she announced. "Those who got here first can go take a dip now if they like, but we promise that everyone here will get a turn."

Several of the crowd stepped forward, unbuttoning shirts and shirking their pants despite the chill of the winter air. Jeremiah Croxton was among them, ever the leader.

Shaking her head in disbelief, Mildred leaned close to Doc and whispered in a low voice, "These idiots are going to catch pneumonia if they're not careful."

Shirking his long, frock coat, Doc turned to look at her, and Mildred saw that there was a fervid excitement in his clear, blue eyes. "No, they will not," he said. "They'll come out of that water young and strong."

"Young and strong and with pneumonia," Mildred grumbled.

While the first two people bravely dipped into the clear waters of the inlet, Eddie pointed to the youngsters who had vacated the pool when they had arrived. "Look at them," he said. "They are the proof that our friendship never leaves you. Our friendship never dies."

Unbuttoning his shirt and stepping out of his pants, Doc Tanner made his way toward the bubbling pool. "Well, in for a penny…" he said as stepped into the water.

Chapter Fourteen

There were bushes and trees around the banks of the stream that Jak used for cover as he made his way along its length, following the departing cart. Where the companions had turned right toward the fabled pool, the cart veered to the left and trundled along a tree-lined pathway that led to more fields.

Although the buildings of the ville were concentrated in a small area, the walls of the ville hemmed in quite a large tract of land, much of it unused.

Occasionally, Jak saw what he took to be a sec man patrolling the banks of the stream, and he obscured his face, looking away or ducking behind the cover of bushes with seeming casualness so as not to be questioned.

When he reached the far wall, Jak was surprised to find how poorly guarded the stream itself was. The people of Baby had constructed high security walls to shut them off from the outlands beyond, but the necessity of the stream had meant that they had left a whole section of wall open. The gap in the wall reached two feet aboveground and was a little wider than the stream itself, perhaps twelve feet across. The low opening had a gauzelike grate over it, with steel bars reaching into the water itself, but, under the surface, their wavering lengths only reached down another foot or so, not all the way to the streambed. If required, Jak thought, he could swim underneath those spikes to freedom.

As well, there were no sec men way out here; it was clear that the villefolk assumed the walls protection enough. Short of driving a flaming wag into them, Jak figured that was a safe assumption.

DOC CAME FROM ANOTHER ERA, a time when nudity was taboo, and for all the sights, both terrible and wondrous, that he had seen in the Deathlands, he had never really sloughed that old morality. Now, however, as he disrobed before this group of friends and strangers and tentatively dipped his right foot into the bubbling water of the pool, he left his old embarrassment behind. Even to Doc himself, his foot looked pale, a sunless, tanless white with thick blue veins visible just under the skin. As he watched his foot enter the water, he wondered why anyone would ever wish to look at his ancient body with anything other than contempt. His *prematurely* ancient body, he reminded himself; the very thing, the very curse, that had led him to Babyville and its promise of renewed vitality. He looked up then, a crooked smile on his old, lined face, and saw that his presumption had been right—the other people in the group ignored him, ignored the "show" he was putting on. They were far too busy removing their own clothes, or staring at the mysterious contents of the bubbling pool.

The five youths who had been in the pool when they got here—Paul's "angels"—were leaving, making their way back to the bridge, wearing the loose clothing that they had left beside the pool, the blankets wrapped over their shoulders. The women used towels to dry their hair as they walked.

The water of the pool was wondrously clear and it appeared to be clean, despite the sulfurous reek that it gave off. Trails of bubbles scurried to the surface, obese, see-through globes bigger than a man's hand, with smaller circles foaming around them. To Doc's surprise, the water itself was warm. Not hot, certainly not of a temperature that his dear Emily would have run for a bath, back when he had been with her in Nebraska, but warm nonetheless. Something below the surface was heating it, in some unspecified way; perhaps the thing that bubbled from under the rocks. Doc peered at the water, looking through the darkness of his own shadow on the surface, trying to discern whatever was underneath, down by those rocks. Magic, perhaps?

The water seemed to call to him then, drawing him toward its rippling surface, and Doc dipped lower, feeling it wash around his legs, and then begin to lap at his body. He sank into the bubbling pool, feeling the water both support his weight and also add that familiar heaviness to his movements. It felt wonderful, a giant's hand wrapping around him, comforting his aching, weary, ancient body. Drifting there in the bubbling water, as it held him, supported him, clamored around him and kissed at his skin, he felt the ache of the journey begin to dissipate. And more; he felt the ache of his life's journey dissipating, too, and without realizing it, he expelled a long, deep breath, as though he was utterly satiated.

The limbs of a tree hung over the far end of the pool, rufous leaves falling from its branches every now and then, wending their way on the breeze to carpet the ground around its trunk. Some of the leaves, Doc saw, fell into the water, and some floated away while others sank to the bottom to join the bubbling rocks.

Beside Doc, two other old-timers were in the pool, a man and a woman, smiling tentatively as they felt

the water wash over their naked bodies. The man was
so emaciated as to appear to be nothing more than a
skeleton with skin draped over it like pink silk. Doc
watched them for a moment, feeling the smile tugging
at the corners of his mouth. They looked relieved, happy.
Like him, they had traveled miles to get here, probably
handed over everything that they owned to try this miraculous gift. Now, the old couple were waist-deep in
water, their ruddy, pink skin so wrinkled and fragile,
bruised and scarred. They stood close, gently splashing
the water up their bodies, watching it wash back to the
pool in clear rivulets. As the water washed over them,
the old man and woman gazed at each other, and Doc
saw a look pass between them, something he recognized
but thought he had forgotten—love. They were happy
here, probably as happy as they had ever been.

Next to the bathing couple, Jeremiah Croxton was
swimming away across where the inlet was at its widest,
just nine feet in all, his patchy white beard dangling
in the water. Croxton looked to the others who remained on the shore. "Come on," he told them. "It feels
fantastic."

Standing along the shoreline, other members of the
crowd were discarding their clothes as Michelle and
Eddie egged them on. Even Mary Foster, the woman in
her thirties who had traveled in Charles Torino's wag,
now pulled off her skirt and grimy blouse with her free
hand, revealing the bandage along her shoulder and neck
where the mutie wolf had wounded her, eyeing the pool
with delight. She passed her baby to Krysty with a grateful smile. "Please hold on to her," she requested. "I just
want to see what it feels like."

Krysty and Mildred watched as Mary sat on the side of the pool and lowered herself in, both feet at once. She smiled as she felt it, giving out a barklike laugh. "It's warm," she said as tears welled in her eyes. "It's… beautiful."

Carefully stepping along the shingle at the bottom of the inlet, Doc worked his way to the center of the pool. The bubbles were more profuse there, blurting from below the surface in a continuous flurry of activity, and he presumed that this had something to do with the rejuvenation process. The bubbles were, after all, the only thing Doc could see that made the pool any different from the rush of the stream. The pool wasn't very deep, and it was hardly big enough to swim, but it had enough room to splash about in, and to cover a full-grown man if he bent his knees a little.

At the center, the smell of sulfur was more intense, making Doc wince a little as he adjusted to it. The bubbles filtered up to the surface all about him. He felt them pressing against his body, clinging to it and walking their way up his planes and curves in their slow, insistent march to the surface. Doc swept his arms around him, twirling in place, brushing at the bubbles and making them pop, and he smiled. Whatever it was, it felt good running up his body. Finally, something good in a world of bad.

Doc glanced to the shore for a moment, barely aware that his companions were still waiting up there. Others were disrobing, lowering themselves into the pool; already there were ten people in there, feeling the rejuvenating power of the stream.

Taking a deep breath, Doc closed his eyes. Then, in an instant, he had bent his knees and submerged himself entirely, dropping under the surface, feeling the water wash over his head. Warm, yet it felt cool against the skin there, cool and refreshing. With eyes still closed, Doc felt the water press against his skin, sealing him inside its grip like a mother's womb, making him feel safe. The bubbles tickled as they ran past him, worked up his body and beyond, up to the surface.

This is it, he thought. *My baptism. A baptism of wonder.*

Standing at the edge of the pool, Ryan made his way across to where Krysty was rocking baby Holly in her arms. "Are you going in?" he inquired.

Krysty cooed at the baby for a moment before she answered him. "What do you think?" she said. "We've come all this way, and Daisy sure seemed healthy enough, right?"

Ryan tapped a fingernail against his lapel pin rad counter. "Radiation's at normal," he said. "Nothing out of the ordinary."

Beside Krysty, Mildred looked at Ryan, concern furrowing her coffee-colored brow. "Radiation isn't the only thing that can hurt you," she said, drawing on her medical knowledge. "You could easily catch something from the water. Ringworm, say. Or you could just slip on a rock. Hey, it happens."

Krysty glared at Mildred. "I thought you wanted to try this," she chastised, though her concern was friendly, her anger just show.

Mildred looked at the pool where a dozen people now bobbed. "Aw, heck—I wish they'd installed changing rooms," she admitted.

WITH THE WALL on his left-hand side, and scrubland on his right, Jak ran the length of the ville's boundary wall, parallel with the dirt track that he had seen the cart following. The sun was higher now, and cover was becoming harder to find.

As he got closer to the curving corner of the ville wall, Jak slowed, glancing this way and that, searching for a hiding place. He was surprised to find that the wall here was unfinished, running only a few feet high. Presumably, most visitors never got this far. Why should they?

Moving out of the shadow cast by the wall, Jak ran across the scrubland and into the nearest field. Root vegetables grew in the field, their bushy clumps of leaves running in jumbled rows across the soil. To his right, Jak could see the dirt path, and up ahead he spotted the cart of blankets that had been hauled by the mule. The cart was stopped at the next field, and Jak could see several figures working there, digging at the land. As Jak got closer, he realized that the cart stood in a fallow field of dirt.

Jak paused, dropping to the ground and watching the proceedings in the fallow field from behind the masking leaves of the crops.

STANDING AMID THE thinning crowd, J.B.'s eyes glazed over as he half watched the oldsters stripping down and getting into the pool. To J.B., they looked like flies rushing to a day-old corpse.

Doc had been one of the first to go in, J.B. saw, brave or stupe or whatever you call that combination of the two that leads to discovery or death. Curious, perhaps.

Behind his wire-framed spectacles, J.B.'s eyes flicked to Eddie and Michelle, their tour guides. The pair was smiling and laughing, encouraging the old folks to dip in the pool. Beside them, Charles Torino had removed his shirt to reveal a tattooed eagle that swooped across the entirety of his back. The locals were all very willing to share, now that they had got their cut of their visitors' loot, J.B. realized. Willing to share this miracle that the girl had attributed to God.

J.B. didn't have much time for that talk, any mystical mumbo jumbo he had encountered had generally served only to obscure the facts. But what were the facts here? What was the pool? How did it work? How *could* it work?

The Armorer felt his legs aching from the long journey in the back of the wag, and his throat felt dry. And he hated to say it, even in his own mind, but he was feeling old. His muscles that never got enough rest, the dull ache across his shoulders from the weight of his jacket and its hidden cache of weapons and ammo, his eyes. Yes, that was the real issue, wasn't it? His eyes felt dry and exhausted, and took longer and longer to adjust each time he removed his eyeglasses to sleep. Age was catching up with J.B., no matter how much he ignored it.

No matter how much you tried to avoid it, J.B. thought, *age did frightful things to a man.* Every person on the planet was dying from that slow disease called mortality.

But the pool…?

JAK COULD SEE THREE youngsters working the soil of the fallow field, the oldest no more than fifteen, and each of them looked exhausted and malnourished. A fourth figure, the one who had led the cart, was a tall man in his twenties, strong muscles bulging along his upper arms. He was talking to the children, barking instructions at them, removing things from the cart, the items themselves obscured by it.

Jak watched for a long while, keeping himself hidden in the shadows until the youngsters finished digging or sowing whatever it had been that they were working at, and the man indicated the back of the cart. Two of the children jumped on the back with their shovels, while the third followed but left his shovel on the ground. The man pointed at the dropped tool, grabbed the girl and threw her to the ground. The girl was forced to pick up the shovel as the man led mule and cart away, back to the dirt road that led to the ville gate. Shovel in hand, the girl ran to catch up with the cart.

After that, there was no further activity in the fallow field. People were working in the other fields, youngsters mostly, like the ones Jak had witnessed, teens and kids. Jak waited patiently, and slowly the winter sun passed its zenith and began its slow death in the west.

WITH A LITTLE GENTLE coaxing and teasing, Ryan and Krysty had done a pretty good job of talking each other into trying the pool. Krysty stripped off and got in quickly, sinking down so that only her head was above the bubbling surface, her prehensile hair floating on the surface around her, a bright red cloud in the shimmering silver of the pool.

"Come on, lover," she called encouragingly as Ryan discarded his own clothes, revealing a strong body, pitted with scars and scratches, old wounds from other days.

There were fifteen folks in the pool now, and Eddie and Michelle kept watch and spoke to the bathers in a friendly manner, answering their inquiries and generally making sure they felt relaxed. The group parted, giving Ryan space to join them.

"See?" Krysty said as Ryan lowered himself into the water. "It's not too cold, just nice."

"I feel like a horse's ass," Ryan muttered as Krysty stroked his scarred shoulder where it poked from the surface. "These people, they need this. I don't."

Krysty leaned forward and kissed Ryan quickly, just brushing his lips with her own. She moved fractionally away from him to look him in the eye. "You've earned this just as much as they have," she told him. "I'll bet you've lived three lifetimes to their one, and I'll bet you'll live six more before you reach their age."

"I don't need to be younger," Ryan said, keeping his voice low as the other bathers swam about them. "Nor do you," he added.

"You won't lose your memory," Krysty told him. "You'll still be the same Ryan on the inside. Just younger. Mebbe it'll heal some of these," she said, indicating the scars on his arms and chest.

Ryan closed his single eye, letting out a long breath. He was thinking about his missing eye and something Jeremiah Croxton had said when they had first met. Could the supernatural waters here be capable of repairing his eye in the same way that they had restored Daisy's youth? When it worked its magic, did the pool repair and replace what an individual had lost, no matter how permanent the loss had seemed?

Mildred sat on the edge of the pool, fully clothed but with her boots off, her feel dangling in the water. From a medical standpoint, the phenomenon was fascinating, and yet she was still wary. What was she waiting for?

The whole of Babyville was monument to this fantastic discovery, a whole society built around regained youth and vitality. Eddie, Michelle, Daisy and the others— they were the litmus test; they were the proof.

As Mildred sat there, feeling the lukewarm water running through her toes, cooling her tired ankles, the blonde girl, Michelle, came over and crouched beside her. "Aren't you going in, new friend?" Michelle asked, a bright smile on her pretty face.

Mildred smiled back. "Not just yet," she said. "Maybe tomorrow, when it's emptier. There'll be time, right?"

Michelle assured her that there would. "Our friends are welcome to remain as long as they wish," she explained. "That goes for you and all of your party." As if that was her cue, Michelle looked about at the few people still waiting uncertainly on the shore. "Where is your other friend, the one with the white hair?"

Mildred thought immediately of Doc, then realized that the woman was speaking about Jak. Yes, where was Jak? "I think he…" she began, wondering what to say.

"He felt ill," J.B. announced, suddenly standing beside the two women, his shadow falling over them. "Been getting that a lot, that's why he came here. I think he went to lie down, back in the room."

Michelle nodded in understanding. "I did notice that he was looking very pale," she agreed.

"Nothing a little rest and some food won't fix," J.B. said with forced joviality. Wherever Jak was, J.B. knew he had to cover for him lest they arouse suspicion in their newfound hosts.

HIDDEN BY THE FALLOW field, Jak remained as the afternoon sun painted the sky with a pinkish-orange glow and dwindled toward the horizon. He had an idea what was in that field, what it was that the children had been burying, but he needed to confirm his suspicion. It made him feel tense just considering it.

Convinced that there was no one watching, Jak crept out from behind the leaves and crouch-walked into the field. The earth was churned up, holding a little moisture but not really muddy.

Jak made his way over to the spot where he estimated he had seen the children digging. He checked around for a moment, making sure he hadn't drawn any particular attention. Then, standing, he toed the ground, scraping aside clods of loose soil with his boot.

Nothing.

Jak looked down, eyeing the soil carefully, running his boot back and forth. There was nothing there. He needed to go deeper, get a shovel or a pick.

He looked up, peering around the field, hoping to spot a spade or pick or other utensil that might have been left behind by the farming children. There was nothing there, just the expanse of naked soil, an occasional green speck where weeds or grass struggled to establish themselves.

Cursing his luck, Jak crouched and began working at the soil with his hands. Perhaps he was in the wrong spot, perhaps there wasn't anything to be found anyway.

Or mebbe, he thought as he reached into the ground and felt something solid there, wrapping his fingers around it, he was holding the wrist of another human being, buried beneath the soil.

He pulled at the wrist and found it wasn't a wrist at all. It was an ankle attached to a wrinkled old foot on one end and a leg that disappeared beneath the soil on the other.

Jak stared at it, wondering what to do.

FLOATING TOGETHER, Ryan and Krysty watched as Doc drifted in the center of the now-crowded pool. His eyes were closed and he had a broad smile on his face.

"You know," said Krysty, her mouth close to Ryan's ear, "I don't think I've ever seen Doc look so happy."

"It's certainly been a while," Ryan agreed.

As they spoke, Doc's eyes opened and he began to push through the water toward Ryan and Krysty, almost as though he knew he was being spoken about. "Is it not marvelous?" he asked, his face dominated by his beaming smile. "No, not marvelous," he corrected with thoughtfulness, "*incredible,* that's the word for it. Utterly, utterly incredible. I never would have believed if I had not seen it with my own eyes, felt these fabulous effects."

Ryan smiled noncommittally. "So you think it's working then, Doc?"

"I can feel it working," Doc said happily. "Deep down inside me, things are feeling stronger and healthier and altogether better than they did when we arrived. It is this pool. I do not know what it is that is in it, but it is like being dipped in a cure-all. Why, I feel ten years younger."

"I'm glad," Krysty said, touching her hand to Doc's shoulder above the surface of the pool. "You deserve it."

At the side of the inlet, Mildred gave J.B. a significant look. "Did you hear that?" she asked. "Doc's feeling younger."

"He doesn't look younger to me," J.B. growled. "I think he's probably feeling delusional, same as he ever did."

Mildred shook her head, chuckling at the Armorer's typically gruff response. "You really don't want to believe, do you, John?"

"If it's true," J.B. replied, "I'll believe it. And I want this to be true as much as that old fool paddling out there in the middle of it, trust me I do."

"Perhaps it's like Krysty said, back in the trading post," Mildred suggested. "We've seen so much that is bad and wrong with this world, why can't there be this one thing that's good?"

J.B. closed his eyes, feeling their tiredness behind the spectacle lenses he habitually wore. "Because long odds rarely work out in your favor," he replied, listening to the bubbling water beside them.

CROUCHING IN THE DIRT, Jak pulled his hand back and looked at the foot that he had dragged up from the soil. The foot was wrinkled and pale, with rough, callused skin on its heel, ball and toes. It was attached to an ankle that, in turn, appeared to be attached to a leg and, presumably, a whole body, hidden down there, under the earth. Right now, it looked strange to Jak, almost comical had it not been so horrifying—a foot plant growing in the field, the ankle and bone-thin leg its stem, the toes its leaves.

As he examined it, a voice came to Jak's ears, calling from far off. He looked up and saw someone waving to him from the dirt track across the far side of the field. The sun was setting behind Jak, just a red line on the horizon now, casting long shadows as it sank. In that warm orange light, Jak could see that the waving figure was that of a child, thin and no more than four feet tall. Other figures, mostly children, were trudging from the fields, walking in the direction of the main ville. "Are you coming?" the figure shouted, cupping his hands to be heard.

Jak held up one hand, palm spread. "Not yet," he called back, trusting the sun behind him would disguise his features, make him appear smaller than he was.

"Hurry up," the child called anxiously. "They're serving dinner in ten minutes, I think."

For a few minutes, Jak watched the young farmhands make their way back to the ville. A sec man came walking along the road, eyeballing the fields for stragglers. Jak lay flat on the ground as the man passed on the far-off road, hoping his prone figure would be mistaken for another mound of earth in the fallow field; the man with the mule had already gathered up the farmhands who had been working this area. There was no reason to suspect someone else would enter once they had left.

After the sec man had passed, continuing his patrol along the dirt track to check the other fields, Jak eased himself up and began hurriedly brushing away more of the soil from the buried figure. The soil fell away, revealing the whole of a woman's leg and pelvis, still attached to something beneath the surface. The leg was that of an elderly woman, old bruises showing on the flesh. The brittle, dry skin flaked away as Jak scraped the soil off, the white specks sprinkling over the dislodged soil like snow.

The sec man came back, and Jak lay down once more until he had passed on his way back to the bridge to Babyville.

BACK AT THE POOL, the air was becoming more chilly as the sun sank.

"I think," Eddie announced, looking out at the visitors wading in the water, "that we should all think about getting back to the ville."

"It turns pretty cold out here at night," Michelle added with a patronizing smile. "Wouldn't want our new friends to catch a chill, would we?"

"Who cares?" Joanna Dougal said, laughing. "We'll all be twenty years younger tomorrow and fit as fleas."

"That's tomorrow," Eddie told her with a warm smile. "Let's get back inside for tonight."

Michelle went over to a clump of nearby rocks and came back with some blankets and towels that had been stored there in a crafted wooden cupboard. She and Eddie held towels and blankets open as each of the bathers exited the miraculous pool.

OVER IN THE WEST, the sun had disappeared, and a thin sliver of winter moon was visible in the darkening blue sky, a silvery gash high on the horizon.

Under the moonlight, Jak dug urgently at the soil with his hands, brushing and shunting the earth away until he uncovered the whole figure of the woman that he had found there under the dirt. She was naked, her thin, emaciated frame somehow unreal, like a thing made of tiny piping held together with whisper-thin sheets of flesh. Her hair was a mess of pure white strands mixed with the deep brown color of the soil that clung to it, and Jak saw now that her hands had been tied. Her mouth was open, and Jak watched dispassionately as a black beetle came flitting out past her pale lips before burrowing itself into the upturned soil. There was a wound at her throat, a thick brown line where a cut had recently scabbed over.

Below the woman, still half-buried in the upturned soil, Jak saw the chest and hands of another figure, and the knee of a third. He worked at the soil a little more, confirming what he had found there, uncovering parts of five bodies before he finally stopped. Some had been tied up and garrotted, two had been shot in the head. All of them were naked, not even jewelery remained. Jak looked up and saw the field, over 150 yards square. There were more bodies, Jak felt, under the surface of that terrible field; he didn't need to look. And every last one of them, he felt sure, was old.

The youngsters wouldn't be here, buried in this shallow grave. No. They were recruited into the death camp that was Baby, forced to construct the buildings, to work the fields; sent out to find other marks who could be brought here, fleeced of all their worldly possessions, handing them over for a false promise of eternal youth. Jak could see it all now, in his mind's eye. Now that he had found the bodies.

Making haste, Jak brushed dirt over the bodies he had uncovered, enough that his work here wouldn't be obvious. Then, he wiped dirt from his hands and clothes and turned back toward the ville.

Chapter Fifteen

Everybody had dressed and, led by Eddie and Michelle, they made their way back from the bubbling pool. The sun set as they walked along the path to the little wooden bridge, back to the main buildings of the ville.

The crowd was in high spirits, and the newcomers all laughed and chatted as they went, all except for J.B. The Armorer was working at his own thoughts like a loose tooth, mulling over his concerns and suspicions in the face of the evidence that the pool had seemingly provided.

As they passed the watermill and came within sight of the accommodation buildings, Ryan made his way over to talk to his longtime friend. His skin smelled of sulfur now, as did that of the other bathers.

"You look worried," Ryan said, keeping his voice low.

J.B. looked pensive as he answered. "Any idea where Jak is?"

"He'll be okay," Ryan replied. "Jak can take care of himself."

"I'm sure he can," J.B. agreed. "I just wonder where he's lost himself. Wherever that boy went, trouble could follow."

Ryan dipped his head in agreement as they entered the accommodation building. "I hear you."

JAK STEPPED OUT of the shadows and walked boldly toward the footbridge that led back to the main area of the ville. As he walked over the bridge, there was a shout and Jak turned as a sec man rushed toward him, ordering him to halt. He was the one that Jak had seen checking the fields. He had to have spotted him and waited after all.

"Hey," the sec man called. "Stop right there, you mutie freak."

Jak ran for the bridge, determined to lose his tail.

WITH JAK STILL MISSING, the other companions sat at a large dinner table in the accommodation building, along with the members of the party that had been to the inlet. Once there, they were served a simple meal of toasted bread and cured meats. Eddie had excused himself before they sat down, but Michelle stayed to answer questions and simply shoot the breeze. She flitted between groups like a butterfly, taking time to speak with each of the visitors. There was a palpable feeling of high spirits at the table, for the various strangers took pains to get along with one another.

As they came to the end of the meal, Michelle had worked her way around to where the companions had gathered. "And how about you?" she asked, fixing her eyes on Doc momentarily before taking them all in. "How did you find the pool?"

"I have to say that I am delighted with everything so far," Doc admitted. "I feel incredible, quite incredible."

Ryan and Krysty nodded their agreement. "It's a refreshing experience," Ryan confirmed.

Michelle thanked them for coming and moved on, making the effort to greet and speak with other diners before they all left to retire to their bedrooms.

Having finished their meal, the companions got up from the table to leave. As they did, Jeremiah Croxton came over to speak to them, shaking Ryan by the hand. "It was good of you to come," Croxton said, smiling in his grandfatherly way. "You did a splendid job getting us here, Ryan, and I really have to thank you for that."

Pumping the man's hand, Ryan explained that they had simply done what was asked of them.

"Do you intend to stay?" Croxton asked.

Standing behind Ryan, Doc made as though to say something, but Ryan's words came first. "We'll see," he said.

As they left the dining hall, Ryan turned back for a moment. Michelle had cornered Croxton and was speaking with him; the conversation clearly had a sense of urgency about it.

The five companions made their way upstairs behind an elderly couple who had been with them at the pool. The bald-headed man showed endless patience with his wispy, white-haired wife, as she slowly climbed the stairs beside him. Each stair seemed like a whole new challenge to her, as though her legs had never encountered stairs before. She looked frail; her limbs were so slender that they seemed almost like something alien, not human at all. The man's breathing wheezed as he reached the top of the stairs, while the woman just seemed to go on and on, never speeding nor slowing, just climbing the stairs at an interminable rate.

At the top of the stairs, the man stood, catching his breath, and watched dotingly as his wife took the final stair in her gradual, meticulous manner. He glanced behind her then and, spying Ryan and company patiently following, he waved. "I'm sorry about this," the old guy said, the words coming amid strained breaths. "Not as young as we used to be."

"Not yet," the lady agreed as she stepped over the final riser and onto the second-story landing.

"There's no rush," Mildred said politely, and the companions waited a moment until the elderly couple had made its doddering way a little down the corridor toward their quarters before they followed.

JAK RAN, TURNING RIGHT and heading toward four buildings that looked complete. The buildings were small, two-story dwellings, little more than huts really, and probably the first buildings to be constructed here by the stream. A tight alley ran between them, and Jak ducked into it, hoping to lose the sec man amid the shadows.

He ran along the narrow alleyway, head down, arms pumping. Behind him, he heard the sound of the sec man's booted feet slapping against the gravel, giving chase.

"Stop right there, White Hair," the sec man shouted from close behind him.

Jak kept running, sprinting around the corner between buildings and driving himself onward. He didn't know where he was going, knew nothing of the layout of the ville beyond what he had noticed earlier as he had strolled to the gates. Maybe he should have made out that he was simply lost, but he didn't want to answer a lot of awkward questions and draw attention to Ryan, Doc and the others. Easier by far to find himself a hiding place and stay there until these sec men lost interest.

Then suddenly Jak found himself out of places to run. The buildings ended and there was just open ville with its cobblestones stretching out before him, a goose squawking defensively at a barking dog.

The voice came from behind him. "Wait right where you are." It sounded both angry and bored—typical sec man.

Jak cast a contemptuous glance over his shoulder, seeing that there were two sec men now, running up the alley toward him. Even in the darkness he could see that the one on the left had produced a blaster, a stub-nosed .38 by the look of it, while the other had his nightstick raised to shoulder height, ready to beat down any opposition. The guy on the right took priority then, Jak decided. He didn't want to get involved in a brawl like this, but he had seen what had happened to the old guy outside the gate, the way they had beaten him, then chilled him, and he knew these idiots were just itching to exercise a little power.

"We saw you in the field," one of the sec men was shouting. "Now, get down on the ground."

Jak bent his knees, holding his hands above his head as though to obey the sec man's orders as the pair closed in on him. Then, with no apparent effort, he sprang up and back, leaping high in the air, his body twisting as he left the ground. Jak's left hand reached high above, grabbing the sill of the second-floor window, and his legs were instantaneously kicking out, running up the side of the building.

The stunned sec men followed the movement, the man on the right swinging his blaster wildly as he tried to track the jackrabbit albino youth. Jak kicked out, his right leg back, his left sweeping outward to land a bone-jarring blow on the jaw of the sec man with the .38. The man cried out as Jak's kick connected, and he tumbled backward, the stub-nosed blaster going off in his hand, its fury loud in the confines of the alleyway.

Shit, Jak thought. Noise like that was the last thing he needed.

As the gun-toting sec man crashed to the ground, the blaster spinning from his grip, Jak landed on both feet behind the other sec man, bending his knees to absorb the impact of his landing.

The sec man swung his nightstick in Jak's direction, but Jak was a chalk-white blur, ducking the attack. The sec man's nightstick hit the wall with a loud crack, and Jak delivered a straight-hand jab slightly below the man's ribs just a second later. With a pained howl, the sec man doubled over, collapsing to the ground between buildings.

Jak spun, his long white hair swishing behind him like a trail of light. The first sec man, the one who had the .38, was scrambling across the ground, trying to reach the weapon. Jak's feet scrunched against the gravel as he ran for the sec man. The guy's hand grasped the handle of the blaster, and he began swinging it around in an arc that would end at Jak's head, when Jak's left leg kicked out and the toes of his leather boot connected with the man's jaw, punting his head like a football. The sec man's head snapped back, cracking against the hard-packed ground as his body slid almost a foot along the alleyway. Jak was on him then, balancing in a crouch, his bone-white hands crossing before his ghostly face.

Dazed, the sec man looked up, a trickle of blood flowing from his mouth where he had bitten his tongue under the impact of Jak's kick. He saw those eerie white hands move before him, then something glinted within them, something that the albino youth had produced from his sleeve like a magician producing a card at the denouement of a trick. The glinting thing passed close to the man's throat and he didn't even feel any pain, so sharp was its edge.

His throat slit, the sec man tried unsuccessfully to cry out as Jak plunged the leaf-shaped blade through his eye socket and into his brain.

The second sec man was just pulling himself up to a sitting position when he saw the strange albino outlander turn from his position crouching over his colleague. There was blood on the albino's hands now, a spattering of scarlet dots that looked dark against his alabaster skin.

Jak powered forward, rushing at the remaining sec man as he tried to recover from the jab punch to his gut. The man looked slow, probably still dazed, with no inkling of what was going on. Jak punched him in the jaw using the hand that held the knife, knocking the man's head back into the solid wall he was leaning against.

As the sec man sat there, his head swaying on his shoulders, Jak reached out with his left hand, slapping the man in the forehead to hold him in place against the wall. Then, Jak's other hand swung forward and his knife slashed across the man's exposed neck.

A moment later, Jak stepped back, watching as the sec man keeled over, leaving a bloody stain on the brick-work of the building he had been propped against. Jak replaced his knife in its hidden sleeve sheath, wiped his bloody hands on his dark trousers where the stains wouldn't show and made his way toward the main yard of the ville.

"SO, WHAT DO YOU really think, Doc?" J.B. asked once they had reached their rooms.

Doc sat on one of the cots, stretching his legs out before him. "I think it could just be the miracle they promised."

Ryan stood by the open doorway, watching as other visitors found their own rooms. "I'm inclined to agree, J.B.," he admitted. "My muscles feel relaxed."

J.B. turned his gaze on Krysty. "You?"

Krysty nodded. "It was pretty sweet," she said.

Taking a place beside Doc, Mildred contributed to the conversation. "That could just be the water," she said. "Hot water can have that effect. It relaxes the muscles. It's a great rejuvenator."

"'Great' or 'magical'?" Ryan asked.

"I didn't see anything there that made me think it was of particular medicinal benefit," Mildred answered, her gaze flicking almost guiltily to everyone in the room.

"Did you smell it?" Krysty asked. "It smelled of something. Not just water. Could that be…?" She trailed off.

"Or what about the leaves?" Doc prompted. "They were falling into the water. Perhaps when they break down they are releasing some kind of chemical com-pound that…" He paused, grasping for the words.

"That what, Doc?" Mildred asked pointedly.

"Well, I do not know," Doc admitted, "but that is not to say it is not doing something. I mean, I feel fantastic, and so did the other people who tried it. You only dipped your toes, and that for just a minute."

"It was a little longer than that," Mildred corrected him. "I'm as fascinated by this apparent miracle as you are, but I just couldn't see anything there to make me believe it could be happening."

The room fell into an uncomfortable silence as everyone considered what they had seen. Finally, Krysty spoke, addressing a question to Mildred. "Then what are we feeling?" she asked.

"Whatever it is you think you'll feel, perhaps?" Mildred proposed. "The placebo effect. Self-delusion can be a powerful force."

Doc laughed harshly. "I am not deluded," he scoffed. "You saw Eddie, Michelle. You have seen the people who run this ville, all of them young and healthy. Daisy was changed here by—"

"She says she was changed," J.B. reminded him reasonably. "We only have her word."

"And that of Mr. Croxton," Doc pointed out.

"Who may have been sucked in with the same lie," Mildred said.

Doc began to respond, and then he stopped himself, biting down on his words. "I see no reason," he said finally, "that anyone would bring people here from far and wide only to   what? Play an elaborate practical joke upon them?"

Ensuring no one was nearby, Ryan spoke in a hushed tone from the doorway. "They're getting everyone's possessions, don't forget."

"And they disarmed everyone at the gate," J.B. added.

Doc nodded. "But if it did not work, the disappointed bathers would surely leave and ruin its reputation with their gossip. I would like to give this some thought," he told the others. "Perhaps it would be best if we all retire for the evening."

The companions split up then, with Krysty and Mildred disappearing to their room while Ryan and J.B. remained with Doc, taking their beds. Soon after, the oil lamps dimmed and the building block went quiet.

SOMETHING CAUGHT Jak's attention as he exited from the alley between the buildings. He peered into one of the windows and heard voices, one of which he recognized.

Jak listened for a moment, before striding down the alley, peering in windows as he passed. The third window showed a group of people sitting around a table, and Jak halted, ducking to the side and listening intently. There were fifteen of them, all young, and they sat around a too-small table chatting and laughing, smoking and drinking. One group was trying to play cards, but the room was too crowded and they kept having to swap cards around a girl, perhaps seven or eight years old, engaged in braiding her friend's long hair.

Jak scanned the faces until he spotted Daisy and Alec, along with the other man who had disappeared with them that morning. They clearly knew the people in the room, and Daisy was engaged in an animated conversation with two boys who looked just about old enough to shave.

Jak watched, wondering whether he should be suspicious.

There was no glass in the window, just wooden shutters that folded open into the room, allowing the night air to flow into the downstairs of the shack. Jak stood there beside the open window, watching and listening.

He saw Daisy greet a young woman of similar age—which was to say, she looked to be about eighteen—with long brown hair that reached halfway down her back, as she entered the room. The young woman was thin, awkward and gangly, and she wrapped her long arms around Daisy, pulling her close in a hug. Standing beside them, Alec scratched at the back of his head as he looked at the floor, embarrassed.

"Daisy Lee, when did you get back?" the dark-haired young woman asked.

Jak pulled back a little more from the window, keeping to the shadows as he picked through the various conversations he could hear, tuning in to what Daisy and her friend said. A little farther along the alley, one of the sec men was still drowning as his own blood filled his throat.

"Hannah," Daisy was saying, "it feels like ages."

"What happened to your hair?" Hannah replied, gently stroking Daisy's bangs out of her eyes.

The young women shrieked and giggled, speaking too fast for Jak to catch. He waited, watching them, trying to make sense of their words in much the same way as Daisy had tried to make sense of his when they had shared a wag.

The dark-haired teen was saying something else now, and Jak half caught the words, piecing them together over the other sounds coming from the room. "How's Dad?"

Jak saw Daisy roll her eyes, biting her lip in a kind of "I don't know" gesture. "We lost the wag, but he's taking it real well," she said. "You'd think he'd be mad as a freaking stickie."

Jak realized immediately about whom they were talking. Jeremiah Croxton had lost his wag in the fight with the nocturnal scalies. Jak and Ryan had come upon the scene of the battle just after J.B. had blown the man's wag to smithereens.

But hadn't the other girl just called him "Dad"? If Jeremiah was Daisy's father, then what had he been doing on this little excursion to the pool?

Warily, Jak made his way out of the alleyway and back toward the accommodation buildings.

Doc stood in front of the mirror in the bathroom once more, running a razor over his chin and jowls. He looked up into the mirror, and his clear blue eyes locked with those of the mirror man for a moment. He was a young man again, the wrinkled lines having ebbed from his face, leaving him a man of thirty once more. He worked the razor through the lather of soap, removing all trace of the stubble.

There came a knocking at the door then, and Doc held the razor steady, tensing momentarily. "Yes?" he inquired.

"Come on, Father," a voice came from the door, "we're going to be late."

"Wanna see Mother," a second voice chimed in, this one high as a piccolo.

Rachel and Jolyon, Doc's children.

Brow furrowed, Doc realized then that he was back in Nebraska. This aging and de-aging was all frightfully confusing.

Out in the corridor, Doc joined his children, feeling the rawness on his jowls where he had just shaved.

"Come on, Father," Rachel said, already so much the grown-up in her ways. "We must not be late."

Three years old, Rachel had dressed in the outfit of a society woman, a somber colored wrap over a black dress that trailed to the floorboards. Beside Rachel, Jolyon was not yet two, and he sat down against the wall, looking up at his father with innocent eyes. Like Rachel, Jolyon was dressed in his Sunday best, a little suit with a white shirt. Evidently, Rachel had tried to tie his tie, but the material looked crinkled and hung askew to the collar.

"We must not be late," Rachel repeated, tugging at Doc's sleeve.

"Just a moment, little one," Doc instructed, giving his daughter a favorable smile as he lifted Jolyon from the floor. He straightened the boy's clothes and retied his tie before the three of them exited the dark house.

It was morning and the sun was bright outside, so bright it dazzled Doc Tanner for a moment when he opened the door. Rachel led the way, trotting along in something that resembled a skipping run, urging her father to hurry as he carried Jolyon in his arms. The streets were sparsely populated, but the few people who passed them stood to one side as Rachel skipped by, tipped their hat and offered a greeting to Doc.

In a few minutes the three of them were at the top of a hill that overlooked the town. "Come on," Rachel urged again, looking at her father with anxiousness.

At the top of the hill, Doc stopped and peered about him. There was nothing here, just a skeletal, leafless tree beneath the gray, foreboding sky. Cawing miserably, a tar-feathered crow landed on one of the tree's spindly branches, and the branch dipped under the bird's weight. Rachel merrily skipped around the tree, giggling as she went around and around.

"I must have quite forgotten," Doc said, "why it is we have come here. Could you refresh your father's memory, Rachel, my dear?"

Still laughing and skipping, Rachel's words came to Doc's ears like the rolling waves of the sea, soft then loud. "We've come to see Mother, of course."

Confused, Doc looked around, feeling the burden of Jolyon becoming heavier in his arms. And then there was a noise, a shuffling from the ground, and Doc looked down just in time to see a crack appear in the dry soil. Doc stepped back, clutching Jolyon closer as he backed away from the opening rent in the ground. "Come over here," Doc instructed Rachel, but she ignored him, continuing her giggling-skipping dance around the lifeless tree. "Rachel, stand over here with me."

Rachel's skipping never slowed, and her words came once more, colored by her giggling. "There's nothing to be afraid of," she trilled. "It's just Mother."

A hand burst from the soil, reaching up into the sunlight. The nails were long and ragged, the fingers bent inward like a claw, and light glinted on the yellow band of metal that was wrapped around the third finger. *Emily.*

Doc stepped back farther, calling Rachel to his side. The soil churned over and over as the corpse that had once been his beautiful wife struggled out of her grave, pulling herself out of the sod. It was Emily Tanner, unmistakably so.

She clambered from the soil, straightening in a series of stuttering, jagged movements, all sharp elbows, shoulders and knees. As Rachel frolicked around the tree trunk, the corpse that had been her mother stood, the moist earth clinging to the tattered remains of her wedding gown, its veil fluttering from the movements of the beetles, maggots and worms that clung beneath it, feasting upon her cold flesh.

She was just a skeleton now, really, the fragile remains of her skin rotten and holed like something eaten by moths. Her once-luxuriant hair clung to her scalp in clumpy strands, and its rich color had faded into a patchwork of tan streaked with white.

Bent over, lopsided, the corpse of Emily Tanner looked at Doc with empty eye sockets.

Horrified, Doc felt himself take another step back, pulling Jolyon close to his chest. What had happened to Emily? When had she become like this? Doc didn't even remember burying her, couldn't recall her death.

At the tree, Rachel finally stopped dancing and skipped over to her mother's side, reaching to tug at the corpse's bloodstained, white dress. Doc watched as the dress split apart at Rachel's touch, flaking to dust in her hand.

"Rachel," Doc said firmly, "come here now. Quickly, Rachel."

Rachel pulled a face and ignored her father's instruction, tugging at her mother's disintegrating bridal gown.

The thought flashed into Doc's mind then, about his dear sweet Emily and what had become of her. Was this the trade he had somehow made, in wishing to be young again? Had she sacrificed herself for his happiness, as he felt sure he would for hers? Was she a moldering thing that he might retaste his youth?

The moving corpse staggered forward, with Rachel chasing beside her, and her footsteps were lumbering, arms swaying back and forth, as though she could no longer balance without great force of will. And then Doc saw Emily's arm strike Rachel as it swung in that relentless, pendulum-like manner, and Rachel's face began to change, to melt away. Doc watched, his heart thumping in his chest, as Rachel, his little girl, hurtled through the aging process, went from three years old to five to ten to a hundred in a matter of seconds. In those brief moments, Doc saw every face the girl would ever wear, maiden to crone, like the phases of the moon.

Jolyon screamed as Rachel's dress slumped to the floor, just bones and dust left inside it. Beside the dress, the corpse of Emily Tanner took another shaking step, and her skeleton hands reached out longingly for her crying son. Doc turned, pulling the sobbing boy away, shielding him with his own body.

With Jolyon clinging to his left side, Doc felt the other weight in his right hand, the familiar weight of the LeMat pistol. He didn't remember releasing it from its holster, couldn't even recall carrying it on this pilgrimage to hell. But he didn't care anymore, he simply knew what had to be done.

Doc raised the percussion pistol, aiming it at the approaching corpse of his dead wife, and pulled the trigger.

AWAKE.

"Come on, Doc, snap out of it." J.B. was above him, shaking the old man ungently by the shoulders.

"Wha—?" Doc struggled, the dream still searing his thoughts like a sizzling cattle brand.

"Wake up," J.B. whispered, his voice low but carrying that definite note of urgency. "Jak's here."

Confused, Doc looked around the room. It was still dark. Ryan was standing close to the doorway, discussing something in a low voice with Jak.

"What's going on?" Doc asked.

Jak looked at the old man and, even in the unlit room, Doc saw the boy's eerie eyes gleaming red.

"Everyone dead," Jak said.

Chapter Sixteen

"I would estimate that there's at least twenty-five sec men here in the compound," J.B. stated, keeping his voice low.

Krysty and Mildred had been awakened to join them as the companions scattered themselves around one of the shared bedrooms to discuss Jak's discoveries.

"We've taken on twice that number," Krysty dismissed.

"I'm talking about the ones I've counted," J.B. clarified, "the ones who are walking around the ville bearing arms. If you include the residents…"

"I think we have to," Ryan added solemnly.

"Then there's mebbe fifty or sixty people here," J.B. finished, running the numbers over in his head. "And we were disarmed at the gate, don't forget that."

"Some of us," Doc said, toying with the swordstick in his hands.

"You don't like the odds," Mildred summarized.

"I couldn't give two hoots for the odds," J.B. grunted. "What bothers me is that they have all the blasters and we've got two knives and a pebble to throw at them."

Doc looked through the open doorway before he spoke up. "You are sure of what you found?" he questioned Jak.

"Buried bodies," Jak said. "Lots. No mistake."

Mildred reached out, placing a consoling hand on Doc's arm. "You wanted this to be true, Doc, we know that."

Doc shook his head sorrowfully. "You must all think I am a damned fool," he said.

"No, we don't," Ryan said immediately. "None of us think that, Doc."

"I would not blame you if you did, Ryan," Doc admitted. "J.B.?"

"You're the smartest man I know, Doc," the Armorer told him. "Even the smartest man gets sucker punched once in a while."

Jak brought them back to the topic in hand—the field of dead bodies and the lingering threat of Babyville. "What now?" he asked.

"They're killing everyone who comes here and burying the evidence," Doc summarized. "We have to stop this practice. We simply have to."

"I agree," Ryan said, "but we need to get our timing right. As J.B. pointed out, if we're not careful we'll find ourselves on the wrong end of a blaster-fight, with no weapons to defend ourselves.

"J.B., how long do you think we have?"

"Eddie and Michelle kept talking in terms of three or four days," J.B. recalled. "That's how long this miracle cure takes to work, they said."

"I guess," Krysty said thoughtfully, "that's to give them plenty of time to chill visitors."

"You don't want to be rushed when you're performing mass executions," J.B. said.

"So, the longer we leave it the more people will get bumped off," Mildred said, irritation in her voice.

"And, if we leave it too long," Ryan added, "they'll no doubt come for us. Fireblast, we may even be the first they plan to off."

J.B. shook his head. "They're cowards. They'll go for the easy marks first."

ELSEWHERE IN THE VILLE, in one of the huts where Jak had fought with the sec men, the majority of the locals were gathered together for an urgent meeting. Eddie and Michelle were among the group, as were Daisy and Alec from the group of travelers that Ryan and his companions had protected.

"I've been watching that one-eyed fella, Ryan, for a few days now," their leader announced, "and I think now's time we got rid of him."

Raising her hand, Daisy spoke up. "I told you that when I first saw him, Pa. That old guy—Doc—he fell for the story hook, line and sinker. But I always thought his friends was too dangerous."

Beside her, the blond-haired Alec offered his thoughts. "There's six of them and they've been disarmed," he said. "They won't cause us any trouble now, Pa."

At that their leader, Jeremiah Croxton, gave Alec a cold look. "They had better not," he said. "We chill them tomorrow morning—first thing—understand? Start with that mutie white fella—Jak is his name. His devil's eyes have been creeping me out since I first saw him, and the little runt's dangerous as forest fire."

"Crazy runt killed my team," a sec man at Jeremiah's elbow whined. "And he saw everything out in the fields, I swear he did."

Croxton bowed his head. "You'll get your chance, Jamie," he assured him. "We'll chill them all."

The thirty-strong crowd acknowledged their leader's request. They may have come searching for immortality, but Ryan and his companions' lives were now numbered in hours and minutes.

OVER BREAKFAST—a simple meal of unleavened bread and goat's cheese—Michelle explained to the tables that three of the "friends" had already left.

"I'm pleased to be able to announce that friends Felicia, Harry and Paul won't be joining us today," she said brightly, giving everyone her perkiest smile. Felicia and Harry had been the elderly couple whom the companions had followed up the stairs the night before.

Everyone looked surprised and Nisha Adams was the first to ask why.

"The pool works differently for different people," Michelle explained. "Some folks are very lucky and they feel the effects immediately."

"So they just upped and left?" Julius asked. "Without even saying goodbye?"

Eddie's booming voice came from the doorway as he strode into the room, with young Daisy and a young man by his side. "If my experience with the pool of youth has taught me anything, it is that life is for living. I imagine that friend Paul and the others felt the same."

Michelle nodded. "It's an amazing experience to finally be young and healthy again. Sometimes people just can't wait to leave."

"I left before dawn when it happened to me," Daisy added. "Just had to spread the word."

At the table, Jeremiah Croxton chewed on his bread and began to chuckle. "Let's hope it changes all of us so absolutely," he said. "And soon. I cannot wait to be running laps of the ville wall, and surely I cannot be alone in that desire."

A number of people at the table chimed in with their agreement, and everyone got back to their meal before their trip to the pool of rejuvenation.

As conversations buzzed around the table, Krysty leaned close to her companions, her voice low. "I liked Paul Witterson," she said sadly. "He didn't deserve…"

Ryan fixed her with his gaze. "Nobody does."

"It's just like we thought," J.B. growled. "They've started closing in, chilling everyone. Old folks in their beds, like shooting fish in a barrel."

As the conversations continued, Daisy and the young man she had entered with made their way across to where the companions sat. When they got up to join the trip to the pool, Daisy stepped close to Jak, smiling up into his sharp, hard face.

"Hi…Jak," Daisy said, clearly feeling uncomfortable under his eerie gaze, "I was on the wag train coming in, you remember?"

Jak nodded.

"I guess you didn't really come here to use the pool," Daisy said.

Jak smiled, shaking his head. "Come with friends," he told her, his explanation typically brief and to the point.

Daisy brushed a hand through her blond locks and glanced at the doorway where the rest of the group was exiting. "There's lots of other stuff to do 'round here," she told Jak. "I could introduce you to people, mebbe find something for you to do. Or someone," she added, giving him a wink.

Jak sidestepped Daisy, making his way to the doorway after his retreating companions.

"Don't run away," she called. "I'm sure we can make up our own fun."

Jak looked back over his shoulder to reject her offer, but instead he saw the blur of the nightstick sweeping down toward him. He leaped aside, fast enough to avoid the full blow of the weapon, catching it on his left shoulder. His arm went dead.

Jak turned to face his attacker. It was the young man who had entered with Daisy, a grim expression on his face. Jak recognized him—one of the sec men he had seen the day before, one of the group who had patrolled the fields. He didn't know it, but this was Jamie, the sec man whose team he had dispatched with such efficiency by the huts.

Jamie snarled, swinging the baton a second time as Daisy cheered him on. Behind him, Jak realized, the doors had been silently closed, his companions urged on. Ryan wouldn't leave him for long, but in the minutes it took for him to get back, Jak could be dead.

The albino teen leaped aside as the nightstick swung toward him again. The weapon smashed against the breakfast table, and the dirty plates and cutlery bounced in place.

Jak's hand reached out, grabbing a plate and flinging it at his attacker. The man ducked the projectile, but when he looked up Jak was on him, his hand slamming into his nose in a straight-armed blow.

There wasn't even any blood. The young scc man, Jamie, just staggered backward and collapsed to the floor. His nose had broken under Jak's swift attack, the cartilage driven up into his brain, chilling him instantly. Daisy stood watching, her face draining of color. The whole nasty business had taken less than thirty seconds.

Jak turned back toward the doors, heading out to tell Ryan and stop this madness once and for all. He slid the door aside and stepped through the doorway, only to find himself staring at Alec, standing there, an arrow nocked in his bow, pointing the weapon at Jak's throat.

Dismayed, Jak halted in his tracks. He hadn't heard Alec approach; the youth had to have been hidden just out of sight around the doorway.

"You don't move," Alec advised Jak, the string of the bow taut, "and you sure as hell don't cry out."

Jak's eyes locked on Alec's, considering his options. He could throw a knife at the young man, but the movement would be too slow. The arrow would be released and would likely strike him either in the neck or face. He could shout, but what good would that do him if the youth chilled him straight after? The locals could cover that up in a minute, say he had been caught somewhere he shouldn't, which wasn't that far from the truth given his excursions the previous day. Or he could wait, bide his time and use this turn of events to his advantage.

"Jamie's dead," Daisy was muttering from somewhere in the room. She sounded distraught.

Silently, his hands out where Alec and Daisy could see them, Jak lowered his eyes in a clear acknowledgment of his defeat. But already, his mind was working at how to elude his captors.

OUT IN THE COURTYARD, the visitors suddenly found themselves surrounded by sec men.

"What's going on?" Julius Dougal asked, shocked by the sudden turn of events.

"Everyone is to return to their rooms," Eddie instructed. And then he walked over to Ryan's group and pointed at each in turn, including Jeremiah Croxton. "It seems we have a traitor in our midst, someone trying to steal the secret of the spring for their own use, make sure no one else gets it."

Croxton looked affronted. "You can't think it's me," he said, startled.

Ryan watched. What was the old man playing at now? He was a part of this, wasn't he?

Obediently, the visitors returned to the accommodation building, suddenly scared by this turn of events—trouble in paradise. Ryan, Doc, Mildred, J.B., Krysty and Croxton were led away, off in the direction of the spring.

Surrounded and outnumbered, the companions were marched past the bridge, the mill working on the other side of the stream there. They marched farther, into the area opposite the pool where Jak had found the bodies. Ryan did a quick head count, there were twenty sec men and women there, young and inexperienced, perhaps, but all of them were armed. The others had remained with the visitors, making sure everyone behaved themselves. And then there was Croxton and another person joined him on the walk, a woman in her late forties by the look of it, probably the mother to some of this little gang of crooks.

They made their way along the dirt track and on into the seemingly fallow field that Jak had described.

The soil was marshy beneath their feet and they saw a cart waiting, with several lifeless figures lying atop it, including the naked body of Paul Witterson.

Croxton held his hand up to halt the party and the sec team surrounded Ryan and his five companions, watching them warily. "Let's stop this pretense, shall we?" he snarled and the sec men pulled away and turned their weapons solely on the companions. "You know what this is about, don't you, Ryan?"

As the man spoke four new figures entered the field—Alec, Daisy and another teenage girl the companions hadn't seen before, and Jak, tangled in a net like a fisherman's catch. Ryan watched emotionlessly as the netted Jak was tossed at the feet of Jeremiah Croxton. The albino teen had been wrapped in a large net, like something a fishing trawler might use, cinching his arms and legs tight to his body. Blond-haired Alec wore his quiver and had his bow resting behind his neck, over his shoulders. Daisy and the other girl looked to be unarmed, and, to Ryan's eyes, unprepared, like a lot of what passed for sec in Baby.

"This is as far as we go," Croxton announced, his expression dark as his eyes met with Ryan's.

Ryan surveyed the field before turning to meet Croxton's gaze. "Nice place you have here," he said. "Smells of something though."

"Death, I should think," Croxton said, with no trace of irony in his voice.

Which confirmed it, Ryan realized—this was the field of buried corpses that Jak had told them about.

Leaning on his lion's-head cane with apparent weariness, Doc looked around at the sec men, addressing no one in particular. "What now, pray tell?"

Croxton was already busy giving instructions to his people, and two of the teenagers came rapidly forward holding five spades between them. The teenagers handed out one spade each to the companions.

"Now, you start diggin'," Croxton ordered, pointing at the soil. "Find yourselves a nice spot, and one for the white-haired freak here, too, while you're at it. You're all going to be spending a long time here. A long, long time. And all of it dead."

Chapter Seventeen

The companions stood in the field of death as the stark, winter sun stared down with its blind white eye. Under the watchful eyes of Croxton and his sec detail, Ryan and the companions dug at the soil with the spades they had been handed. All except for Jak, who remained caught up in the net, lying against the ground.

"So, why the big ruse?" Ryan asked as he dug at the soil. "Getting picked up by your own men, I mean."

Croxton laughed. "You think I wasn't looking for an excuse not to bathe with those ugly old folks again?" he challenged. "When I came up with the idea of the spring, I should have said it only worked on pretty virgins, I swear to you. Hindsight is a pain in the ass, ain't it?"

Ryan said nothing.

"Guess I don't have to tell you folks that though," Croxton said. "Not now, anyway. Welcome to Babyville, the greatest little carnie show on Earth."

Krysty yelped in surprise as her spade struck something, and she turned the soil carefully to uncover a human skull, tattered remains of flesh still clinging to the yellowing bones.

Croxton laughed when he saw. "Looks like you found yourself a bunk mate there, Red," he said.

Krysty's emerald eyes burned with hate as she glared at him.

His foot on the horizontal edge, Doc shoved the end of his spade into the soil, feeling the anger welling within him. "You have quite the scam going here, Mr. Croxton," he said. "I very nearly believed it."

"Very nearly?" Croxton challenged.

The trace of a smile crossed Doc's lips. "For a while," he admitted.

"I worked in the carnie for a long while," Croxton said, "going hither and yon. Saw a lot of this country, up and down like that, and I always saw the same thing. People looking for dreams to believe in. Just like you, Doc Tanner.

"Keep digging," he added after a moment. "My story ain't that long and, even if it were, I can still reminisce after you all have been chilled."

Doc and the others continued to dig while, over in the netting, Jak watched with his fiery red eyes. While everyone else's attention was on Croxton, Jak worked a blade from his sleeve and set to work on the netting.

"The thing about the carnie," Croxton continued, "is people—marks—love a good scam. Can't get e-freak-ing-nough. Bearded ladies, elephant men, this and that and mutie something or other. Look at this idiot dance, look at this old robot speak, look at this mule count on his clip-clopping hooves. Doesn't even need to be believable. In fact, most people love the unbelievable shit more, because they want to believe that mebbe it could be. You come up with a good scam, and I am talking about a *real* good scam, and people'll do all the work for you. They don't even know they're doing it, they just fill in all the blanks themselves. A bubbling pool that makes folk young again? You have to be a fucking moron to buy in to that. But people want to believe, you see? Like you wanted to believe, Doc."

"The placebo effect," Mildred muttered as she dug her grave.

Two feet into digging his own, Doc looked up at the man, checking the surrounding sec men from the corner of his eye. He knew the others would be doing likewise, waiting for an opening, one last chance. The longer they could keep Croxton talking, the better chance that he and his people would be distracted, that Ryan's group might make their bid for freedom.

"And where," Doc asked, "did you find all these people to staff your...whatever you call this?"

"Theme park," Mildred proposed bitterly. She could see now how the whole place was organized like some perverse holiday camp. A ghastly holiday camp where every visitor ended up dead.

"These folks?" Croxton asked, his gaze taking in the sec men and women who stood beside him, watching the diggers. "My kids, mostly, or kids from the traveling show that I picked up over the past couple of years. Good kids, they know how a scam works, know how to play their parts, how to hustle. Put the pretty ones out front, 'cause everybody likes a little shine on the surface. They had you, didn't they? For a while?"

Doc nodded begrudgingly. "For a while," he acknowledged.

Ryan didn't bother to look up from his digging as he addressed Croxton. "But why did you choose us?"

"When I saw you folks take on those wolf hounds," Croxton stated, "I thought you were something real special, something I could use. The way your team fought, like some well-oiled machine. That took my darn breath away. I need people like that, people like you, to make this ville strong. People who can lead."

Croxton took a step closer to Ryan, addressing his speech to the one-eyed leader of the group. "But I watched you and your redhead there and I came to realize that you are one of the rarest of things in the Deathlands—a man with principles. When I watched you two bury that baby, I knew it was over. Should have left you there and then, but I hoped I was wrong. Then your white-faced freak boy goes snooping around—" as he said it, Croxton took a step toward Jak and kicked him hard in the side "—and ends up chilling two of my people who got close to him. My own kids. That's just plain unfriendly."

Jak snarled as he rolled in on himself, stifling the pain in his side where Croxton's boot had connected.

Croxton looked regretful as he spoke now. Ryan continued working at the soil, digging his own grave, now almost two feet down into the ground. As he dug with the spade, he felt its weight, judged its heft in his hands.

"So," Croxton continued, watching Ryan shovel aside another clump of soil, "if it makes a whole crap of difference, you have earned my respect, Ryan, you and your companions here. I am real sorry I got to chill you now. This here is the future, and you could have been a part of it."

Ryan tossed soil aside with the spade, glancing up at Croxton. "Well, for what it's worth, Croxton," he said, "I thought you were a pretty stand-up guy, the way you herded those people, led them here, took care of them and kept their spirits up. Reminded me of my father, and he was a great man. I'm not half of what he was. I guess you, too, could have been something truly great if you had tried. Turns out, like most everything else around these parts, you're rotten to the core." As he spoke, Ryan stepped out of the grave and swung the heavy steel blade of the spade at Croxton's form.

Croxton leaped back, and the spade swung just short of his legs, missing him by two inches. "Ha-ha," he mocked. "You have got to be just a little quicker and a little less obvious than that, Ryan, my boy."

The sec men turned their weapons at Ryan, every one of them watching him, daring him to continue. But Ryan ignored them, his lone eye focused on the spot where Croxton now stood.

"Less obvious," Ryan repeated. "I'll remember that."

Assured that he had the upper hand, Croxton chuckled at Ryan's bravado. Abruptly, his laughter turned to an agonized scream and, as everyone in the field turned to see what had happened, Croxton fell to the ground, howling in agony. Beside him, still bundled in the netting, Jak turned the knife in his hand, twisting the razor-sharp blade into the old man's leg, ripping a bloody line through his Achilles tendon.

"Fuck!" Croxton shrieked as blood spurted from the wound. "My leg! My fucking leg!"

Inexperienced, the teenage sec force reacted in confusion. Many of them just watched, dumbstruck, as Croxton rolled on the ground. Some had the presence of mind to turn their weapons on the culprit of the vicious attack as he lay within the net. It didn't matter, the scene had been set for the endgame, and none of the sec team had kept their attention on the main threat.

Twisting the top of his sword stick, Doc pulled out the hidden rapier blade from within its black sheath, lunging at a sec man who was now firing his blaster at Jak. The man's blaster spit bullets uselessly into the soil as he was pinioned on Doc's blade thrusting into his back.

Realising the threat behind them, the others in the sec force began to turn, blasters and clubs ready, but the companions were already on them.

Ryan held the spade in a two-handed grip, wielding it like a bo staff. He jabbed the spade's handle at the gut of a young woman to his right and, as she crumpled, he swung the other end high, sweeping the edge of the blade across the face of a young sec man, splitting his mouth open in a spume of blood. Beside Ryan, Mildred swung her spade like a club, working its weight and length to knock a sec man in the head, and his companion across the arm, knocking one man to the floor and forcing the second to drop his blaster as he fell reeling sideways.

J.B.'s attention was on the blasters, and he swung his spade at a sec man holding a remade Heckler & Koch MP-5 machine pistol, rapping the man across the legs so that he lost his balance. J.B. stepped forward, grabbing the foot-long muzzle of the machine pistol as the sec man tumbled backward, kicking the man in the chest and wrenching the weapon from his grip before he could depress the trigger. An instant later, the Armorer turned the blaster on the fallen sec man, flipping the safety to single shot and pumping two bullets into the man's prone form before turning the weapon on another enemy target.

Tossing her spade aside, Krysty dived to the churned-up ground as two sec men turned handblasters on her. Her vibrant red hair had made her the most eye-catching target in the grim field, and it was simple bad luck that two of the sec team had both selected her as their target of choice. Krysty rolled across the ground as bullets dug into the soil all around her. Then, one of the sec men fell under a swift burst of fire from J.B., and the other—confused—turned his weapon in the direction of J.B.'s attack. In that moment, Krysty sprang from the ground like a panther, her right arm reaching around the sec man's throat and pulling his head back. His blaster fired twice before Krysty broke his neck, both shots flying wide of their intended victim.

After running his rapier blade through the first gunman, Doc had found himself fending off three attackers at once. Two were armed with knives, one a vicious-looking machete, while the other swung a nightstick with wild abandon. Doc thrust and parried, finally drilling his blade through the torso of the attacker with the smaller of the two knives. As the knifeman danced at the end of Doc's blade, the other two piled upon him, forcing him to the ground.

"Come on, you old bastard," the man with the machete goaded as Doc fell. "Let's see how tough you are without your sword."

Doc cried out as the nightstick thrashed against his ribs, and he thrust a sharp elbow into his attacker's face. The nightstick man's nose exploded in a shower of blood, and he seemed to forget his attack for a moment as he reached for his ruined face. Doc ignored him, turning his attention to the other attacker, the one with the machete. The curved blade whizzed through the air, and

Doc rolled out of its path, hearing the rush of the blade as it cleaved the air just a fraction of an inch from his left ear. The sec man crouched before him, raising the cruel blade over his head in readiness for another swing at the old man. On his knees now, Doc clenched his fist and swung it at the machete wielder's face, connecting with the man's jaw in a solid crack. Machete man fell backward, and Doc scampered over the ground to deliver another solid punch to the man's face, followed by a third.

"A bit of the old-fashioned," Doc snarled as the sec man fell into unconsciousness.

Behind Doc, the man with the nightstick had forgotten all about his bloodied nose and was rushing to renew his attack on his foe. As he swung the nightstick at the back of Doc's head, something solid slapped against his raised hand, and his whole arm went numb. He turned to see Mildred standing over him, hefting the spade in her hands ready for a second blow. Then, the spade's metal blade crashed into his head and his vision blurred into darkness as he lost consciousness.

"Come on, Doc," Mildred instructed. "No time to rest."

WHILE HE HAD BEEN lying on the ground, Jak had been working at the strands of the net with one of his hidden blades. When Ryan had tricked Croxton into stepping close enough, Jak had seized the opportunity, lunging at the man and cutting a mean wound as high as he could reach in the Croxton's leg. That had been the catalyst, and, as soon as the battle had kicked off, Jak had found himself rolling to avoid bullets and kicks as he clambered out of the net through the hole he had cut.

Now, Jak was a little way from the main battle, finding himself a little space so that he could better use his throwing knives. Alec, Daisy and the other young woman, the one he had identified previously as Hannah, broke from the main group to follow Jak, and Alec raised his bow, the string pulled taut as he targeted an arrow at Jak's skull. Daisy and Hannah stood at Alec's side as he let the arrow fly, and the shaft tore through the air toward the albino youth.

Jak let himself fall backward, his arms whirring as he flicked the two knives from his hands. The spinning knives cut through the air as Jak dropped to the ground under the arrow's path. As the arrow zipped overhead, Jak's knives connected with their targets—Alec's right wrist and his forehead. The former had been a security measure on Jak's part, just in case the forehead blade had missed. Jak leaped back to a standing position as Alec fell to the soil, two leaf-shaped blades embedded in him.

Still standing beside the fallen teen, Daisy and Hannah were now in openmouthed shock. Daisy reached into her bag and pulled out what looked like a sharpened screwdriver as Jak closed the distance between them at a dead run. He was on Daisy in a flash, his right fist swinging at her breastbone as his left hand revealed another blade. Before Daisy could react, Jak drove the blade into her right eye, rending a bloody line across her face before slashing through the eyeball with the knife's sharp edge.

As Daisy fell, Jak dropped with her and his leg swept out at the other young woman. Jak's foot connected with the side of Hannah's knee, and her leg buckled, dropping her to the floor.

The blonde girl was shrieking herself hoarse. Jak approached Hannah where she lay in the dirt. Her leg now lay at an awkward angle where his kick had connected; her kneecap had popped out.

"Please," Hannah begged as she lay there before the albino outlander. "Please don't kill me."

Jak looked down at her pitifully. He wasn't known for his mercy, but he could see she was out of commission, a mixed-up child in way over her head. "Daisy lives," he said. "You, too."

With that, Jak walked over to the corpse of Alec and pulled his blades free. Behind him, Hannah sobbed as she crawled over to where Daisy lay. "It's okay, cousin," she was saying, trying to hush the screaming girl. "It's over now."

Jak took off at a run back to the main field of battle, just twenty feet away.

JEREMIAH CROXTON WAS running, the pain of Jak's knife cut searing through his leg. He ignored the battle raging behind him now, knowing in his gut the likely outcome. He had seen Ryan's companions fight with mutie wolves and those crazy nocturnal creatures they had run into in Tazewell; they were soldiers, warriors whose minds were at their sharpest in the heat of battle. And his kids, the ones he'd produced with his own loins and a handful of women he'd met on the road, the ones he'd come to use to populate this little venture—they were nothing but cannon fodder. Chilling unarmed old folks was one thing, any brat could do that. But Ryan and his people— they were something special.

Croxton had a solution to that, though. Up in the old watermill he had stashed an old Russkie AK-47, ready for emergencies just like this one. He'd mow the lot of them down if he had to. There were kids here, orphans that had been incorporated into Babyville as slaves to work the fields. Those kids had no one. Once all of this was over, they would turn to him and, if he kept a low profile for a while, he could raise them into his own personal army and start the whole Spring of Eternal Youth scam somewhere else. Screw that. Once Ryan's people were dead he could keep the operation right here, who'd ever know?

The wooden bridge was just ahead of him now, and Croxton forced himself onward, feeling that dreadful burn in his leg where the albino freak had knifed him. Didn't matter, not now. "Give me a blaster and a target and nothing'll get in my way," he told himself, his breath coming heavier and heavier. He regretted his pretense of innocence while out on the road now, looking for marks. *I should have carried a blaster from the start,* he cursed in his thoughts, *lived like a lord.*

Croxton's feet pounded on the wooden planks as he ran across the bridge. Once over it, he turned and made his way toward the mill. There was no one around, nobody. The night before, Croxton had ordered almost everyone to come chill Ryan and his companions, even the sec team on the main gate. He knew Ryan was dangerous, and he hadn't wanted anything going wrong. In spite of himself, Croxton almost smiled at how wrong things had turned out. Funny that.

Croxton panted as he climbed the wooden steps over the waterwheel and pulled open the door to get inside the mill. As he did so, he heard a noise behind him and he turned. There, sprinting across the bridge like a runaway train, his feet slamming into the wooden structure, came Ryan, his single eye trained unwaveringly on Croxton.

"There's nowhere left to run," Ryan called when he saw that the old man had spotted him.

Jeremiah Croxton ignored the one-eyed man, shoving his way past the door and into the mill.

USING THE HECKLER & KOCH, J.B. mowed down the last few sec men with any fight left in them, driving short bursts of bullets at the first few until the others finally saw the foolishness of their attempt. As one, the handful of remaining sec men and women threw down their weapons and held their hands where the companions could see them.

J.B. turned around checking everyone was okay. "Think we're about done here," he announced, then he realized that Ryan had disappeared during the scuffle. "Anyone seen Ryan?"

Mildred looked off toward the main area of the ville. "He ran after Croxton," she said. "Maybe someone should go after them."

J.B. swiftly ordered Krysty join Mildred in the search. Jak picked up a blaster from one of the sec men and headed after them a moment later. "Might need backup," he said.

That left just J.B. and Doc standing guard over the eight conscious locals who had tried to chill them. Good odds.

RYAN RAN THE LAST FEW YARDS across the muddy path before coming to a halt at the bottom of the wood stairs leading into the mill on the stream's bank. His hands were empty, and he reached down and pulled the panga from its sheath at his boot. Though not ideal, the eighteen-inch machetelike blade made an acceptable combat weapon.

The one-eyed man watched the stairs for a moment, acutely aware that the higher ground made for an ideal spot to ambush him. After a moment, Ryan made his way up the stairs, the panga held ready in his hand.

At the top of the stairs, Ryan warily nudged the door open, letting it swing inward while he stood to one side in case of attack. Nothing happened. Standing beside the door, blade at the ready, Ryan could hear the sounds of the great millstones turning, grinding wheat into flour as the huge wooden wheel below his feet turned in the current of the stream. The water splashed from the struts of the wheel, and there came the continual hissing and creaking just below where Ryan stood.

Slowly, carefully, the one-eyed man popped his head over the lip of the door, before ducking back.

Again, nothing happened.

Tentatively, his senses on high alert, Ryan risked his head over the threshold, peering into the dull interior of the shacklike mill. Bulging sacks lined one wall, and filled several chairs. The bulk of the room, however, was taken up with the milling machinery. The heavy grindstones whirred around, crushing grain to dustlike flour beneath them, but the sack that had been placed to catch it had been knocked over, spilling white powdery flour across the floor. The millstones continued to turn, and flour trickled to the floor in a continual white stream, like grains of sand through an hourglass.

Ryan hunched, dropping his head so as to make a smaller target of himself as he stepped farther into the

room. His attention was drawn across the room, and
he spotted Jeremiah Croxton's balding head behind a
clump of filled sacks. As Ryan took a step toward the
man, his panga raised, Croxton turned and saw him, his
face twisted in anger.

The former carnie blasted at Ryan with some kind
of automatic weapon. The sacks in front of Croxton
exploded in a burst of wheat grain and clouds of beige-
white flour, the billowing dust obscuring the room like
a fog as his stream of bullets ripped through the sacks
toward Ryan.

The one-eyed man dived to the floor, scrambling and
rolling as he made his urgent way toward his adversary.
At the far wall, Croxton continued to drill bullets into
the flour-filled room, sweeping the muzzle of his blaster
left and right as he tried to locate his target through the
white clouds obscuring his vision.

The sound of the blaster was loud in this enclosed
space, its echoes rebounding from every surface. Nar-
rowing his eye against the onslaught of the flour cloud,
Ryan searched for the telltale flash of the blaster through
the sheet of white that obscured both men's vision. He
located the spitting red-gold flashes from the weapon,
watching from the floor as Croxton swept the room
again and again. The old man was on the move, clearly
trying to find his way to the door and out to freedom,
and his shots were whizzing over Ryan's head. Crouching on his haunches, the one-eyed man judged the distance to his foe and, drawing back his right arm, tossed
the panga. End over end, the long blade flew away from
Ryan's powerful hand, disappearing into the cloud of
white as Croxton's stream of blasterfire continued to

sweep the room. Then there was a cry and the volley of bullets went from horizontal to near-vertical, drilling into the ceiling of the wooden mill as Croxton fell.

Ryan was on his feet immediately, running across the room, eating up the distance between himself and his opponent. The blaster stopped spitting bullets, and Ryan could see the dark shape of its muzzle poking through the settling cloud of flour. He drew back his fist and swung at the form waiting in the whiteness behind that dark, steel muzzle.

Croxton grunted as Ryan's punch slammed like a jackhammer into his chest.

Ryan brought up his other fist in a follow-through, the sound of Croxton's groan confirming his opponent's location. Ryan's fist connected with the side of Croxton's head in another solid blow.

The dust was settling, and Ryan could see his opponent now, his round face and clumpy beard turned ghost-white with the explosion of flour, like some awful impersonation of Jak Lauren. Ryan's panga was embedded in the old man's breast, far to the left, too far and too high to have hit the heart. Ryan swung his right fist again, knocking Croxton's head back on his neck.

Croxton staggered backward, crashing into the wall behind him. Bullet holes riddled the wall, and the wooden boards creaked, complaining at the stress of the impact. Ryan swung again, driving his left fist into the old man's gut, forcing him to double over.

"This is as close to eternal life as you'll ever get," Ryan snarled as Croxton floundered against the wall of the mill.

"Dammit," Croxton grunted, struggling to catch enough breath to speak. "It doesn't have to be like this, Ryan. We could still work together. What d'you say?"

"Since you just tried to chill me and my friends," Ryan responded, "I'm disinclined to accept your offer."

"Too bad," Croxton spat. He held an AK-47, and now he swung it at Ryan, knocking the man away from him.

A moment later, Ryan found himself struggling for balance as Croxton brought the length of the Kalashnikov rifle down on him, driving the butt into the back of his head. Ryan slumped to the floor, landing amid the sprinkled carpet of strewed wheat and flour. He saw the shadows move as Croxton pulled the AK-47 around to shoot him, heard as he fought with the oversize weapon in such close quarters. The whole operation took less than a second, any quicker and Ryan would already be dead, a bullet to the back of the head, catching a one-way ride on the last train to the coast.

Ryan kicked off from the floor, driving himself forward and up at the figure looming over him, driving his head into the man's gut, just below his ribs. Together, the two of them plowed onward, Ryan's powerful legs driving him, Croxton crumbling over the man's attack as he staggered backward, the AK-47 blasting random fire into the flour-filled room.

A cracking noise sounded behind Croxton, and both men felt something split and break as the wall of the shack gave way. The wood of the wall was old, and it had been abused by the bullets and the pounding that Croxton's form had given it just moments earlier. The wall splintered, no longer a solid barrier.

As wood fell all around them, Ryan and Croxton tumbled out of the shack, plummeting into the stream with a colossal splash.

KRYSTY LED THE WAY as she, Mildred and Jak ran through the field and headed for the wooden bridge leading back to the ville. As they reached the bridge, they saw the wall of the watermill give way and two grappling figures drop through the gaping hole in its side.

"That's Ryan," Krysty barked as the two men splashed down into the water.

Without a moment's hesitation, Krysty arched her back and dived into the rushing stream.

DOC AND J.B. MADE the sec team kneel in the dirt, while they disarmed them, heaping their weapons out of reach in one of the freshly dug graves.

Standing before the defeated locals, Doc returned his rapier blade into the sheath of the swordstick with a flourish. Other than the older woman, they seemed to be mostly teenagers or folks in their early twenties, all of them young and fit.

"Young bunch of whippersnappers, aren't they?" J.B. observed. "You'd think they could take an old man."

"Experience should never be underestimated, John Barrymore," Doc told J.B. as he looked over the dejected locals.

"Sure, Doc," J.B. agreed, "but this is one experience I'll be damn glad to put behind me."

"So say we all," Doc assured him as he walked past the group, knocking the last few weapons aside with the tip of his cane.

As he passed one of the group, there was a sudden movement and the man closest to Doc leaped at him, driving something at his leg. Doc fell to the ground, howling in pain as Eddie, the young man who had played the role of founder of Babyville, took another swing at him with a rock the size of his fist.

Doc struggled, rolling aside as Eddie slammed the sharp rock into the ground where Doc's head had been an instant before. As the blond-haired man continued his attack, Doc reached up and grabbed his wrist. Together, the two of them wrestled for the rock, Eddie driving it at Doc's face while Doc struggled to push it wide of that target. "John Barrymore?" Doc pleaded as the pair fought on the ground.

CROXTON HIT THE WATER with a crash, and its surface felt like a solid block slapping into his back. A moment later he was below the surface, the breath bursting out of him and water filling his mouth and nostrils. Above him, he saw the one-eyed man open his mouth, unleashing a stream of bubbles as his own breath burst forth with the impact.

Croxton realized he had dropped the AK-47 in the fall, as it was no longer in his hand. Improvising, he rabbit-punched at Ryan's side, driving his round fists through the water, feeling the liquid's subtle resistance leech the momentum out of the blows.

Croxton's chest was hurting already, and he felt a cough ripple through him where it was trying to expel the water he had swallowed. Ryan didn't seem to be doing much better, still struggling under the surface before him. Croxton watched as his scarred adversary swam toward the surface, and he lashed out with his leg, kneeing Ryan in the crotch, forcing the man to blurt out the last of his breath.

As Ryan flipped over himself under the water, Croxton searched around for the AK-47, determined to use it to finish off the man. A red cloud of blood was obscuring the water, and Croxton realized with horror that it was his own, pumping from the knife wound in his chest. The panga was still there, half of its long shaft buried close to where his left arm met his chest. As he looked, Croxton's eyes lit on something else, something large and mechanical beneath the surface of the stream—the waterwheel. Its wooden blades cut through the water, rotating around as it dipped close to the bottom of the stream.

Croxton surfaced then, drawing a long, desperate breath of air, feeling nauseous with its intake. Beside him, swimming about three feet away, Ryan surfaced and struggled to do the same. Croxton's hand lashed out and he tried to punch Ryan in the face, but the impressive man was just quick enough to avoid the blow. Instead, Croxton's arm caught Ryan across the throat, knocking the one-eyed man back and below the water's surface once more.

Ryan's vision blurred for a moment as his head dipped under the water, and then he saw the huge wooden wheel turning unstoppably with the current of the stream. It was just a foot away, and he was perilously close to getting his head snagged by it. He felt the old man's arms against his chest, shoving him closer and closer to those churning blades, driving him nearer to his doom.

Blindly, Ryan lashed out, reaching for Croxton, grasping to pull himself away from the blades of the waterwheel. His hand grabbed at something solid, and he realized it was the handle of the panga, the long knife that had embedded in Croxton's chest. Ryan grasped the handle, twisting it, driving it deeper into Croxton's chest as the old man pushed at him with all his strength.

Ryan looked up and saw that his head was now just inches from the whirring blades of the mill's wheel as they cut through the water. Then, suddenly, Croxton's strength faltered, and a wash of red filled the water as Ryan felt the knife blade pull free.

But it was too late; Ryan felt the sagging weight of the old man pushing him onward as they tumbled into the blades of the waterwheel.

THE ROCK DROVE into the ground beside Doc's head a second time as Eddie shoved it at the old man's face.

"Die, old man," Eddie demanded through gritted teeth. "Die for me."

Doc didn't reply. He was too busy trying to keep that lethal shard of stone from hitting him as Eddie tried again. And then, there was a sudden burst of blasterfire, and Eddie's head exploded in a plume of brain, bone, blood and flesh.

Doc looked up as the lifeless body fell on top of him, its formerly handsome face now a splatter of blood and brain matter. The Armorer stood over him, the Heckler & Koch MP-5 held firmly pointing at Eddie's wrecked head.

"You okay, Doc?" J.B. asked.

Doc took a breath to calm his racing heart. "Never better," he said with good humor as the sense of relief washed over him.

J.B. turned back to check on the other prisoners, and saw the blood-soaked Michelle—their once pretty tour guide—reaching for the pile of discarded weapons. The Armorer pointed the machine pistol at her head. "You want to risk it, girl?" he challenged.

Michelle stopped and glanced up, realizing that J.B. had spotted her. She shook her head and edged her hand back away from the weapons.

"Good girl," Dix told her. "I don't know much about eternal youth, but I can tell you one thing," he added, his gaze taking in all of the prisoners, "chances are you'll live a whole lot longer without a bullet in you. We clear?"

The defeated group agreed, accepting its fate once and for all.

RYAN'S HEAD AND SHOULDERS careened between the swishing blades of the waterwheel, and he felt the water churn as he was dragged between them, the deadweight of Jeremiah Croxton pushing against his body.

If he was caught up in those blades, Ryan knew the force would break his neck, snap his spine or simply decapitate him before he could extricate himself. He gritted his teeth as he waited for the inevitable crush of the wooden blades. And then…

Nothing.

Ryan felt his lungs crying for oxygen. He had been under the water too long, exerting himself against the bastard-mad Croxton. But the waterwheel hadn't cut him in two, hadn't broken his neck or snapped his spine. Instead, he felt Croxton's heavy, lifeless body falling away as strong hands reached for him, pulling him from the water.

"Breathe, Ryan," a woman's voice urged. "Just concentrate on breathing."

Ryan struggled to draw a breath, coughed and spluttered as it tore against his lungs. Then he felt himself being tipped as water surged up his throat and into his mouth. He vomited, bringing up more water, surprised at how clean it tasted in spite of everything.

Mildred was beside him, Ryan saw now, holding his head to make sure he didn't choke—or drown—on the water he had swallowed from his savage dunking in the stream. It had been her voice advising him to breathe, he realized as clarity returned to his whirling mind.

Ryan's body shook as he coughed up more of the water, spitting it in a gush onto the muddy bank of the stream. He looked up and saw the familiar red hair of Krysty, Jak crouching beside her, and he realized with a start that she was doubled over, shaking as she struggled to stand upright.

"What happened?" Ryan managed. "Is Krysty…?" And a coughing fit took him once more.

Krysty looked up, her vibrant hair falling over her face, and Ryan saw the smile on her lips. "I'm fine, lover," she told him, though her voice was softer than normal, weaker. "Just had to stop the wheel turning."

The Gaia power, Ryan realized. Krysty had called on the incredible surge of strength that the Earth Mother granted her, using it at the crucial moment to halt the vast waterwheel, holding it in place against the pressure of the current until Mildred and Jak could pull them both from the stream. She was weak now from the exertion, but Ryan knew that she would recover.

As the ticklish feeling in his chest began to ease, Ryan looked past Mildred and the others, his lone blue eye scanning the stream. "What happened to Croxton?" he asked, his voice sounding raw.

"Dead," Mildred assured him. "You chilled him."

With that, Mildred plucked something from the soil beside her and handed it to Ryan. It was the panga, a mixture of blood and soil staining its length. Taking it, Ryan leaned across and held the blade in the stream, watching as the current washed away any trace of Jeremiah Croxton and his foul Babyville.

Chapter Eighteen

The companions regained their weapons from the sentry post, which had been left unmanned while Croxton's people attempted to take down Ryan and the companions. They also saw to it that the remaining weapons were distributed among the old folks who had been drawn to the Babyville scam, once they had captured or chilled the last few sec men who had been left guarding the accommodation buildings. Some of the oldsters had trouble believing they had been duped, but all of them realized that they had had a narrow escape once they were shown the field of corpses that lay so close to the supposedly mystical pool.

"You're in charge now," Ryan told Patrick Clifford and his wife as the weapons were redistributed.

"What about the locals?" Patrick asked.

"They're locked in one of the accommodation buildings," Ryan told him. "Give them a chance to cool off. I don't think they'll give you much trouble now. The fight went out of them once they heard Croxton was dead. Most of them would probably be grateful of some medical attention."

Holding her husband's arm, Sara Clifford looked around the ville, at the half-constructed buildings and the farmyard animals that ran between the buildings. "It's not such a bad place," she decided. "We could make a go of things."

"Croxton's vision was a thing of evil," Patrick added, "but he managed to create the start of something impressive here. We could set up a committee, figure out what needs to be done."

"Start with building a nursery for the kids," Sara said. "They shouldn't have been made to work the fields like that."

Patrick agreed and Ryan felt a sense of relief at leaving these people in charge.

"You might get a few visitors for a while," Ryan pointed out. "Probably a few of Croxton's scam artists still working the farms and villes hereabouts, trying to find easy marks to bring here and chill."

"They're in for a surprise then," Mary said firmly as she came over to join them. She held a 12-gauge shotgun in her hands, and she looked a whole lot more determined than Ryan had ever seen her before. "We've already got us a new sec man for the gate."

Ryan smiled as he saw Charles Torino following her, carrying a giggling baby Holly in his arms. He had recovered his Taurus blaster, and it now sat snugly in his belt, ready for a quick draw. "I only said I'd do it so I didn't have to change the baby," Charles admitted, but Ryan saw that self-deprecating smile tug at the man's lips.

"You okay, Charles?" Ryan asked.

He nodded. "Your healer there—Mildred—she fixed me up with something to ease the coughing. Guess that's all I can ask for. At least till the next miracle spring comes along."

Ryan was gratified. Babyville had been a horror show, a one-man death camp with kids being turned into slaves to work the land. Now it had been passed into the hands of good, honest people with the wisdom to build something worthwhile, and the empathy to take care of one another, perhaps even to rehabilitate lost souls.

Scratching at his head, Doc wandered over to join the group as the last of the weapons was handed out. "John Barrymore is looking to get going," he told Ryan.

"Doesn't surprise me." Ryan nodded. "It's not like J.B. to stick around any place too long."

Patrick reached out to shake Ryan's hand, then Doc's. "Thanks for all you've done," he said. "If you're in these parts again, you know you're welcome here in Baby."

Sara shook her head. "Now, Patrick, that name has got to go. Whoever heard of a ville called Baby?"

As Sara, Patrick, Mary and Charles began to discuss new names for their ville, Ryan and his companions walked toward the high gates. By mutual consent they decided to help themselves to a buckboard wag, two horses and as many provisions as they could grab in ten minutes that would sustain them during the overland journey to the next redoubt.

Krysty pulled herself close to Ryan as, beneath the midmorning sun, they headed away from Babyville. "Do you think they'll be all right?" she asked.

Ryan shrugged. "They've got fields with rich soil, they have shelter and they have…something else, too."

"Nobility?" Krysty suggested.

"Yeah," Ryan agreed. "And mebbe that's what's needed to build a better future out here."

Jak walked beside the wag, picking the leaves of plants as he passed them, while Mildred, walking beside him, gazed up into the winter-blue skies, enjoying the feel of the wind blowing on her face.

Behind them, Doc turned to J.B., who was sitting in the rear of the wag.

"Well, John Barrymore," Doc began, "is it not time for you to say 'I told you so'?"

Shaking his head, J.B. looked Doc. "When we were ambushed back there and everything was about to go to hell," he said, "you stood up and fought just like the rest of us, Doc. So, the way I see things, either you've been lying about being an old man all this time or that dip in the magic spring did you some good."

"You had to step in when Eddie attacked me," Doc pointed out. "You saved my life."

"Well," J.B. said, shrugging, "I figure you're too young to die. Just yet, at least."

"Just yet," Doc agreed with a laugh.